THE HEART IN EXILE

RODNEY GARLAND was the pseudonym of Adam de Hegedus, about whom little is known; the few available details of de Hegedus's life are recounted in the 1995 Millivres reprint of *The Heart in Exile*. Born in Budapest in 1906, de Hegedus came from a middle-class, intellectually inclined family and originally intended to pursue a life in the Hungarian diplomatic service. Visiting London on a short stay in 1927, he decided instead to follow a career in journalism, and, after a stint in Paris, where he claimed André Gide as a friend, he returned to London and settled permanently.

De Hegedus served briefly in the Second World War before a nervous breakdown led to his discharge; afterwards, he worked as a van driver and resumed his writing career. Under his own name, he published several volumes of autobiography, fiction, and nonfiction, including *Hungarian Background* (1937), *Don't Keep the Vanman Waiting: A Chapter of Autobiography* (1944), *The State of the World: Reflections on Peace and War in our Time* (1946), *Rehearsal Under the Moon* (1948), *Strangers Here Ourselves* (1949), *Home and Away: Notes on England after the Second World War* (1951), and *Struggle with the Angels: A Novel* (1956). But his sole success was *The Heart in Exile* (1953), published pseudonymously, which ran into at least four London editions and was also published in America and reprinted several times in paperback.

De Hegedus was apparently a lonely man, and his end remains shrouded in obscurity. It is believed he committed suicide in London in 1958.

THE HEART IN EXILE

A novel by

RODNEY GARLAND

"In youth despair is overwhelming.
There is then no tomorrow, no
memory of disaster survived."

A. N. WHITEHEAD.

With a new introduction by

NEIL BARTLETT

VALANCOURT BOOKS

The Heart in Exile by Rodney Garland
First published London: W. H. Allen, 1953
First Valancourt Books edition, 2014

Published by Valancourt Books, Richmond, Virginia
Publisher & Editor: JAMES D. JENKINS
20th Century Series Editor: SIMON STERN, University of Toronto
http://www.valancourtbooks.com

ISBN 978-1-941147-12-2 *(trade paperback)*

Cover by M. S. Corley
Set in Dante MT 11/13.2

INTRODUCTION

Gay men have always been modern; that is, they have always been
seen as a symptom of society's latest crisis, from Petronius' *Satyricon*
to Fellini's, from Christopher Marlowe's *Edward the Second* to Derek
Jarman's. Talking about us has always been a way of talking about
how social values are being challenged or corrupted or changed for
the better. This way of looking at our lives is not peculiar to theo-
rists or artists; we ourselves see ourselves as permanently novel.
We are, we think, literally recreated each generation.

This means that we have (or have had, at least until very recently)
a very odd relationship with our own history. Because we have so
often been omitted from the official record, we feel original. This
has been particularly the case since we decided in 1969 that all
cultural babies had to be thrown out with the historical bathwater
and the world re-invented the name of Gay Liberation. At that
particular point in our history, we needed to be free to re-imagine
ourselves—to be free, if you like, to imagine ourselves living lives
without precedent. Nothing, of course, could be further from the
historical truth. Even before 1969, the beginnings of modern gay
culture—the first gay play, the first gay novel, the first gay politician,
the first gay bar—were being pushed back by our historians every
year. We now know (for instance) that the first professional comedy
in English (written in the sixteenth century) has gay obscenities in
it; that there were more gay bars in New York in the early 1920s
than in the early 1970s. And what about the "gay novel"? I wonder
where we will eventually decide that our first true representative
in English prose is to be found? Renault's nurses? Wilde's Willie
Hughes? Dickens's wonderful Tattycoram? A minor homoerotic
beauty lurking somewhere in Smollett, in an Elizabethan Cer-
vantes, or even in Lyly?

So, *The Heart in Exile* is by no means the first example of a
gay novel, but it is certainly worth reprinting and rereading as
a reminder that popular fiction which explores our lives is not a
new idea—and it was popular, being reprinted three times in its

first year. Queens and those who find queens fascinating (i.e. just about everyone who reads books) have long been a staple in novels which mix the conventions of the crime thriller and the "problem play" of the nineteenth century; genres whose main task is the entertaining exposition of a dark secret. One of the great pleasures of Hungarian Adam de Hegedus's novel (published under the discreetly queeny British pseudonym of Rodney Garland) is that it is fearlessly true to type, an unselfconsciously perfect example of the genre, studiously placing itself as it does precisely halfway between the sensationalism of *Dorian Gray* and the journalistic documentation of the Wolfenden report and then wrapping the whole thing up in the would-be sophisticated tones of a minor rainy-afternoon Celia Johnson vehicle. Literature never does this sort of thing as well as a good read.

Like the film *Victim*—the screenplay for which was written eight years later, in 1961—it has a one-line plot; a crime (a suicide) becomes the pretext for the examination of the explanation of the "crime" of homosexuality. In order for the crime to be solved, the reader must be taken by the hand and led down the various garden paths of a more or less systematic exploration of our twilight world. The book is a perfect crash course in the prehistory of British gay culture—every cliché and every theory is there. The locations are classic—a queer pub, the House of Commons, Scotland Yard, a "theatrical" party—and in each one, there we are, ready to give ourselves away; to be identified and to be explained. All of our symptoms are dealt with in turn—self-hatred, bodybuilding, interior decoration, a taste for Philpot, Gingold and guardsmen. As in *Victim*—where Sylvia Syms comes to understand Dirk Bogarde's torment through teaching art therapy to disturbed children—psychiatry is there to provide a truly modern touch, and of course to justify the swathes of up-to-date but barely-digested sociological and psychological "theory" concerning the "problem" of homosexuality.

Before we dismiss all this as "out of date", it is worth remembering that the form is still with us—it is a distant ancestor, for instance, of the journey-through-the-underworld narrative of Alan Hollinghurst's *The Swimming Pool Library*, and in hands as accomplished as those of crime-writer Ruth Rendell, for instance, forays into the hidden gay world which stay well within the confines of this genre can still not only provide us with thrills, sentiment and colourful minor characters but also with genuine insights into the ways our contemporary queer world does—and does not—work.

The pay-off of such narratives is supposed to come at the end, when the mystery of the crime is solved, and the mystery of homosexuality is dissolved in a concluding argument for rational tolerance. The real pleasure of this particular narrative, however, is in its details, not its conclusion—in the assembling of the evidence, so to speak, not in the identification of the culprit. It is thoroughly entertaining to hear de Hegedus trying in all earnest to explain the latest technical terms of 1953—pouf, butch, trade, haveable, camp, drag-party. And it is completely fascinating (for this reader at least) to spot the first signs of what was later to become clone culture—lumber-jackets, check shirts, white vests, tattooed forearms, leather jackets, body-building. If anyone ever tells you that the style was imported from America in 1972, lend them this book and ask them to read it carefully.

Is it any good? Well, the post-war queen is of course an acquired taste—personally, I love them, from Mary Renault's *The Charioteer* to Terence Rattigan's *The Deep Blue Sea*—from Fred Ashton and Bobby Helpmann to Douggie Byng and Oliver Messel to Julian and Sandy—ad infinitum. But with historical hindsight (or a proper sense of camp, if you prefer to call it that) two things entitle this book to retain its place in our library. The first is its straightforward and too-easily dismissed assumption that the destruction of life is a given of the historic British gay experience. It is an assumption that I tend, rather to my surprise, to now share, and it was this that made me re-use names lifted from this novel in my own *Ready to Catch Him Should He Fall* as a small repayment of a debt. The second thing (and this, I think is what really makes it worth rereading) is the agenda of questions that the relationship of the narrator and his 'friend' raises. Why is it that the ideal boyfriend is butch, but always on his knees; loveable, yet both stupid and ignorant (such a rare combination of qualities in real life); why is he passive, grateful, fabulously domestic; and why, best of all, does Garland specify that he has no gay friends at all—why is he, in fact, not a boyfriend at all, but a wife? And why is it that in Dr. Page the figure of the virtuous—even abstemious—homosexual; the homosexual who longs to be married; the homosexual who isn't a queen; the homosexual who knows about such things as rough trade but doesn't do them himself; the homosexual who never has to fight for his life or living; the homosexual who doesn't make a fuss in public—the homosexual who is, in fact not, in any meaningful *social* sense of the word, a homosexual at all—is still, seventy years on, so entirely recognizable as a liberal dream of who and how some people still want us to be.

Strange how potent cheap fiction can be.

NEIL BARTLETT
Brighton

March 12, 2014

NEIL BARTLETT is the author of *Who Was That Man?*, a ground-breaking study of British queer culture which was published in 1988. His third novel, *Skin Lane*, was shortlisted for the Costa Award; his most recent, *The Disappearance Boy*, was published by Bloomsbury in 2014. His website is www.neil-bartlett.com.

THE HEART IN EXILE

AUTHOR'S NOTE

BOOK ONE

One

I opened a window and we could hear the muffled sounds of Kensington from beyond my quiet street. Resting on the couch, Miss Wilkins' old-fashioned, pointed shoes stood like two sentries at ease. They glittered in the glorious sunshine of the summer afternoon. I could not help smiling at her hat on the radiogram, as I resumed my seat behind her pillow.

Miss Wilkins and I had been "free associating" for ten months now, three times a week. I knew that her hand-washing obsession had become less pronounced and that she was no longer as frightened to touch door knobs as when she first came to me. She also talked less about irrelevancies than in the past. I dare say she got a certain amount of comfort and confidence from being in positive transference with a safe male, and perhaps the outlook for her wasn't as poor as I had felt, even six months ago.

Maybe it was the warmth and the peace of the day that were encouraging me; the weather had been wonderful for the past week and I had been feeling very happy all day without any particular reason. It was one of my good days, when work is easy and the future and the past are forgotten.

"Any dreams lately?" I said.

"I don't think so," Miss Wilkins said eagerly.

"Then what about the dream you had the last time? You didn't tell me all about it."

". . . Which one?"

It was obvious that Miss Wilkins knew very well which dream and fairly obvious why she had shied away from it three days ago. As dreams went, it was a perfectly "standard" dream—a handbook dream if you like—of obsessive-compulsives. Thousands of people like Miss Phoebe Wilkins dream the same dream every night.

"You were being chased over open country," I said, "by a tramp.

3

You were running wildly, but finally he caught up with you. I asked you what he looked like and you said his face was blurred. Now try to remember what he looked like."

After a short silence she suddenly said, "I don't know." She sounded petulant. "Is it so very important?"

"Of course it is. You may as well try to look on me as a policeman. I must identify the tramp in order to catch him, you see. And I must catch him, because he's a nuisance. Now try to think what he looked like? Would you say he was young?"

"Mm, yes . . . fairly tall . . ."

"As tall as I am?" I was feeling a little uneasy.

"Oh, no." Miss Wilkins suddenly giggled and I felt relieved.

"Well," I said, "we're getting on."

"It's funny. At first I thought it was Mr. Mainwaring. But you wouldn't know him. . . ."

"Who's he?"

"A clergyman. But I haven't seen him for a long, long time. Must be quite an old man now. . . . You see it was he who prepared me for my confirmation. . . ."

I made a quick note on my pad. This was becoming interesting. I said: "At first you thought it was Mr. Mainwaring. Then what happened? Did you make a mistake?"

"I must have done."

"So it was another man, after all?"

"Well, not exactly. . . . I should say a mixture of two men."

"Who was the other?"

". . . I . . . I don't know."

"Miss Wilkins," I said in the tones of Infinite Wisdom, "we shall never get anywhere if you are not perfectly truthful. And the point is that your condition is improving. Now come on, who was the other man?"

Miss Wilkins didn't reply. But I had an idea.

Ten minutes later, after a short, gentle battle, I saw that my original guess was correct. The other man was her father. I was feeling hopeful, very hopeful, and it seemed that Miss Wilkins was feeling happier. Her treading-on-coalholes compulsion was still worrying me, but we could start exploring that next week.

"Well," I said, "that's about all for today. I'll see you next Thursday."

Miss Wilkins got up from the couch, put on her hat, and I showed her out; then I went back to the desk and made a few notes. Another indication of her improvement was that she no longer wore gloves all the time to protect herself against contamination. More than this; lately she had, quite on her own, offered me her hand, or three fingers anyway.

It was a quarter to six, and the new patient was coming at six. I remembered that, but I had forgotten her name. I reached for the diary and saw Terry's schoolboy handwriting: *Miss Hewitt 6 p.m.* She had rung last night, when I was on my way to dine with Weblen. Terry had asked whether Friday morning would suit her, but she had said it was urgent and wanted to come earlier.

I was wondering who had sent her, the hospital, her G.P. or possibly some other patient. Very likely a G.P. Another Miss Wilkins, I thought; but the prospect at the moment was not displeasing. Miss Wilkins was getting on well, and her previous doctor had given her up. The only thing that made me doubt that Miss Hewitt's case would interest me was her sense of urgency. It was my experience that the patients whose cases really excited me professionally— with the exception of Dighton—never said things were urgent. They usually accepted, even asked for, an appointment in the distant future, often rang up later to alter it and sometimes even failed to turn up for the first appointment.

As I put Miss Wilkins' file back into the cabinet, I saw the two empty teacups on the desk. I took them into the kitchen. Terry, in his dark blue singlet, was busy peeling potatoes.

"Did Miss Hewitt say yesterday who sent her?" I asked.

Terry put the knife down. "I'm so sorry. I forgot to ask." His face turned crimson. Serious concern made him look incredibly young in spite of his build.

"It doesn't really matter," I said. "Forget it. . . . I mean, *don't* forget it." As I put the cups on the draining board, I saw his smile, the coral gum over his strong white teeth. The only thing, I thought, was that if I took on Miss Hewitt, I must fit her in at an earlier hour. Three times a week I already had Dighton coming after six and I wasn't anxious to have any other late patients. If

Miss Hewitt worked all day and couldn't come earlier, she would have to go somewhere else. I had eight patients in all; definitely enough.

"A cup of tea?" Terry said.

"Well, we're eating in an hour's time, aren't we?" I said and remembered that we had thought of going to see a film. Then, as the idea of a glass of sherry crossed my mind, the bell rang. It was only five minutes to six. "She's early," Terry said and jumped to dry his hands on the towel by the sink.

"You carry on," I said. "I'll answer it."

As I opened the front door, I realised that my preconceived ideas about my new patient were wrong in every conceivable detail. The woman who stood there was young, about twenty-five or so, tallish, with broad shoulders and expensively dressed. "Dr. Page," she said, a little abruptly I thought.

"Yes," I said. "Will you come in, please."

I looked at her back as I let her into the consulting-room and I felt it was not only nervousness that made her look ill at ease in her high-heeled shoes, the smart costume and the impossible hat. "County," I thought, but she's made up her mind to be smart. Who on earth could have sold her that hat? She had probably insisted, brushing all arguments aside.

But there was little determination in her voice as she now suddenly said: "It was very kind of you to see me at such short notice, but it's urgent."

"I see," I said. It's always urgent, or nearly always. "Will you take a seat, please." I pointed to the armchair. She carried a large and expensive handbag, and now I saw her pearl choker. I had never had a rich patient before. Nervous insomnia, I thought suddenly, and I took my seat at the desk. "First of all," I said, "may I know who sent you to me?"

"Oh, I'm not ill," she said, shaking her head slightly; but she didn't smile. "As a matter of fact, I'm not feeling too well," she corrected herself shrugging a shoulder as if to say that that was beside the point, "but I came to see you about a personal matter. . . . You knew Julian Leclerc. . . ."

Just as she said "personal matter", a barrel organ in the street outside began to play a jazz number, slightly out of tune. On most

occasions in the past I would have been irritated by such an inter-
ruption, but as I jumped up without saying excuse me, I felt with
my heart in my throat that the barrel organ was a heaven sent
opportunity; a lifebuoy, a glorious release. I hoped all she had read
on my face was annoyance.

"That's better," I said after I shut the window and my heart was
no longer thumping as I sat down again. "You mentioned Julian
Leclerc. I was very sorry to read about it in the papers. . . . A week
ago, wasn't it?" I added, and immediately felt that my voice was
false, that I was hamming it. I was looking at the desk, trying to
avoid her eyes, and a sudden fear made my heart thump again. My
throat was dry. "I hadn't seen him for a very long time," I said.

"Then I was wrong." Her words came fast and loud with childish bitterness and I saw at once that she noticed nothing unusual
about me, that her embarrassment was greater than mine. "I
thought you were his doctor. . . ." She was blushing in confusion.
"But you *did* know him," she said, almost imploringly. "You did
know him, didn't you?"

"Oh, yes," I said, but my voice seemed too loud with relief. "I
knew him for quite a long time. We met a few years before the
war. When we were both students, you see. . . ." I was sitting
against the light all the time; she couldn't have seen my face. "But
what gave you the idea that I knew him?" I asked. What indeed?

I thought my voice was fairly calm now, but she must have
interpreted the question as suspicion or disapproval, because like
lightning she picked up her handbag from the carpet and opened
it. She said nothing. She was trying to prove a case. She took out a
large, grey envelope and handed it to me, as if it were a passport.
The envelope had my name and address on it, and in the corner
my telephone number was scribbled in pencil. The envelope was
empty and unused.

"I found it on his desk, inside the blotting-pad," she said anxiously, like a child. "There was nothing else there, except writing
paper and some luggage labels." Her hand, a large hand, like a
man's, was trembling. She was trying to prove that the passport
was genuine. She seemed to feel inferior and almost apologetic.
"We were engaged to be married, you see. . . . This envelope was
my only hope of finding out why Julian killed himself. . . ."

"Why do you say he killed himself?" I said. It was now that I began to feel ashamed of my earlier fear, which obviously had been unjustified. "There was an open verdict, wasn't there? I read the case in the paper. An overdose of sleeping tablets. . . . If people only knew how dangerous . . ."

"Everybody thinks it must have been suicide," she interrupted. Her voice was peevish again; it was now a voice that disliked contradiction. Almost angrily, she shrugged a shoulder. "At least, *I'm* absolutely sure. They didn't ask me much at the inquest. I was so ill. But I knew how upset Julian had been in the last few days." Her voice suddenly dropped and she shook her head slowly. "I'm *sure* it was suicide. Only perhaps, out of consideration for me, he made it look like an accident. But people will talk. You can imagine how I feel." I saw her chest rising. "We were in love, about to decide the date of our wedding, then he suddenly kills himself. . . . And it was in *every* paper. . . ." She began to sob.

She looked quite ugly now with the tears streaming down her face, and I saw for the first time that her skin was not too good. I rose and offered her my handkerchief, but she shook her head and reached for her handbag. "I'm sorry," she said.

"What on earth for?" I asked. Partly from habit, I placed a hand on her shoulder. Her shoulders were padded.

I think we both felt relieved. "I've made such an exhibition of myself," she said, explaining the obvious. "But I just couldn't help it."

"Exhibition," I said. "Come now. . . . Nothing could be more natural." She said nothing, but dabbed her eyes; I noticed that her eyelids were already pink. "I'm not only a doctor, but a psychiatrist. Everybody who comes here has some trouble. . . ."

"My first idea," she said staring at the damp handkerchief in her hand, "was that you were an ordinary doctor. You know . . ." After a moment's glance at the ceiling, she found the word she wanted: "I mean, a family doctor. I thought perhaps Julian was ill." For the first time I was conscious that the barrel organ was no longer playing outside.

"It just doesn't make sense," she said. "I mean, why did he want to contact you? Had he written to you before?"

"Never," I said, but as I walked back to my chair I felt somehow that my answer was unconvincing, although it was true. Julian had never written to me. I picked up the envelope. "This, I take it, is his handwriting?" It was large, with the capitals printed. I knew much less about handwriting than I ought to have known.

"Yes."

"Did he ever mention my name to you?" I said.

"No."

"There was no reason for him to have done so," I said. "The last time I saw him was about a year or so ago. Quite a chance meeting. At the Underground station at Hyde Park Corner." I remembered the occasion. Julian had said he would come and see me "one of these days." "Professionally." But I decided I wouldn't tell her that. In any case, he might have been joking. "It was only before the war that I really used to know him," I said.

"Not since then," she nodded. It was a statement, not a question.

"Well, I met him once or twice during the war. Quite casually. I suppose he was abroad most of the time, wasn't he? I was working at a hospital in London. Not much opportunity of seeing him or anybody else. Then I went to America after the war. . . . But surely you must know a number of people who knew him really well?"

"That's just the point. I don't." She shook her head helplessly. "I tried to think of people all day yesterday. His father's had a nervous breakdown. He lives in the country. Julian's mother has married again and lives in Kenya. There's only his partner, Peter Mohill. . . . Perhaps you know that Julian was a solicitor. . . . Mr. Mohill was extremely kind to me; he helped me during the inquest; told me there would be hardly any questions. He was there when the police looked through Julian's things. But they found nothing except the sleeping pills. The jar was empty. . . . Peter gave me lunch afterwards, but it turned out that even he knew next to nothing about Julian. Or that's what he said." She shook her head. "Maybe he knows much more than he wanted to tell me. . . ." Suddenly she looked up. "I say, do you know Roger Temple?"

"No. Who's he?"

"He was in the Guards with Julian. They are neighbours of ours."

I was more interested at the moment in Mohill.

"Why did you think Mohill knew more than he would tell you?" I asked.

"Oh, it was just a feeling." She raised a hand slightly, and her thumb became curiously eloquent. "Maybe I'm wrong. I'm quite often wrong in my feelings. But sometimes, you know . . ."

"You hadn't known Julian long, had you?" I said.

"I suppose not," she spoke quietly now. "Actually, we'd known each other for about six months, but I always felt as if I'd known him a long time. Once or twice, in the early days, I told him that. He said he felt the same way about me. And it was true. I knew it was true." She was looking at the floor. "I feel I knew him quite well. At least, that's what I used to feel. It's only now . . . I mean, it's so awful to know that Julian had no intimate friends; at least I've never met any, because there's no one I can talk to about him. I can't find out about him from anybody." She was looking straight at me now. "Julian knew dozens of people. He was very popular. But he had no real friends. . . ."

"Perhaps he didn't need them." I said. "And if he was in love with you . . ."

"Maybe." She suddenly looked away, but she didn't say what I expected. "My parents want me to go back to the country or to go away for a time. My mother has rung me up four times since Monday, but I can't rest till I find out what happened. I must know." She shook her head. "Even if the evidence damns me in the end. . . ."

"What do you mean," I said. It was an alarming decision, but this time I felt I was in full control of the situation.

"I have a dreadful feeling that it must have been partly my fault. Something in me that came between us. . . ."

"Why do you say that?"

"Because I'm more than certain there was another woman."

I saw that she was watching my face when she said that, and she noticed my surprise, but I was confident that she didn't know what it was that surprised me.

"Another woman?" I said.

"Yes. And if that's so, it must have been my fault. . . ." She broke off abruptly. I was about to say, "What makes you think so?" when she spoke. "I really don't know why I'm telling you all this . . . the more so because you didn't know Julian well. . . ." She had been addressing the carpet.

"I can tell you why," I said. I spoke fast. I mustn't allow her to go now. "Because you simply must tell someone. It would be unnatural if you didn't talk about it. And . . . there are situations in life about which it is easier to talk to strangers. . . ."

How often I had employed that cliché—how often! I had first used it at school, the precocious child I had been. But all the same I knew that I was not "just a stranger", but a "particular" stranger to whom people talked without reserve, and in whom they confided at once. I had known that practically all through my life. This was, I suppose, what was known as a "social asset"; about my only one. It had great value in my profession, I carried it like a skeleton key. But I had had it all my life. Perhaps it was my enormous curiosity about people, their minds, their actions and motives, that some-how luckily conditioned my behaviour and, in the end, perhaps even my voice and looks.

"You see," Miss Hewitt said—and I wasn't quite sure whether she had heard and understood me—"like Julian, I have very few friends. . . ."

I nodded. It was a sympathetic nod, I saw to that—an approving nod, a bedside nod, if you like. Her statement, in so far as it concerned Julian, was completely untrue. Julian had a wide circle of friends, acquaintances, and admirers, even though, for a very good reason, he had kept this fact a secret from her. I imagined, however, that she herself didn't make friends easily.

She was now fumbling in her bag and took out a leather ciga-rette case. "Want one?" she said.

"You have one of mine," I said. I pushed the box towards her. "I've smoked too much today already."

"Dr. Page," she said. "You said you were a psychiatrist. . . . That's not why I came to see you in the first place."

"I am." I was feeling my own warmth. This was better than I had expected.

For a moment she was silent; then she looked away, and, raising her voice a little, "Could you please give me treatment?" she asked. "As a private patient, I mean. I'm on the verge of a nervous break-down. Perhaps I have one already. . . . I feel awful. . . . And I don't know any doctors, except our own in the country, and he wouldn't understand. . . . I know it's expensive." She suddenly looked at me. "Treatment, I mean. But I can easily afford it." Abruptly she looked round the room as if to indicate that she could easily afford me. It was a simple room that contained just a few pieces of furniture I had bought after the war. Instead of the close-fitted grey Wilton I had always wanted, it had a shabby Indian carpet, and the steel filing cabinet was an eyesore. She ignored my only two worthwhile things: the Rouault drawing above the mantelpiece and the Chinese horse below it. There was a purse-proudness in her brief stocktaking and a slight ring of the cash register in the words "I can easily afford it", but I knew it was sheer despair. She was trying to use the one single weapon she had. "Will you take me on?"

"Well, of course," I said and immediately I saw the relief on her face. "Mind you," I continued, trying not to show how pleased I was that she had saved me all the trouble, "I don't know if there's much need for treatment. You are at present in a nervous state. But everybody would be under the circumstances. I'm not sure you are on the verge of a . . . nervous breakdown, but in any case I shall be glad if I can help you."

"You see, I can't talk about this to anybody else," she said. That was her way, I thought, of saying "Thank you". "When I had lunch with Mr. Mohill, I naturally didn't even hint at the idea that there may have been another woman, or anything like that. I mean, he either wouldn't have believed me, or he wouldn't have told me if he knew. And I couldn't possibly talk about my suspicions to Julian's father, even if I could get to see him. Or to my own parents. . . . In fact, it would be awful if they found out. . . ."

"But why do you think there was another woman?"

She reached for her handbag again and took out a sheet of yellow writing paper. "You won't tell anybody?" she said, clutching the paper like a schoolgirl.

"How could I? For one thing, I'm supposed to be your doctor. . . ."

"I'm sorry." She handed me the letter, which I read.

"Where did you find this?" I asked. I made no other comment.

"It was in the blotting-pad on his desk." At first she tried to avoid my glance, but now she was looking at me. "Yesterday morning . . ." She shook her head. This was obviously a habit of hers. "I wish I hadn't looked. But one is . . ."

"The most natural thing," I said.

"You have to agree it's very painful." She made an impatient gesture towards the letter. "I mean, the writing. It's uneducated. And there's a spelling mistake, I think. The whole thing is so vulgar. And her name. Gina. Italian, or God knows what. A waitress. . . ."

"It may not mean a thing," I said. "Just because she speaks of 'good times we had'. Completely meaningless words. Besides"—I raised the yellow sheet in the air—"they may refer to a time when Julian didn't know you. After all, there's no date on it. It may have been written a long time ago. During the war . . . years ago. . . ."

It was amazing how cool I was, how very cool, because now I was no longer thinking of the letter and the things it really conveyed to me or of the pretence I had been keeping up. Pretence was easy for a man like me, it was second nature; a great necessity, sometimes a lifeline and always self-defence. I was thinking of the young woman facing me. I found myself wondering how people could have behaved in a crisis before cinema-going became a habit. Everything Miss Hewitt said, every intake of breath, every modulation of her voice, every gesture seemed to have been conditioned by the screen. Her feelings were genuine, the problem was genuine and so were the pain, the burning doubt and the shame, and yet her emotions found expression in the manner of a talented amateur imitating her favourite film star.

"If so, why did Julian keep it?" she asked now.

"Just by chance. It may have been in the blotting-pad for years and years. You didn't find anything else?"

"I didn't look very thoroughly. I . . ." Here she broke off abruptly. "In any case, you'll help me, won't you?"

"I shall do what I can."

"Did you know anybody who knew Julian?" she said. "Mutual friends."

I had to say something quickly now. "Let me see," I said and I felt I was hamming it. "I think I know one or two. I haven't seen them for a long time, but I can try to contact them. . . . In any case," I said, changing the subject, "I shall try to give you some sort of treatment. You haven't been sleeping well lately, have you?"

"Well, the first two nights I didn't sleep at all, and since then . . ."

"I know," I said. "I shall give you a prescription for a harmless draught." I took a sheet of notepaper and decided that one grain of Persomnia was about her dose, then I printed my name above the address. Since I write very few prescriptions, I always used my private notepaper. "Here you are," I said, and pushed the sheet of paper across the table. "I should like to ask you a few questions."

"What would you like me to tell you?"

"You said you saw Julian the night before he died."

"Yes. Last Thursday."

"And he was very upset."

"Well, it's difficult to say. He had been very upset the last few weeks, but not on the last evening. In fact, he was very sweet. Or perhaps he was just acting, I don't know. . . . I think so. We had dinner at the Berkeley. He ordered champagne and we danced; then we went home. I asked him to come in, but he said he had to get up very early the next day. So I gave him a lift to his place. Then he said something, which, looking back on it, was very significant. He said 'Thank you for a very lovely evening'. He'd never said that before." She shook her head. "At least never the way he said it that night. Then he kissed me. . . ." She was looking at the floor again. "It was a very strange kiss," she said. "He gripped me by both shoulders so much that it almost hurt me. Thinking back on it, he must have felt like crying." She shook her head. "A man crying. Then he suddenly turned round, opened the door of the taxi and got out. He slammed the door, didn't give my address to the driver and ran up the stairs. I had no time to think much because the taxi-driver pushed the glass back and asked me where I wanted to go. I told him, but as he drove me home I felt Julian had behaved in an odd way. But that was all. I wasn't really upset, because he'd been so nice during the evening. I thought he was getting over the trouble he'd had the last couple of weeks. When I got home I noticed he'd bruised my lip." She paused for a few seconds and I avoided her glance on purpose. Suddenly she said, "If only I could get myself to go to a detective agency," she said. "I've been think-ing about it the last two days."

"It would be worse than useless," I shouted; then I took a grip on myself. "Worse than useless. They charge you fantastic sums and can't find out anything. For one thing, you can't investigate things when the man is dead. You can't follow him and the clues you have are insufficient. Besides, I shall try to find out what I can for you. And I can do it as well as a detective."

"I wish I had really gone through his desk," she said. "Look." She suddenly raised her head and I noticed again that she had no lipstick on. "I have the key to Julian's room. The caretaker gave it to me. He thought I was a relation. Could you very kindly come with me some time and look through it?"

"I think *I* ought to go," I said, "but not you. You must not go there any more."

"Perhaps you are right." She shrugged a shoulder like a little girl who has been told off, and I began to feel where I was with her. "The address is sixteen Hans Terrace. It's just behind Harrods. Julian's flat is on the ground floor at the end of the passage as you go in. Nobody would notice you. The front door is always open and the caretaker's usually out in the morning." It was clear that she was now trying to persuade me, not even guessing that I needed no persuasion, that on the contrary I would have tried my very best to persuade her to give me the key. "Besides, should anybody notice you, you could always say you went to fetch a photograph for me. . . . Incidentally," she gave a little sigh, "I really want my photograph back. It's on the mantelpiece. In a brown leather frame. Could you please bring it back." There came a pause. She added: "Only please take it out of the frame and leave the frame there. . . . Could you kindly do that . . . ?"

Was she already trying to get rid of Julian's memory while consciously trying to find out why he had died? 'And leave the frame there', that was almost a conclusive indication. It was not just a sense of propriety. It seemed she didn't want anything to remind her of him.

"How are you feeling now?" I said a little later.

"A lot better than when I came in, but of course . . ."

"I know. But don't worry. You will be all right." I almost added: "sooner than you'd imagine."

"When can I come to see you again?"

I looked at the engagement book, though I knew more or less

precisely what engagements I had in the next few days, now that my lectures were over. "I'd better telephone you in a day or two."

She wrote her telephone number on a visiting card which said *Mrs. Herbert Hewitt*, and under it *Miss Hewitt*, and the address in Hampshire; a visiting card which I thought had gone out with the war.

II

"Dinner's ready," Terry said a little later. It was some time before I realised that he was now wearing a cowboy shirt of red-and-green checks.

"How much?" I asked, pointing to the shirt.

"Thirty-two and six." He sensed I was feeling troubled and that I was just making conversation. He washed his hands at the sink, then replaced his watch on his wrist.

"I couldn't get decent mushrooms," he said quietly as he served the soup. "This is tinned."

"I'm feeling rather tired," I told him a moment later.

"So you don't want to go to the Odeon tonight?"

"If you don't mind, Terry. You go. You don't mind going on your own, do you?"

"Well," he said, a little confusedly, and I remembered at once it was I who had suggested we ought to go to see that particular film.

"You'll tell me all about it," I said.

He continued to smile shyly, but a sudden look of alarm crossed his face. "You're not ill or anything?" he asked me. He pushed back his chair, walked over and put his hand on my forehead; the smell of washing soap came to my nostrils.

"No," I said. "Just a little overworked. I didn't sleep too well last night. . . ." This was untrue, but I hoped it sounded convincing. I liked Terry very much and trusted him more than I did most people, but it was important that he should not know what was worrying me. "How brown your arms are," I said.

"I peeled very little this year," he replied. He went back to his chair.

"Did you go to the Serpentine today?" I asked.

"For about an hour. There wasn't much sun."

"Many people?"

"The usual crowd. Mostly men who have night jobs."

"We must go there again one day," I said. "Only the water's so dirty."

III

I refused coffee and returned to the consulting-room, where it was quiet and rather stuffy. I opened the window and stood by it for a time. This was an occasion when I was feeling in need of a friend, but no friend existed. When it came to a personal crisis, one usually found oneself alone. This is what I usually said to people, but it was only true in relation to people like myself. I couldn't say anything to Terry, not only because I was alarmed, but rather because Miss Hewitt's visit had provoked in me a mad mixture of emotions, of which alarm or fear was only one constituent. There was curiosity, a sense of shock, a sense of shame for a childish anger, which I had thought I had forgotten some time ago, and—most important of all—a sense of shame for the original cause of that anger. It was love—love which I had long forgotten.

Love, I thought, and a vicious circle suddenly closed. I was alone because I was almost incapable of love, because I was suffering from a stunted heart; not a disease, a condition, and fairly common. I knew how common. I had a well-developed body, a well-developed mind, but my heart was small and stunted.

I could be good, understanding, charitable, helpful, that was my reputation, I knew. Considering the man I was, it was surprising how few people I hated. I could also be brave, there was no doubt about that. On certain occasions, it seemed, I had been almost insanely reckless—when it came to sex, to be precise—but when it came to love, I suppose I had been a coward. This had all started long ago, of course, and in later years cowardice had become "reasonable precaution". I presume I had learnt to live without love. I didn't miss it. I felt, in fact, that its absence gave me strength. To admit one's weakness was a sign of weakness. Now, I wasn't so sure, and I felt the need for a friend.

Yes, I suppose, I could have discussed things with Terry. The story was complex and madly incoherent, but Terry might have understood. He wasn't intellectual, but he felt deeply and instinctively, and might even have helped. In fact, I owed him some confidence. He had told me all about himself: private and intimate things. And I had told him nothing about myself, beyond a series of vague commonplaces. Did Terry feel in his own way how mean I was? Perhaps not. But I knew all the time that, if I really revealed myself to him, he would discover how confused, weak and frightened I was, and it might destroy his respect for me; a respect I needed, because I liked him.

I heard his footsteps along the passage and the sound of the front door shutting behind him. I turned round.

In front of me on the desk was the letter on the thick, yellow notepaper, and the key to Julian's flat. I read the letter again.

> *"The same bloody adress.*
>
> *"Dear Jul,*
>
> *"This is just a letter to say hullo and thank you again for the good time had last week. I am now back on the old job but like I said previous I shall be in Landon again in two months time look forward to see you then.*
>
> *Cheerio till then,*
>
> *your friend, Gina."*

I had formed an impression already as to the type of man who had written the letter. That it was a man was obvious from everything about it. It was obvious to me *before* I'd read it. Only one point puzzled me, the signature. It had misled Ann Hewitt and was the one thing which didn't fit in. *Gina.* He was certainly not the sort of person who might have used a woman's name as a nickname. But I was already comparing his "i's", his "n's", and his "a's", and in less than a minute I saw that the last letter was not an "a", but a distorted "g". *Ging.* So the signature was "Ging", short for "Ginger".

It was five days since I had seen the news about Julian in the paper. It had shocked and rather pained me for a moment, then a minute or two afterwards a patient had come in and I had forgotten it. But the shock had returned the same afternoon, while I was going through the notes for my final lecture. I remember that I'd closed my eyes and went back in my mind more than ten years. I suddenly saw the barber's shop in Knightsbridge, with its view over Rotten Row, and I began actually to smell the lotions, the shampoos, the damp towels. Then someone telephoned me, and while I was still on the line, my next patient arrived. Later that evening, I thought of contacting Bobby Sillock to enquire what could have happened. Bobby had known Julian well and would probably have told me all the facts, but I hadn't seen him for quite some time. That phase of my life was perhaps over; in any case lately it didn't interest me. So, I let the matter drop. I was then, as far as I can see now, far more curious than concerned.

The next day, it seems, I didn't think about Julian, but he returned to my mind while Miss Mayhew, lying on the couch, mentioned the word "suicide". "My mother often thought of suicide, you see," she said in her wooden voice. "But that was after we moved to Morden . . ." and for a moment I smelled the damp towels and heard the buzz of the electric hair-dryer in the barber's shop. Then, noticing that she was silent, I said, "Yes. Please go on, Miss Mayhew. We are getting on fine." And, until today, that was the last time I had thought of Julian.

It is difficult to know how I would have reacted later to his death had Ann Hewitt not called and brought me the envelope bearing my name and address. Of course, I should have thought about him in the days, weeks, months, even years to come, but the emotions I had felt when I first saw the news in the paper would have faded. For that matter, they had begun to fade already until Ann's visit revived them.

I thought I had successfully put aside what was troubling me, but now, after her visit, I knew that the thing was not over, in fact it was very real. I again felt the shock and the pain that had come to me five days earlier, only this time they were stronger, particularly the pain. I was curiously excited emotionally, and, for the moment, I was not feeling alarmed. What on earth could Julian have wanted from me? We hadn't seen each other for six or seven months, and then only for a couple of minutes, casually at Hyde Park Corner Tube Station.

Until today I had attributed no importance to that meeting, as, after all, I didn't know it was to be our last. But now I remember that cold morning just around Christmas when I had last seen him, hatless and without an overcoat. "How are things?" he asked. "One *has* to be well"—this was a cliché I sometimes used—"when one's dealing with so many sick people." He smiled. It was then that he said, "I'll come and see you one of these days. Professionally." Many people say things like that to psychiatrists as a joke, and I quickly replied that he would find my charges moderate.

I don't remember what he said to that, but perhaps his remark hadn't been a joke, after all.

When had we last met before that? I tried to think, but couldn't remember. It was probably just before I went to America, because after my return I seldom visited the places where, during the war, I'd occasionally bumped into him—pubs, night-clubs or parties. On those occasions we rarely spoke more than a few words. This wasn't perhaps from reserve or embarrassment, but as likely as not because we each thought the other was tied up with a different circle of friends. But we did talk, I remembered, at Bobby Sillock's party, just after the war. We were sitting together and Julian said he had heard I was a capable psychiatrist, especially with shell-shock cases. I was a little embarrassed partly because of the praise and partly because this was the first serious talk we had had in four or five years. I wondered at the time whether he remembered our first meeting, and whether he knew that he had played a more important part in my life than I in his.

I looked at the envelope again. I couldn't say when my name had been written, recently or several months ago. The fact that there was only an envelope and no letter was not necessarily difficult to explain. He may have looked me up in the telephone directory, addressed the envelope and left it on his desk to remind himself to write to me. People do that sort of thing fairly often. Then he decided to ring up instead. In that case the unknown man with the "nice voice" who had telephoned the night I had a wisdom tooth out and refused to give his name to Terry, may have been Julian.

I got up and looked through the pile of newspapers on the bookshelf. I found the one. *Solicitor Found Dead.* It was six days old, and the telephone call had been made eight days ago. It must have been Julian; I was fairly certain now. But what on earth could he have wanted? Did he want to come as a patient? Did he want me to help him in connection with some . . . well yes, perhaps, scandal? I had in mind that in certain circumstances a doctor's testimony, if he says he has been treating someone, occasionally influences a magistrate to put a man on probation instead of sending him to prison.

I lit another cigarette. These were the most likely possibilities. There couldn't have been anything else. I had to be a realist. It was no use romancing. If the situation were reversed and Julian had read of my suicide, his feelings, no doubt, would have been very different from mine. It was true, of course, that I knew my feelings about him and I didn't know his about me.

I never knew them. The most agonising thing in fact was that I knew so little about him and the time had come, now that he was dead, when I should like to have known more.

IV

In the darkness of my room I again saw the barber's shop where my mother had taken me when I was very young. I remembered the engravings and the cartoons on the walls and the special atmosphere of the place and how I used to listen to the talk of the Guards officers. The nice, elderly Jew, Mr. Studd, who is dead now, was working on the nape of my neck, and I could see the King's cousin dozing in the chair next to me.

Then I recalled the time, years later, when suddenly somebody said, quite loudly, "Hullo, Tony," and in the mirror I saw a young man in a chalkstripe flannel suit, who smiled at me. "I'm glad to see you," he said and almost collided with someone vacating a chair. He had to move. "I won't be long, Tony," he said, and waved to me as he went up to the chair by the window. This was the second time we had met, and he now called me by my Christian name. I felt curiously excited. He didn't say, "Will you wait for me?" He just said, "I won't be long." I decided to wait and tried to think hard and even anxiously of his Christian name. What did they call him, the Pooles at whose house we had met some three weeks earlier? His surname, I knew was Leclerc.

I thought back on our earlier meeting. It was at a lunch party somewhere near Regent's Park, given by Mrs. Poole for her daughter Delia, but we stayed on till tea. There were Martin and Delia Poole, then two girls I didn't know, a funny-looking young man in black jacket and striped trousers, and another young man who stammered and talked about skating. Then there was Leclerc, wearing the same smart grey flannel suit. Because there were more boys than girls, I was seated next to him, and we talked nearly all through lunch. He was a couple of years younger than I, about nineteen, and I noticed he had a tiny impediment in his speech, as if he had a small lozenge in his mouth, but I felt it suited him. When he laughed, he showed all his teeth, which were very white. He was a likeable person, and I somehow felt I was impressing him. I impressed very few people in those days.

"Will you be requiring anything, sir? Brilliantine, razor blades, shampoo?" Mr. Studd was speaking discreetly in a dubious undertone as if offering hashish, opium, cocaine. I said no, and he wrote out the bill. After I'd paid at the cash desk, I sat down on a chair behind the King's cousin, who was now awake and talking at the top of his voice to M. Philippe about a horse. I looked through the illustrated paper. There were photographs of people I had never known and never shall. I read the review of a new play, then I heard the assistant say, "Thank you, sir," and Leclerc came over. We walked out into the warm afternoon.

"I wanted to contact you," he said, "but Delia didn't know your address and Martin's away. I thought you might have liked to come down to our Commem Ball. You could have stayed with me in College. It was quite fun. . . . Are you doing anything this afternoon?" he asked.

Well, a medical student is always doing something while other students are on vacation, and I hadn't done well lately, especially in pathology. Moreover, my finals were not too far away, but it was Friday and an exceptionally beautiful day, and I liked Leclerc's company even if I didn't know his Christian name. "Nothing in particular," I answered.

"It's such a glorious day and I have a car. I thought it would be a good idea to drive down to the river and have a bathe. Would you like to come?"

"That would be grand," I said. "Thank you very much."

Leclerc's car was an old red sports affair, that made a lot of noise; I later discovered he had borrowed it from one of his Oxford friends. We collected bathing trunks and towels on the way and left for the riverside. We hardly talked till we reached Olympia. I didn't know whether I envied or admired his maturity. Although two years my junior, he was so much more decided, so much more adult, sure of himself and such a good driver. Like many people at the age I then was, I felt Leclerc had achieved far more than I had.

He asked me if I saw many plays and said he was very keen on the theatre. At Oxford he was more interested in the Dramatic Society than in his studies. He wanted to be an actor, but of course his father wouldn't hear of it. His father was in the Army and wanted him to be a soldier, but somehow gave way and allowed him to go to Oxford instead of Sandhurst. We came to Hammersmith Bridge and suddenly, with excitement, I remembered that his Christian name was Julian. I decided I must show him that I, too, knew *his* first name. The opportunity soon came.

"You spent some time in Germany," he said, and again I was rather thrilled. It was obviously the Pooles who had told him. So they had been discussing me.

"I was partly educated there, Julian." I had said it. "At a co-educational school in Wuerttenberg," I added. I decided not to tell him yet that my mother was Swiss or why I wasn't sent to a school in England, except for two years.

"So much the better for you," Julian said; "I wish they hadn't sent me to Harrow of all places."

"I've just read somewhere that half the Cabinet went to Harrow."

"And nearly all of them sent their sons to Eton," Julian laughed. "But frankly, English education makes you so narrow. . . . I wish I could speak German. . . . I suppose you can pass for a German in Germany."

"I think so," I said.

We changed in the car. It was still very warm when we entered the water. Both of us were very white. I noticed that Julian was trying to show off a little and I was pleased. The current was unexpectedly strong, but we got across, and he couldn't beat me.

"You're a good swimmer," I said with the generosity I felt I could easily afford.

"Coming from you . . ." Julian said. He laughed, I thought, a little uneasily. "You have a swimmer's long muscles."

"I've been swimming practically all my life," I said. "We used to live on the river when I was a child."

"D'you play tennis?"

"So-so. I haven't played for ages and I get so little chance. I sometimes play squash when I have the time. We have a very good squash court in the hospital."

We swam across again, then we allowed the river to carry us downstream a bit. A pleasure steamer passed and rocked the waters. It was suddenly cooler now, and a few minutes later we got out and walked back to the car.

"Shall we go to Maidenhead for dinner?"

"Yes," I said. It was obvious I wouldn't be doing any work today. Perhaps it was better. I should have a clear head tomorrow.

We went to a riverside restaurant that was fairly empty. Towards the end of dinner a swarm of mosquitoes began to play around the lamps.

"They eat you alive in Venice," Julian said. "You have to sleep under nets."

I hadn't yet been to Venice then. I said: "They carry all sorts of diseases. Malaria."

After dinner there was an argument as to who would pay the bill. "Please let me pay my share," I said.

"Certainly not. It's my party," he insisted.

"But you provided the transport." I was thinking fast of possible arguments. "I'm older," I said, a little stupidly.

"Oh, cut out the prep. school stuff," he said, and grabbed the bill.

We talked continually as we drove back. He asked me if I went to many dances; I said no, and he changed the subject. He asked me about Germany. Whether I had been to Berlin. He said he had heard so much about it. Then we talked of Reinhardt. I told him I'd seen one or two of his productions in England and I said my mother knew Reinhardt's wife. Then we talked of doctors who became playwrights and novelists. Then the subject changed to

Germany again. He said he had made up his mind to take German lessons.

I reflected as we drove through Kensington that I would suggest we went to a play together some time the following week. He was pleasantly unlike most of the people I knew, who were largely medical students. I somehow felt we were in many respects similar, even in looks perhaps, in spite of the two years' difference between us. Knightsbridge Barracks came into view. He suddenly said: "It's very early yet. Would you like to come up and have a drink? I can drive you home afterwards."

We climbed the stairs of a block of flats near the French Embassy. There was a smell as we entered the sitting-room, a smell I knew, a pleasant and impressive smell even though it was a little stale. I had no name for it then, but now I call it "Country Gentry". The sitting-room too, in the very heart of London, somehow suggested the country. It had mahogany furniture and a couple of old paintings: family portraits which always look more exciting if the lighting in the room is insufficient. "My people went away for the week-end this afternoon," he said. "I stayed on because there's a dance tonight. But I'm glad I met you. You really don't care for dancing?"

"Well, I haven't much time, for one thing. . . ."

Julian opened the cabinet and asked what I wanted to drink. I said whisky. I was getting more and more conscious of the smell in the room. It took me to an unfamiliar landscape where I felt instinctively at home. One window was open and it looked on the courtyard, beyond which, judging by the traffic sounds, must have been Hyde Park. The grey muslin curtains were still, and it was rather warm. I drank my whisky standing.

"You're six foot one," Julian said when we were having our second drink.

"So are you," I said.

"I don't know if I'm dizzy or dreaming, Tony, but I feel we are very much alike. I don't mean brains, because you're clearly superior, but looks. We might pass for brothers." He finished his drink.

"Well, that's precisely what I've been thinking on the way back. Except . . ." I said all that very fast, and now I couldn't continue, I couldn't tell him what I had felt. It was stupid and embarrassing.

"I know," Julian said. "I don't mind. You happen to be good-looking."

"Certainly not," I said, and I felt my laughter was forced, because, if anything, I thought he was far better looking than I. But Julian was already standing by me and my heart began to pound violently, because I was suddenly aware of some special and intimate bond between us. I had never previously had this feeling, except perhaps in my dreams, but I knew that this time I was not dreaming and that dreams sometimes come true. I couldn't fight against it and I didn't wish to. Perhaps sensing my embarrassment Julian put his arm across my shoulder, as if to reassure me. I heard his wrist watch ticking at the back of my neck. As I turned round, I realised that his face, like mine, was hot. He hadn't begun to shave yet.

"Did you know?" Julian said quietly, but he said that much later, or so it seemed to me. I was then sitting in an armchair. He was on the arm. Neither of us dared to look at the other.

"Yes," I said.

It was many, many months later that I understood what Julian had meant when he asked me that question, and the answer was no. I merely said yes because I felt he wanted me to. After that we were silent for quite a time. My mind was in a turmoil. It was wrong, the whole thing was wrong. Perhaps not so wrong as funny, yes, it was really funny and ridiculous. Then I suddenly caught his eye and thought again that he was far more adult at nineteen that I at twenty-one, far more mature, daring, brave, independent. And there was not the slightest doubt about it, he was better looking than I was, and now I felt he didn't realise it, and that made it even better.

But later, after Julian had driven me back to my room, I didn't feel it was wrong. I had no guilt, no doubts, no uneasiness. In fact I felt a curious sense of release. I felt I had suddenly grown up. Until quite recently, even a month or two earlier, the thought of my own virginity had impressed me. This was not connected with religion, for I didn't then believe. Not even with the fact that I had seen so many syphilitic ulcers in hospital. Perhaps it was because I had developed slowly or because of my desire to get on in the world. I had very little money and I wanted to make a career. I had no emotional interests, and consequently I had no envy of fellow students who had affairs with nurses or waitresses. In fact I looked down on them. They usually failed at examinations, they had no culture, no class; they were inferior. One was "nice" to them, of course.

Looking back on it—as I did often enough—my emotional life was unusually retarded. I grew up when I was twenty-one, suddenly, and the process of maturity after I met Julian came very fast. I had no more dreams, no debates, no internal arguments. At one time, when I was fifteen, I had formed a sentimental attachment for a boy I had known in Stuttgart, and the memory of it had made me a little uneasy from time to time. After I met Julian it vanished for ever.

The next morning I felt a different man. I went to the hospital fairly early and I was pleased that nobody noticed I hadn't been there the previous day. When I talked to the other students, I had an almost irresistible impulse to tell them what had happened the night before. Then I looked up the number in the directory and rang Julian. I asked him to lunch and afterwards we drove out again.

That summer Julian and I saw quite a lot of each other. He took me to the river and the sea and I gave him squash lessons. A few times we went to the theatre and one evening he took me to dinner with a friend, a stockbroker who had a very attractive flat off Park Lane and who said an affair like ours was the most beautiful thing on earth. He was some ten years our senior and I forgot what his name was and haven't seen him since. Then I met another friend at a dance, Hugh Harpley, who made me laugh.

Once Julian asked me to spend the week-end at his parents' house in the country. It was near Ware in Hertfordshire. I met his father and stepmother. He was rather gruff and she kindly and stupid. I believe Mrs. Leclerc died suddenly during the war. The house had exactly the same smell as the flat in Knightsbridge and there was, I felt, something intriguingly sinister about the red walls, the dark passages, the trees outside and a strange picture in the dining-room. At that time I knew nothing about Fuseli and his school, nor were the nightmare painters as fashionable as they are now. "We brought it over from Ireland," Colonel Leclerc said.

He was a spare man, a few inches shorter than us and not a bit like Julian. He had thin lips and a frowning expression. I imagined he was short-tempered. It may have been his leg, of course, for I noticed that he walked with a slight limp; rheumatism, or a war wound?

Julian had already told me that his mother had run away from his father, and I then told Julian that my parents too had been divorced, except that my father hadn't remarried and my mother was dead.

Then with the summer our affair was over. Julian went back to Oxford and later I heard that he was all the time in the company of a new friend, a Canadian who was very good at athletics. By that time I was in love with Julian, but I only realised it when he left me. I was badly hurt and one evening I cried, but soon afterwards my father came to London, took a flat in Earl's Court and I went to live with him.

In those days I took a violent dislike to Julian and to love-life in general, and my reaction to being thrown over was to concentrate on my studies. As a result, I passed out well. It was, I was sure, partly due to Julian that I decided to specialise in psychology after I qualified. But I am not sure whether my resentment towards him was the cause of the violent reversal which took place in my emotional life. I soon began to look back on the whole business with Julian with nausea, and I decided to be "normal". I had an affair first with a girl student, then with the secretary of one of my professors. I enjoyed sex with them, I was quite proud of this, but they couldn't stimulate my mind, nor was I capable of loving them. But this was not because they were women.

Then my resentment against Julian began to fade with the years. The war came just when I qualified and through a lucky chance Howard Weblen took an interest in me and I began to work at his clinic at St. Gabriel's. He even secured my exemption from the Army.

My father was killed in the second year of the war, and immediately after I became "Abnormal" again. This second change in me was due to many circumstances. For one thing when I had been psycho-analysed by Pollner at the hospital, it transpired—as I already knew—that I was bisexual. For another there was my father's death, which—among many other things—meant that I no longer had any fear of being discovered by him, and finally there was the revolutionary climate of the war. There were many people into whose emotional life the war had brought a violent change. In many ways war meant freedom. The fears of peacetime gave way to more actual and threatening fears.

At that time I was involved with the professor's secretary, and she gave me up. "You only want one thing," she said and it was perfectly true. A month or two later I was introduced to a young actor and we started an affair. It was not satisfactory and soon came to its end. Then at Marble Arch I met a Serviceman, who was stationed near London. I liked him very much. And his matter-of-factness was as shocking as it was fascinating; perhaps he wasn't an invert. I never found out, because a few months later he was posted away.

I began to drift after that. Little by little I became as promiscuous as others were. For close on three years I seemed to be making up for my long virginity, for the discipline of my student years. It was a new freedom for me. I became a member of the "underground", which in wartime London came as near the surface as perhaps it had ever before come in the course of English history. I became the habitué of certain pubs, certain night-clubs, got invited to certain parties. I had no less than fifteen affairs in three years.

Immediately after the war I went to America and spent a year working at a New York hospital. To say that America had a decisive influence on me morally would be untrue. The change in me had perhaps more to do with time than with place. It happened that while in America I had reached a certain point in my life where I had to take stock of myself. The underground was almost as close to the surface, in New York at least, as in London, but the atmosphere towards it was far less tolerant. In any case the war was over and the uncertainties were as different now as the dangers. I was also very interested in my work, which I found absorbing.

But all this may have had little to do with it. I happened to be in America when I suddenly began to feel the necessity for religion. It was strange, for there was apparently nothing unusual among the things that had happened to me to have provoked it. There was no hard blow, no miraculous escape, no particular revelation. It just came out of the blue, overnight as it were and without apparent reason. It happened, of all places, on the Lexington Express as I was going home. I had never denied the existence of God, but I had taken little interest in the polite social rituals of the Church in which I had been brought up. But that night in the empty coach as the train was speeding nervously towards Grand Central, I began to feel strongly that there was a Divine Order, and because I acquired a belief, I acquired a stronger moral sense too. Protestant morals, among which I had grown up, were a little harsh; the Catholics were somehow more human. I felt this perhaps because a Catholic priest once told me that they never took such a serious view of a homosexual affair as they took of adultery between a man and a woman. It was, of course, immoral just the same; a sin. Then I began to argue. If God had made me—and I believed that he had—then there could be no objection if I tried to be happy according to my own nature. This was an old line, a very old line and a half-truth. Finally, I arrived at a conclusion. There was no sacred love and profane love; there was only one love, and it was sacred. And as long as one loved and shared and cherished, the object of love was immaterial.

I brought this change in my emotional make-up back with me to England. After my return I received a few invitations to parties. Out of boredom I visited the old haunts and some new ones. I found the parties dull and strained and the pubs sordid and un-interesting. If I had found somebody with whom I could have fallen in love and settled down, I should perhaps have been happier, but I didn't. I decided it was my fault: perhaps I gave all my sympathy to patients. Besides, I was very busy now. Weblen wanted me to assist him with his lectures at St. Gabriel's and he helped me to build up a private practice.

I took a flat in Kensington and looked round for a woman who could act as a receptionist and do the cooking also. Just after I had placed an advertisement in the paper, the registrar at the hospital recommended Terry. Terry had been a male nurse from Stockton-on-Tees, who had been working for some time at St. Gabriel's and wanted private employment. A meeting was arranged. I recognised him as someone I had seen in the hospital quite often, a nice, even-tempered young man of twenty-five, serious, reliable. I had been thinking of a woman, but decided on the spot. That

Terry was an invert was fairly clear to me at once, and this was an advantage. I felt that my withdrawal from the underground was temporary. The invert who abstains from sex is a well-known type; some say that one in every five are that way, but I didn't know if I was really one of them. One evening I might bring somebody back with me, and this wouldn't embarrass Terry.

As it happened, I brought nobody back for the whole of the following year.

Terry was the pleasant housewife type. He had known what he was since early childhood and accepted it. He was cheerful, hardworking and tidy, and not in the least neurotic.

Terry and I had few discussions about our private lives. Little by little he told me about his early years, a touching story charmingly and intimately related. I felt I ought to have told him more about myself. Actually I didn't, but as it happened there was no need. Terry had a rare gift of intuition and sometimes I felt certain that he knew how I felt at given moments. I rather thought he had had no affair with anyone since he had come to live in my flat. He had few friends, all of them normal, and he seldom saw them. His life was work: cooking, mending, sewing, the patients, the theatre and physical exercise. He was quite a good swimmer and he soon took to weight-lifting three nights a week.

V

Terry opened the door. "May I come in?" he said.

"Do."

"How do you feel?"

"Much better," I said. "How was the film?"

"Oh," he smiled gently, "a little sad." I noticed he wore his brown corduroy jacket over the check shirt I disliked. "But you may like to see it. It goes the other side of the river next week."

I remembered it was a film version of Stendhal's *The Scarlet and the Black*, which I wanted to see, just out of morbid curiosity. Stendhal via Metro-Goldwyn! But then it could have been ruined even by a French company. "Somewhere there," I pointed to the bookshelves, "I've got the novel, if you want to read it."

"I'll take it tomorrow," Terry said. "Do you want a glass of hot milk before you go to bed?"

"No, thank you," I said.

"Well, good night."

"Good night, Terry."

I saw the letter, the key and the envelope on my desk and I knew I would not sleep easily, apart from the fact that it was a warm night. Tomorrow morning I should go to Julian's flat and look over it. I ought to have gone tonight, except that it was rather late; more people were likely to be at home, and I might have been seen.

It was a quarter past eleven. I got up and went to the bathroom. The point was that, when all was said and done, I knew little about Julian. Since our affair I had seen him perhaps a dozen times in all. The first of these meetings stood out. It was one evening during the first year of the war when we suddenly confronted each other at the *Cambridge Surprise*, a Soho pub with a reputation. Julian gave me a pleasant nod. This was our first meeting in three years. He was in battle-dress, having a drink with a sailor, and expressed no surprise at seeing me there. It was clear that Julian didn't know that at that time I was still something like an outsider, an outsider at least in Soho pubs with a reputation. It was also clear that Julian didn't realise that between our affair and about a month or two before we saw each other at the *Cambridge Surprise*, I had been having affairs with women. A few minutes later he disappeared with the sailor. Though I needed guidance in the underground, I felt it was perhaps better I should find someone else, and soon enough I met Bobby Sillock, who told me all there was to be known.

I took a sleeping pill after I had brushed my teeth.

Two

To get into Julian's place was as easy as Ann had told me. It was in a private house which after the First World War had been turned into flats. The front door was open and I could at once see the white door at the end of the passage. I walked past the shiny wooden board which said that Captain W. Maxwell, R.N., was in, Mrs. H. T. Milman out, Mrs. E. Probyn out, Mr. N. J. Leclerc in. It was a place where one would seldom meet anybody in the passage or on the stairs, and it was clear to me why Julian should have chosen to live in a quiet, semi-deserted house full of widows and retired Service people.

There was just a bed-sitting room, a bathroom and a kitchen, and as I went in I saw that the window looked on to the backs of other houses.

The first thing I noticed was the white Edwardian rococo mantelpiece with Ann Hewitt's photograph in a brown tooled-leather frame. It was obvious that the room had been tidied up. The divan bed, in which Julian had been found dead by the charwoman, was made, and the red metal waste-paper basket with the hunting scene on it was empty. But there was already a little dust on the writing desk.

The walls were shiny and light green and quite bare except for two Cecil Aldin reproductions and a crayon drawing of Julian in Army uniform. If it had not been in his room I wouldn't have recognised it as Julian, except perhaps for his eyes. The room gave a masculine impression in negative good taste, extremely English and genteel, without the very slightest suggestion of Julian's emotional life. The furniture was his and it seemed as if most of the pieces might have originally been in his rooms at Oxford. The only really "good" thing in the place was a Regency corner cupboard with a semicircular door. It contained a few bottles, most of them half empty.

There was a little dust on the old-fashioned radiogram over which stood a shiny, metal stork, the emblem of a legendary pre-war racing car. Above it hung a small miniature of Julian's mother. The resemblance was unmistakable. When he was young Julian had looked exactly like her.

Nor did the books give the slightest indication of Julian's real personality. The top row consisted almost entirely of law books, the *Oxford Dictionary* and a volume called *With Silent Friends*. On the second row there were practically all the books of G. M. Trevelyan, the second volume of the Greville Diary, a few books by Maurois and Arthur Bryant, *Cassell's French Dictionary*, the history of the Coldstream Guards. The fact that he had the one-volume Havelock Ellis and Walker's *Physiology of Sex* in the Penguin Edition, was completely meaningless; practically everybody above a certain level has read them.

People sometimes leave things in books, so I went through all of them, but the search yielded nothing beyond a telegram from his father many years old and a few notes in the law books in his own handwriting.

Nor was there anything of interest in his clothes. I examined his four suits, all slightly countrified, chalk stripe flannels and a Glenurquhart check. His black jacket and striped trousers were missing. He had probably been buried in them. There was a pre-war dinner jacket and tails, a much-worn blazer with regimental buttons, and the "British warm" which had been converted to civilian use. There were a dozen ties, including the Old Harrovian and the Brigade of Guards; the rest were all foulard with tiny, Landed Gentry patterns. I felt no embarrassment as I went through his clothes while I was searching among his private effects, and even had I not been so curious I should not have been in the slightest embarrassed. I found nothing I was looking for, but Julian was somehow still around. It was perhaps the smell in the wardrobe: his personal smell which I somehow remembered, the smell of tobacco, good soap, the perspiration of a healthy body. I noticed there was a used shirt on top of the clean ones, one that would "do" once more, a blue-and-grey check flannel. For a moment I hesitated, but then nobody could see me; I held it to my nostrils and Julian was alive once more.

But time was getting on. I went to the writing desk. There was nothing on it but an old copy of *The Spectator*, an inkstand, the blotting pad where Ann had found the envelope, and a spectacle case. I had not realised that Julian must have taken to wearing glasses. I took them out and held them in front of my eyes: they were very weak, for reading when your eyes feel tired.

There were some more law books in the drawers and copies of the *Law Journal*, a few sheets of writing paper with the embossed heading of the Guards' Club, bills, mostly paid, an invitation to a dinner party at Ranelagh, a broken-down cigarette-lighter, tennis balls, and his medals—among them the Military Cross. There was his cheque book. Electric company £2. 17. 5., Inl. Revenue £57. 10., Cash £10, Ldry £2. 13. 8., Law Journal £1. 15. 0., Harrods £18. 7. 0., P.M.G. £6. 15., Cash £15. The last entry was rent £35, obviously for a quarter, and I saw that Julian had paid his rent a week before he died. There was nothing else in the drawers.

I looked round again. The most disappointing thing so far was that I had not found an address book, which would obviously give indications, perhaps even valuable clues. It seemed quite unlikely, impossible, even sinister, that Julian had not possessed one. There is hardly an adult of a certain position in life without an address book, especially a man with Julian's fairly tidy nature. Perhaps— the idea came suddenly—he kept it in his office or in the country, though both were unlikely. Did he destroy it before he died? I saw that the fireplace was boarded up and the electric fire stood in front of it. The waste-paper basket was empty.

There are, of course, hundreds of ways of destroying an address book. And if he had destroyed it, which was very likely, what else went with it?

I knew for certain that the police hadn't taken it away. Julian's partner, the solicitor, had told Ann that the police had searched the flat in his presence and found nothing, except the tube containing his sleeping pills. That was all they took. Apparently their routine experience told them there was "no suggestion of foul play" as the saying goes, and they were not concerned with the question whether it was suicide or "an overdose of sleeping tablets".

Suddenly I felt uneasy. Clearly the police hadn't removed the envelope with my name on it, for Ann had found it several days after the flat had been searched. But had they made a note of my name? Perhaps not, because if they had they would have inquired immediately. But one never can tell and men like me always feel unsafe.

I shrugged a mental shoulder. A man searching my flat would have found nothing compromising either, except perhaps my address book, which could have provided a clue or two to my past. It wasn't so much that I was careful, though I suppose I was, but I never kept letters and photographs. Many people do, perhaps just because it's unsafe. Hubert Tull, the K.C. who died recently, had his bedroom practically papered with photographs of boys and young men, Rodney Croodie had an almost unique pornographic library. Other people kept love-letters, diaries, sometimes in code language, sometimes openly, or went in for art photos: male nudes on glossy paper. It was true that it was usually the middle-aged and the timid who collected art photos of nude men or women. A photographer I heard about was doing quite good business out of the likenesses of young and not-so-young athletes in various Greco-Roman poses with oil on the body. Though the photographs were used as erotic material, they made me laugh when they didn't disgust me. The bodies somehow looked artificial, if not diseased; no classical athletes had such inflated chests and such unnaturally slim waists and their faces would never reflect such strain, which in itself was tragi-comic.

On the door I saw hanging a riding mackintosh, almost white, but with a red flannel lining, and a bowler hat. The hat was fluffy and looked hard and heavy. From Lock's, I thought, but I didn't bother to look inside.

The narrow door on the right opened into what must have been a large Edwardian bathroom, but half of it had been partitioned off to serve as a kitchen. A foulard dressing-gown was hanging on the door. It had a polka-dot pattern; blue and white. By the window, there were two brown cowhide suitcases piled on each other, much used but expensive, with the faded initials N.J.L. on their side. One contained Julian's Army uniform in moth-balls, the buttons almost rusty, and his Sam Browne belt. The other was empty.

I suddenly caught sight of my face in the shaving mirror: it was pale, and cold, and expressionless. The small cabinet behind the mirror yielded none of the things I vaguely expected and looked for, nothing except collar studs and razor blades. On the shelf above the wash basin, were his razor, two tooth-brushes, toothpaste, shaving soap, a brush and a comb. It would have been difficult to find anybody who had less toilet articles than Julian. I finished with his kitchen in less than a minute. I was now back in his room again, standing by the bathroom door, just looking round. I saw his slippers under the divan and a rolled umbrella in the corner. I had plenty of time, but my search was unproductive. It came to me suddenly that Julian was gone for ever. The finality was frightening. But I soon realised that I was becoming morbid. It was not often in my uneventful life that I came face to face with drama, and I was perhaps getting enjoyment out of trying to torture myself. He was gone indeed, but a man doesn't die when his heart stops beating, and Julian Leclerc for the time being was still in the room. His flat, his personal effects, survived him, but then he was still very much alive in people's memory. His father, his mother, his relations, his friends. Friends, friends, friends. I suppose "friends" was the only word to describe them discreetly, noncommittally. Some of them, I was sure, didn't even know his name, and remembered him just as Julian or even perhaps under some code name, as if he were a spy. Ginger was one of the friends. Who was he? And who were the others? Young Servicemen, years older now, no longer good-looking, out of uniform, perhaps married: former sailors, soldiers and airmen. What would be their reactions now if they knew that the man who loved them and whom they loved for a brief period had suddenly committed suicide at the age of thirty?

What were the real limitations of immortality? My thoughts suddenly turned to Ann Hewitt and I was sure that despite her present and understandable nervous state, she would forget Julian more quickly than many people would, myself included. At that moment, as I turned towards her photograph on the mantelpiece, I felt that I was a little in love with Julian.

Then I noticed for the first time that there was a cigarette box beside the photograph. It was almost fascinating in its vulgarity. It was of shiny metal, cheap, shoddy and with a jazzy design, the kind of thing one might win at a fun-fair. Nothing could have been more out of place in this conservative, reticent room with its Cecil Aldins, its country suits, its Harrow and Guards ties. It seemed obvious that someone had given it to Julian and that he had kept it for emotional reasons. There was a shilling piece inside it.

Ann's photograph, taken by a society photographer, showed her in a silk dress, possibly dark blue, with small white patterns. She was wearing a pearl choker. It was her hair in the long bob that gave the best clue to her identity. She looked stiff and ladylike, but her face—an ugly face in real life with a good deal of personality in it—was now completely stereotyped. It was the angle, of course, and the lighting. The man who had taken it must have thought that Ann wanted, above all, to look like a lady; he may have been right.

It occurred to me that, after removing the picture, I ought perhaps to put the frame into one of the drawers, because it would look strange and guilty standing empty on the mantelpiece, apart from the fact that it would betray my visit. Also it was probably not Ann's sense of propriety that made her want her photograph back and not the frame, but she really wanted to get rid of Julian's memory.

I undid the two metal clasps at the sides, holding on to the glass, since I knew from experience that sometimes it isn't stuck fast to the frame and falls out. As I opened the frame to take out the photograph, a blank postcard fell swiftly on the carpet. With fingers slightly trembling, I picked it up and turned it round. I knew at once that my instincts were correct, and I was glad I hadn't allowed Ann to come back with me to the room.

He was what in these days some people call the Butch type, with a pleasant, open face, decidedly serious; a face which laughter sometimes doesn't suit. I had to discount the slight alarm in the eyes facing the camera lens, somewhere, I imagined, in the Charing Cross Road, but the eyes were light-coloured and large and I saw how long the eyelashes were and how generous the lines of the mouth. The nose was broad, very broad, almost flat in the middle. But apart from these features the face, just like Ann's on the photograph, was a little stereotyped. If Ann's photograph looked "postwar upper middle class", this young man looked post-war working class. Except for the features, he need not have been English. At first glance, he could have been any variation of Atlantic Youth—American, French, English, the prototype being Guy Madison or

Burt Lancaster. Clearly, either he or the photographer had tried to give him the look of a popular young film star of the day. It was true that the hair-style helped. I only saw the front, but I knew what the back must look like. It was a "snazy" haircut—the sort that includes cut, shampoo and set—and his thick and rich, light-coloured hair lent itself perfectly for the purpose. There are only about a dozen hairdressers in London who understand the trick, one or two in seedy West End streets, the rest in Camden Town or Stoke Newington. They are expensive and there is usually a queue of cyclists and barrow-boys outside them.

Was this "Ginger"? In real life his hair might have been reddish and, masking the top of the photograph with my hand, I tried to work out what he must actually have looked like. I was sure now that he was English, more likely from London than the provinces, and I was sure he was "normal". He wore a dark jacket—obviously "semi-drape"—a spearpoint collar and a dark tie in a Windsor knot. He was the type some middle-class inverts look at at street corners with nostalgia, a type sometimes dangerous, but always uninhibited. He would spend a good deal of money on clothes as dramatic as his haircut—more than people like Julian or I or anybody in our social group. We would not be allowed to call attention to ourselves in such blatant if successful ways as Ginger. As so often, I began to wonder whether these young, metropolitan working-class males effect this remarkable self-dramatisation for their women. Maybe, I thought, but it was doubtful. They wanted to assert their personality and wanted to be admired by both sexes.

I put the postcard into my wallet, then I took the old copy of The Spectator from the desk and slipped Ann's photograph into it. I shut the door behind me without looking back.

II

The patient was already waiting for me as I came in. It was Gordon, a boy of fourteen, a shy Jewish child from Bayswater, who was afraid of the dark. Terry was entertaining him, playing some records on the radiogram; they were having a cup of tea.

"Well, Gordon," I said. "How are we?"

"Very well, Dr. Page," Gordon said. He spoke like an old man with little love for humanity.

I was feeling, not for the first time, that Gordon had an almost greater confidence in Terry than in me. This wasn't because Terry was a trained and skilful male nurse, but because he loved children and they knew it instinctively.

"Any calls?" I asked.

"No." Terry shook his head. He patted Gordon on the back, then switched off the radiogram. As usual in the morning, Terry walked about in his woollen socks.

"Goodbye, Gordon," Terry said now and gave him a nice smile. I again noticed his strong, white teeth.

"Well," I said to Gordon after examining his file, "would you like to draw a picture for me?"

"Yes, Dr. Page," he replied with almost superhuman dignity and took out a large propelling pencil which could write in four colours. I handed Gordon the copybook, from which I detached his previous drawing. I remembered that he had last been to see me the previous Monday. I scribbled Monday's date on the drawing and put it among my notes in the file.

For a time I stared at these notes on Gordon, but I knew them backwards. His mother had brought him to me a couple of months back on a recommendation from Raymond Dunkley. The symptoms were clear and the mother was unusually intelligent and helpful. But one couldn't get much out of the boy. He was most self-reliant. After the first visit he came on his own and was not hostile to me, but when it came to his daily life, his family life, all I got were monosyllables and a raised eyebrow over eyes which looked tired and very, very old. I tried the inkspot test, his reactions were interesting but inconclusive, then I tried word-association, introvertive response and several other tests before I suddenly struck oil: from a casual remark I discovered that Gordon liked drawing, and had in fact some drawing talent, so I gave him paper and pretended I was not in the least interested in him. On paper he certainly was not monosyllabic or tongue-tied. Once you understood his symbols you could interpret his mind fairly easily. The method, of course, wasn't new. Stowasser had been doing it for years when I worked under him in America.

I looked up Bobby Sillock's office number in the telephone directory. He was in when I phoned.

"Would you like to dine with me?" I said after a minute or two.

"Not tonight. It's Friday. . . ."

"Are you washing your hair?" I asked. I decided to be light-hearted. "I didn't necessarily mean tonight. What are you doing in any case?"

"The rounds."

"Oh, yes, the rounds. The *Black Rod* . . ."

"You're out of date."

"Well, what's new?"

"The *Lord Barrymore*'s about the only place. Why don't you come along tonight? I shall be there round about nineish."

III

The *Lord Barrymore* was a pub near Regent's Park. The building looked old, possibly Regency, and the furniture was massive and Victorian. There was a lot of pretty, rococo, carved glass over and behind the counter and a number of mahogany chairs with red leather upholstery. Until recently it must have been a nice, friendly local institution, never perhaps very full, except on special occasions, such as after a match at Lord's or the Arsenal. But in the last few months it had apparently become a meeting place—one of them at least—of the unorganised but world-wide underground society of which I myself was an associate, if not a member. Once during the war in a pub full of Allied soldiers Bobby Sillock called it the "Homintern". I laughed—one nearly always laughs at a good pun—then I saw how untrue it was. Although their emotional lives are illegal and generally unacceptable, inverts are not a conspiratorial society, perhaps because like criminals they have only an identity of aim, but no identity of belief. It is true that national frontiers do not separate them, maybe not even class frontiers, but individual happiness, even if it is particularly difficult to come by, is no sufficient basis for an ideology, any more for that matter than are sin or virtue. Homosexuals recognise each other easily, but for the most part they lead parallel and incommunicable lives, more so even than a group of "normals".

These meeting places of the underground changed all the time, like the publishing offices of clandestine newspapers, and the changes were usually abrupt. The underground took up a pub, and met there regularly, which meant that a good deal of the undesirable element came too. First of all the "obvious", young and not-so-young pansies, who either couldn't conform or didn't wish to. This may have been due to social background: they had never had any training in discipline and they had little to lose. A few drinks did the trick; they got into high spirits, let their hair down, and screamed—and the underground was given away. Another unpleasant element that was often attracted to a pub of this sort consisted of those who lived on the fringe of the underworld: the near-criminal, the delinquent, the deserter.

As a consequence, the pub in question soon gained an unsavoury reputation. It was raided by the police. Names and addresses were taken, one or two wanted persons were detained and the publican was told to be more careful in future, otherwise his licence would not be renewed. He heeded the warning and, if next day a too obvious-looking person turned up, he refused—with a heavy heart—to serve him. A few days later the pub was "clean" again, which meant that it was empty: the clientèle dwindled to a few locals, postmen, commissionaires, charwomen and some respectable married men from other districts, who didn't want to visit pubs in their own neighbourhood.

The underground, fairly well used to abrupt changes of their meeting-place, took up another pub after the raid, and the same cycle of events was repeated. It became crowded and famous, then notorious, and did very good trade; then it was raided and became empty again. In and near the centre of London there were comparatively few pubs which had not at one time or another been taken up by the underground. One of the best—and now highly respectable—pubs in the West End had been a notorious haunt of the underground of the eighteen-eighties and, in turn, an old and highly respectable place had become notorious during the war. This was the *Poulteney Wheel*, which I myself used to visit at the beginning of the war.

During week-ends the crush was so great that it was occasionally impossible to get in. The word would go round in Army camps, at seaports, in air bases, that in London a good time was yours for the asking, and the name of the *Poulteney Wheel*—among others— became a kind of evil magic. The war had made most members of the underground profiteers in an emotional bargain basement. The young Servicemen were far from home, neighbours, friends. For some of them this was almost tragic; for others it opened up possibilities which had never existed before on such a large scale. The war broke down inhibitions and the element of danger made sex rampant. Public opinion was lax and the understaffed police had many other things on their hands. Normal relations—that is, women, dance-halls, cinemas, hotels, meals—cost money, whereas the underground offered hospitality, which to the young provincials who had not "been around" seemed lavish. In many cases not only did their week-end trip to London cost them nothing, but they often departed with money or gifts. All that was needed was a certain lack of inhibition, and the inculcated belief that sex with women was either immoral or dangerous or both.

But that is to put it unsubtly. The Second War marked the end of the individual's power of influencing history and the beginning of a collective world. This gave rise to personal frustration and a new sense of self-importance. The young were living mostly in exile, but exile gave them possibilities of which they had seldom dreamed before. Everything around them became slightly abnormal, the new occupation, the environment, the dress they wore, the physical and emotional climate. The concrete things of the past, like postal addresses, time-tables, road-signs, became less probable and friendships became all-important because it was unlikely that they could last. Nearly all of them, willingly or unwillingly, became creatures of the moment, living in an everlasting present; the past had vanished, the future was uncertain.

I entered the *Lord Barrymore* a few minutes before nine. It was reasonably full. As usual, practically everybody looked at me as I came in, but I knew they would, and I didn't pay much attention.

Inexperienced people, outsiders, usually became puzzled when by chance they entered a pub taken up by the underground. If the sudden gaze of uneasy or expectant eyes did not disturb them too much they could not help becoming conscious that the atmosphere verged between strain and exaggerated hilarity. But perhaps strain was more predominant. The average English pub is about the friendliest institution there is, especially in the poorer districts. It is not a railway compartment: an exercise ground for reserve.

The queer pub is different. Comparatively few people come alone, except if they happen to be regulars. The usual custom is to come in pairs, then ignore each other for most of the evening, except when the strain becomes too great. If one talks to an unattached person there is usually tension. The man is ill at ease, it takes time to sum you up and the process occupies most of his mind and renders him tongue-tied. He doesn't know whether you are a plain-clothes man or not. This, of course, is usually easy to decide; your age, your clothes, your appearance give the information in a few seconds. But there are other considerations: he doesn't know what you demand; he can guess, but only trial and error can supply the answer.

Sometimes, of course, it is difficult to decide whether the other is "trade" or competition. He may look very young and poorly dressed; last year he may have been trade, but this year he may have changed his status. And then you become a nuisance because you tie him down when he wants to be free to make his own overtures to someone else. Without knowing it, you may be intruding. He might well have been on the verge of speaking to someone when your intervention ruined his chances.

My technique was a gentlemanly disregard of the stares, open and concealed, as I entered the pub. I walked up to the bar. A woman who looked like the landlord's wife came up to me at once with a friendly smile and some slight curiosity, which indicated that the pub had not been a haunt of the underground for long. I ordered a bitter and took it to a table near the entrance by which there were several empty seats. By that time I had already looked over most of the people.

There were about thirty. A few were locals and almost painfully normal. I saw two or three railwaymen around the dartboard, an elderly caretaker and a couple of young soldiers: local boys on service leave. The rest were underground: a few obvious ones whom I had never seen before and a small group of the semi-obvious whom I seemed to remember in other pubs during the war; a little older, probably more seasoned, if not wiser. Though I didn't look in their direction, I knew that the three people standing by the empty fireplace were discussing me.

It was when I sat down by the entrance and took out my cigarettes that I realised I had no matches on me. There were no less than ten people, maybe fifteen, smoking around me, but in a place like this it was out of the question to ask for a light unless one knew somebody. The legitimate phrase, "Could you please give me a light?" was, in these surroundings, a recognised approach and a too obvious one at that. I walked up to the counter and bought a box of matches. As I returned to my seat, I reflected that the place was full of strategic points from which operations were being carried out. As it happened, I was not the only observer. I had already noticed him in the mirror as I ordered my drink: a middle-aged man by the door, talking to the elderly caretaker, and smoking a pipe. The man had actually been pointed out to me a year earlier, somewhere in the West End, but there was not much need for this. I was pretty good at spotting plain-clothes men, even the new type who is specially chosen because of his unofficial looks. I had something in common with a criminal, who instinctively senses a "grass".

But unlike a criminal I had a certain detachment, and I began to wonder what it was that gave him away. I looked at him in the mirror. Perhaps the fact that it was difficult successfully to appear uninterested. The man standing there in his grey suit, pint glass in one hand, his pipe in the other, overacted his unconcern. It would have been quite admirable on the stage, but not here in real life. He pretended he was absorbed in the caretaker's talk, but he hadn't yet learnt how to see without looking.

I was sure that most of the underground, here at least, saw through him fairly easily, and, being better actors by necessity than he was, it was difficult to know whether they were much perturbed by his presence. There was a group of four men around the bar: clerks or shop assistants who, I presumed, lived on the other side of the river. They were laughing now, but there was something in their laughter that suggested that few unpleasant things could be laughed out of existence.

One of the two sailors who had been standing by the bar now went to the lavatory and it seemed obvious to me at least that someone sooner or later would follow him. It was actually one of the small men: he looked like a waiter in civvies. In a minute or two they both returned, talking as if they had known each other a long time. They joined the group of three, then a minute later the sailor summoned his mate. The first stage of the operation was completed. The man would now stand them a drink, then he would find out whether they were ready for the second stage. I began to concentrate on the two soldiers now, who had just been served. One of them seemed to have "been around", not perhaps an invert, but a type known as "haveable". His mate, the younger and more attractive of the two, was apparently new at the game, and somewhat bewildered. He was a mixture of uneasiness and expectation, a young boy from the provinces, perhaps a bit anæmic to begin with, but put right by the healthy life in the Army. It seemed that his mate was putting him through his paces, for a minute or two later they went over to the benches and sat down quite close to two men whom I remembered having seen before.

Two more people entered now, middle-aged businessmen, and as they walked to the bar they took a brief inventory, almost like housewives at a remnant sale. Then one of them gave a nod to the group of pansies who stood around the fireplace.

Theirs was the least interesting group. It may be that I am too severe in my judgement of them. I try hard to be understanding, but I shudder from them. It is not only that they give the game away, but it is my experience that such people are usually unintelligent, verbose, neurotic and generally tiresome. They are not much good at their jobs, because they are too temperamental, devoid of discipline, unable to work long hours, unable to concentrate, full of either self-pity or of that peculiar parody of self-righteousness which would be ridiculous if it were not so pathetic.

On the whole I think they belong to a group of people who are stunted if not destroyed by inversion. They have no other interests and their impulses are for ever crippled. They are out of their depths everywhere, except in each other's company, and they are more feminine than most women, the "modern" woman in particular.

I can't laugh at them, perhaps because I'm not normal, and I am painfully aware that, since they are conspicuous, the whole of the underground is associated with them. For that matter, they don't mind ridicule; in fact, they realise it is a protective armour—to laugh is partly to forgive. Nature has been unkind to them and they try to restore the balance through the easier and less efficient of two ways. Instead of physical exercise, which could help, they resort to plucked eyebrows and an excessive application of the wrong shade of rouge.

A man came in now in a hacking jacket. He was an almost successful imitation of the minor public school type and a fairly successful one of a normal individual. He looked round as if searching for someone in particular, though it was obvious he just wanted to see if any possibilities were present. He was already on the verge of leaving when the swing doors opened and a young soldier came in. He was tall and attractive, with the assurance of his youth and strength and that trusting air which is sometimes the hallmark of provincials. Hacking Jacket quickly changed his mind. With measured steps he walked towards the bar, timing it carefully so that he should get next to the soldier, as if by accident. The performance was so polished and competent that I myself got up and, on pretence of ordering a fresh drink, stood behind them.

When the landlord came up to them, he turned to Hacking Jacket first, but he, in turn, indicated the soldier. "This gentleman came before me." The soldier smiled. "Ah don't mind . . . pint of mild an' bitter, please." I didn't hear what Hacking Jacket ordered, but he soon turned to the soldier and enquired whether he was on leave. The soldier said: "No. I'm stationed in Lundon." I was wondering what he was doing in this particular pub. Had he heard about it from his mates or was it just a chance visit? I knew that this was the exact line of thought that was exercising Hacking Jacket's mind. Apparently it was a chance visit. The soldier had been calling on a friend in the neighbourhood and had found the friend was out.

By the time the landlord had returned with their drinks and taken my order, Hacking Jacket was already disserting on London. It was part of his sales talk. His diction was as competent as his choice of subject and I had no doubt that, within an hour or so the article in question would be sold. I got my drink and went back to my seat.

All this was sordid from beginning to end. There had never really been a time when I had not regarded places like this as sordid, but in the past there had been a sense of curiosity, a sense of adventure, some cynical amusement and intermittent desire. Now it was merely repellent. It ought not to have been, if I had been normal, because a psychiatrist is a man who deals with more dirty linen than most other people, and he is detached. But I was not normal and not in the least detached. I thought I had said goodbye to these places, but I was wrong. I was here in this sink because I was involved, because I was afraid. It was ironical that I should feel afraid, long after I had given up this special world, or at least its more sordid aspects, but there it was. And mine wasn't an unreasonable fear, like Miss Wilkins' of dirt, Gordon's of darkness and Miss Mayhew's of confined places. On the contrary, mine was a reasonable, justified fear of getting into really serious trouble because of my past.

It was now about fifteen minutes since the two soldiers had sat down next to the two middle-aged civilians, and after a long preparation the older and more forward of the soldiers entered into conversation with the man on his left. I didn't hear his opening gambit, but he probably said, "It's getting crowded, isn't it?" After a time he introduced his young friend, to whom he was trying to be helpful and whom he had probably already initiated. But it seemed that he was trying also to work a contact for himself. In a temporary lull I caught the words in a Midland accent, "We're stationed at Gravesend," and I imagined that they were on leave and looking for a place to sleep. The second of the middle-aged men now entered into conversation with the younger of the two soldiers. Probably a small trader around forty-five, he was the type whom upbringing and experience had made somewhat shy, and I felt that the horn-rimmed glasses he wore were to some extent a means of protection.

The detective now said goodbye to the caretaker and with over-dramatised unconcern ambled out of the pub. He almost bumped into Bobby Sillock.

Bobby was less happy entering the bar alone than I had been.

He was tall and very thin and he looked obviously upper-class and slightly older than his real age. Everybody stared at him as he entered and I noticed that he tried to appear at ease without much success. The sailors, now in the middle of a group, looked at him with an enormous interest, and the two soldiers on the bench with an almost undisguised curiosity. The pansies by the fireplace, knowing at once that Bobby would despise them, and resenting this, looked at him with an ill-concealed spite and envy.

I got up as he was making his way to the bar. "Hullo," I said. "I'll get you a drink."

Bobby Sillock was a stockbroker with literary interests whom I had met during the war quite casually. We had struck up the nearest approximation to a friendship. It was he who told me about the underground when I was new to it and I in turn treated one of his young friends for neurosis. A kindly man by nature, he went out of his way to advise me about the small investments I possessed.

"I'm a little late," he said, glancing at the clock. "I met a young man on the bus, a veterinary student. Extremely nice. I asked him to come here tonight, but he said he had to meet a friend. So I walked with him a bit when we got off the bus. I think he knew what I was after. Anyhow, he's the enthusiastic type. I gave him my telephone number. He said he'd ring me tomorrow. . . . Well . . ." Bobby smiled, "what's happened to you? People don't just go into retirement like that. In any case, you've chosen about the worst moment to come back. London's dead."

We sat down at my table. Bobby began to toy with his drink. He didn't really care for alcohol and sometimes he poured the contents of his glass untouched into his friend's. "You've probably heard that the *Poulteney Wheel* has been raided. And another pub in Bermondsey. There's a new morality drive going on."

"With the same chances of success as the previous ones," I said.

"Just about. And nowadays nothing gets into the papers. It may be because they're so small and hard-up for space or, as a journalist put it to me, because the queer world has no circulation appeal for the general reader. I must say the Sunday papers look quite bare without their juicy bits. You always found them on page five. It was my Sunday-morning treat. *Scoutmaster Detained*, or clergyman facing *Grave Charges*. I'm certain they are still busy detaining scoutmasters and preferring grave charges against vicars, but nothing gets into the papers. All you get today are cosh attacks, armed robberies and breach of promise. . . . I'm told they arrested four men last week, somewhere in North London. Rather a nasty case. One's apparently a cinema manager, but there isn't a word about it in the papers. . . ."

He took out his cigarette case and offered me one, then looked round. "This is quite a nice pub," he said; "or, rather, it was."

"How long has it been in circulation?" I asked.

"Oh, since the *Welsh House* was raided. About three months. . . ." The door suddenly opened and three sailors entered. One was quite young and, I suspected, Bobby's taste. I thought this was the moment to inquire about Julian, before Bobby got up and began to "case" the scene with a view to operations.

"By the way," I said, "you knew Julian Leclerc."

Bobby nodded. "Yes. A tragic story. I've been wondering what could be at the bottom of it."

I tried hard to hide my disappointment. I had been on fairly intimate terms with Bobby Sillock. I liked him and think he liked me too. Indeed, our relationship could well have been described by outsiders as "friendship". Yet I couldn't bring myself to tell him—or anyone else for that matter—why I was inquiring about Julian.

"When did you see him last?" I said.

"About . . . oh, six months ago at a restaurant in the City. He was with some people, clients, I suppose. . . . But"—he seemed to think—"I did see him later. Soon after, anyhow, at the *Aldebaran*. He was with Rodney Croodie. I suppose you know that Croodie is out of jail. He lives in the country now, but comes up for occasional week-ends. I thought Julian had changed quite a lot since the war. He was still remarkably good-looking, but not so full of life as he used to be. I suppose it was strain. . . . You see," he said slowly, "the trouble with all people like Julian and you and I is that life is made extra complicated for us. We don't like people like ourselves. We don't want anybody who shares our standards, I mean educated, middle class and so on. In fact, we want the very opposite. We want the primitive, the uneducated, the tough. Then we are surprised that satisfaction is so difficult to obtain and that our affairs don't last. They don't last because we don't share the same culture. Things are far easier for people who are attracted to others like themselves. Possibly younger, but from the same background. They are usually happy. There are hundreds of dons, museum officials, clergymen, civil servants like that. They settle down to a happy, married life with younger friends. I suppose they go to drag-parties and dress up like Indian snake-charmers or Carmen Miranda, but they don't hunt and tour the pubs. . . ."

I saw the red light. Bobby was getting depressed. Quickly I said: "You know that Julian was engaged to be married?"

"Yes. Well, there you see. He was trying to get away from it. And he might have succeeded. . . ." He shook his head briefly. "There may have been some scandal. You never know. I don't know who the girl was, but her people might have put a detective on Julian. That sort of thing has happened quite often." Bobby flicked the ash off his cigarette. "At times Julian was quite indiscreet. I remember when he came back after Dunkirk there was a terrific party at Croodie's house and Julian practically raped a Canadian soldier. That was the second time I met him."

"Was Croodie a friend of his?"

"Well, he was very keen on Julian, but I don't think Julian played. And one can't blame him." Bobby shrugged a shoulder. "I mean, I saw Croodie the other night standing in front of the London Pavilion. Completely sozzled. One tries to be nice to him, but occasionally he's impossible. I'm really not the man to criticise others, but I think Croodie asked for what he got. . . ."

"Who were his other friends?"

"Croodie's?"

"No. Julian's."

"Oh, Tidpool, I suppose, and Everard and that awful Hugh Harpley. You know, this is the third suicide of people I've known since the war. There was a boy called Fabre I used to know. An actor. You must have seen him around during the war. He jumped off the roof of a block of flats in Hampstead. Then, another boy, only six months ago, shot himself. Pat Frazer." Bobby raised an eyebrow. "Julian, of course, was older, but still young." He looked away. "Why do young people kill themselves so easily?"

"Because they have a greater capacity for despair," I said. "No experience of disaster survived. . . ."

But Bobby was not listening to me. I saw Hacking Jacket and the soldier making their way out of the pub, which was now getting quite crowded. That was certainly quick work. The whole operation hadn't taken more than half an hour. They would take a taxi or a bus and in another half an hour's time they would be in each other's arms. As they passed us, Hacking Jacket nodded to Bobby.

"Who's he?" I said.

"His name's Ralph. Quite an enterprising chap. He's an engineering student or something, and he supplements his scholarship by acting as a procurer to two men, who don't want to appear. Did you see the soldier? Nice type. Ralph must have picked him up for old Senlis or for a music publisher he knows. Both are rich and don't want to bother. They pay Ralph a regular salary and he dishes up the boys. But I think he vets them first. He told me in as many words that he is working his way through college thanks to this spare-time occupation.

"After all," Bobby said, "there are several boys who use their immoral earnings to further their career. Winter kept one: a nice, reliable type, half-normal, an accountant. He's married now and Winter went to the wedding. Matron of honour, I suppose."

He offered me a cigarette. "Well," he said, "how are things with you? You've been hiding yourself for some time now. . . ."

I had a sudden idea. I took the photograph I found in Julian's flat from my wallet and carefully showed it to Bobby.

"Now I understand," Bobby said.

"D'you know him?"

"No; but I wouldn't mind."

It wasn't the words that made me sick, but the tone.

Three

It was ten minutes to eight the following evening and Terry and I had just finished our dinner. "Coffee?" he said.

"Yes, please." I looked at my watch. "But it'll have to be ready very quickly."

He jumped to his feet. "I quite forgot about the appointment." He put the coffee cups out. The kettle was already boiling.

Ann Hewitt had telephoned me in the morning, before I had a chance to call her. It was obvious she couldn't bear the suspense, the more so because she had nothing else to do. I, too, was anxious to see her and hear the rest of her story, but being Wednesday I had to see her after dinner. Even so, I couldn't keep Dighton behind for a chat, as I usually did after the session was over, just talking away as one does with one's most interesting patient.

I noticed that Terry was a little surprised, as this was the first occasion since he had been with me that I was seeing a patient after dinner, but I knew he wouldn't make a comment. We very seldom discussed patients, although we quite often talked about psychiatry, when Terry occasionally came out with a surprisingly intelligent observation.

I was far less certain whether Terry had guessed what had been on my mind during the last forty-eight hours. This was very unlikely, particularly as I must have seemed to him thoroughly absorbed—as I was—in the conversation we had been having at the table about his bicycle, which had been rebuilt. Before I met him I had never realised there was a world of cyclists which was far more exclusive if not more snobbish than the world of motorists. They belonged to clubs, they met at various places and they talked cycles. Terry's was a "Romer", an alloy-tubing job that cost almost as much as a cheap second-hand motor-bike. The technical discussion was a great relief to me.

II

"Here's your photograph," I said to Ann. "Just as I expected, I found absolutely nothing in Julian's room." The lie came out naturally and convincingly. I was now sure of myself; I knew where I was with her. But all the same, I had somehow to find out whether she had ever seen Julian with any young man of Ginger's description, even for a moment, even if she attributed no importance to it. Julian, after all, would have had enough skill to pretend successfully that the young man was an errand-boy, a servant, a former batman, if Ann had ever seen them together. "I'll give you an envelope to take it home," I told her.

"Thank you," she said. "You can't imagine how anxious I was waiting for you to telephone me. . . . You must forgive me. . . . I'm very grateful to you"—she said this without conviction—"but I have absolutely nobody with whom I can discuss these things. And I must. You were so right about it. I mean, I always knew I didn't get on with my people, but now that I'm in the worst mess of my life, I'm more conscious of it than ever." She suddenly raised her voice, "Mind you, they are extremely nice. They always have been. My mother's telephoned four times since Thursday; she wants me to go home, but I said I wanted to go and stay at a nursing-home. By the way"—she suddenly looked at me—"I hope you won't mind, but I told Mother about you. I had to. I said you're looking after me and that I must obey your orders. I said you're a famous specialist. Was that all right?"

"A slight case of misrepresentation or overstatement," I said. "Otherwise perfectly all right. But you must really follow my instructions."

"That's very kind of you," she said, having obviously listened only to my first sentence. "Because I really couldn't face them. Not now. You see, it isn't exactly *me* not getting on well with them. . . . I don't know. . . ." Impatiently she stubbed her half-smoked cigarette in the ashtray. "My parents are old people and I'm an only child. Father and his brother are in business. I don't expect you know Boardman's Entire; it's a Hampshire beer. . . . It's actually ours," she said a little uneasily, "but Father's about to retire. When I said he was an old man I meant sort of mentally. He's sixty-five and his health is good, but he's very restless. . . ." Here she hesitated for a second or two before continuing: "Father's always been very religious, but during the war he joined a thing called Zion's Messengers. It's a new sect. You've probably never heard of them." I had, but I didn't smile. "Well, my uncle and Mother approved of his joining. They thought it would keep him quiet. He only spends two days a week at the works. Since the war his eyesight's been bad, so he can't go out shooting and all the rest, but actually he's become much worse lately. He tells people that the end of the world's coming. All these wars and the atomic bomb. . . . All you have to do is to read Revelations; you find all the prophecies there. Recently he hasn't talked about it so much, because I suppose he's afraid of people laughing at him, but he does write letters to his friends, asking them to read certain passages in the Bible. I don't know. . . . Revelations, chapter five, verse four, or Jeremiah, chapter two. . . ." For a moment I saw the shadow of a smile flitting across her face. "We're all certain he's spending a lot of money on the Messengers," she said.

"And your mother?" I asked.

"She's been an invalid for many years now. In a way. I say, is it true some people escape into illness?"

"Of course," I said. "Fairly common."

"Well, you see, I shouldn't be surprised if Mother is persuading herself that she's ill. I mean, there's nothing really wrong with her, except high blood-pressure and some mild stomach trouble. Sometimes she feels very well, then a few days afterwards she just doesn't want to get out of bed. Of course, the state of the country worries her far more than it worries Father. I mean, he thinks doom is inevitable wherever you go, but Mother's been thinking about going to Kenya. . . ."

She broke off abruptly and it was only now that I discovered that I had been making shorthand notes of what she had said, as I always do with patients. It was force of habit. But perhaps they might be useful.

"Please go on," I said.

She remained silent for a moment, then she spoke very suddenly: "Of course, I don't know whether it wasn't my fault." She shook her head. "I'm afraid it must have been."

"What?"

"The whole thing with Julian. You said that letter I found must have been an old one. A girl he knew before he met me. Well, it may have been, but quite frankly, I can't get away from the feeling that it was somehow my fault. . . . I . . . I don't know how to put it. I didn't feel this at the time, except once, when I proposed to Julian, but I only felt, you know . . . funny, for a short while. I thought it was a little humiliating, afterwards I mean, but Julian was so nice about it, I forgot the whole thing. Any case I was very happy. Julian was fond of me. . . ." She began to cry.

"All right," I said. "Would you like to lie down a bit?"

She shook her head, took out her handkerchief and dabbed her eyes. We were silent now. So she proposed to him, I thought.

Suddenly and very abruptly she spoke again: "I don't know if I told you this the last time. Julian was very upset in the last few days." She shook her head. . . . "Well, really weeks." She looked at me a little angrily.

"You did; but please try to be a little more explicit. There's no hurry. You can stay as long as you like. Cigarette?"

She shook her head. Then she smiled faintly. "Well, I did tell you that Julian used to ring me up regularly in the country, and he either came down for almost every weekend or else I came up and saw him in London. He spent all his free time with me. Then just about three weeks . . . or a month ago, something happened to him, must have, but I don't know what it was. It was a Saturday and I was expecting him for the week-end and he rang up and said he couldn't come, but would telephone me later. Actually he only telephoned me on Monday. He said it was some difficult business affair which he had to settle. Incidentally, at the time I caught a chill and was in bed, but a few days later . . . Wednesday, I came up to London.

"I rang him at the office and he took me out to lunch. I noticed he looked worried and nervous. I didn't want to say anything, but in the end I did, and he said he was going through a difficult patch, but it would sort itself out and he didn't want to talk about it. It was business, anyhow; nothing really personal. I asked him if he'd like to come down to the country for the week-end. It would have done him good, get his mind away from things. He didn't answer me straight away. I thought he hadn't perhaps heard what I'd told him; then he suddenly said that what he really wanted to do was to go away for a time. Abroad, you see.

"I thought it was the strangest thing to say. I said: 'You mean without me?' He didn't say anything for a while, and I had a dreadful feeling that he was going to break off the engagement, but I felt so upset I couldn't say anything. I was completely speechless. I almost cried, then he shook his head, and said 'No, not without you. In any case, I can't go.' Well, that was a great relief. I said, 'I wish I could help you. I don't mind anything, as long as you're happy.' I said that almost too loud. We were at the Colony and it's always full, but I didn't mind, and Julian didn't mind either. He said 'You're very, very sweet.'

"Then soon after that he had to go and as we walked out I said: 'I forgot to tell you, Uncle Graham's succeeded in getting me a new car. It was very difficult but he knew some people in the car business. It's going to be delivered very soon and it can do eighty cruising, but I won't let you drive it till you get over your problem.' Because he might have smashed it up, you see. 'I'm going to leave you in peace for a few days, in any case. Then you ring me up when you feel well.' I thought that was the best way to face things and I saw that Julian was impressed. He had no idea of my tremendous self-restraint." She looked at me with unmistakable pride. "I mean there are women who would try to worry the life out of the man they love with questions and crying and writing letters and ringing up. Mind you, it's only natural. If you're in love. Well, I drove home and for three days I didn't bother him, but I rang him on Saturday and said I'd come up again a week or so later. 'How are things?' 'The same as usual. I've been very busy.' 'The main thing' I said, 'is not to worry.' 'I won't if you don't.' 'In any case the reason I'm ringing up is that I saw Uncle Graham and he said he'd like to see you on business. You mustn't tell him, but I think he's very dissatisfied with his lawyer and he's looking for another one, a younger man. Promise you won't tell him that I told you?' 'Of course not,' Julian said, but I couldn't say whether he was interested or not. So difficult on the telephone. I mean, I couldn't tell him that it meant quite a lot of money, could I? Father once said that our lawyer was making quite a comfortable income out of the works alone. I don't know much about business, but I knew Julian wouldn't have liked it. It's sort of humiliating."

"I quite agree," I said. "Tell me, how was that interview you had with your uncle? Was it really he who proposed it?"

"Well, yes. I mean, he'd met Julian and liked him very much. So did my aunt. Actually, it was I who brought it up, I think." She looked at the ceiling for a second, "I don't remember."

"It doesn't matter," I said. She was far shrewder than I had originally thought. Of course it was she who had brought it up. "What I really want to ask you," I said, fast, "is what happened after that? I mean, after you told him about your uncle?"

"Well, I was at home trying not to worry and keeping back my impatience. It was the stupidest thing to do. All that self-restraint." She raised a hand. "I feel now that if I'd really let myself go and stayed in London or if I'd taken Julian away for a time, things would have been different. Mind you, I'd been thinking about it, but in the end I decided that I mustn't show him that I was going to pieces because of him. That would never do. Men don't like it. . . ." I wondered who had briefed her how to handle Julian. She had said she had no woman friends, and that her mother was not very practical. I began to suspect the influence of Sunday newspapers and their "psychologists".

"Anyhow," Ann Hewitt said now, "the new car arrived. I telephoned Julian from the country to say I was coming up again on Thursday for the day and would he like to lunch with me. I called for him at his office. He liked the car very much, but I could see he still looked worried. I didn't say anything though. We went to the Colony, and during lunch I said: 'Shall I leave the car with you, in case you want to come down for the week-end? In any case you ought to have a talk with Uncle Graham, or are you still busy with the other thing?' He said, 'It's very sweet of you,' and I thought he meant yes; then he said 'I don't know. . . . You'd better take it back. For the time being.' Then he suddenly took my hand and he said, 'You'll have to get used to me, Ann. It's hard, I know. When I'm in trouble I never tell anybody about it. It may be silly, but it always works out in the end. That's my experience. In any case you've been far more considerate to me than I deserve. But I have to dash off. I'll give you a ring soon.'

"Well, I thought that was very sweet and I was relieved, but a couple of days later I began to worry. For one thing, Julian didn't ring up as he'd promised and I felt it was quite awful that lately it was always I who had to telephone him. In the end I rang him and said Uncle Graham was expecting him to talk things over. Julian was rather abrupt on the telephone. Not rude, but he said he was just going out on a court case. I tried to be calm, but this time I didn't succeed. The next day I came up and rang him, but he said he couldn't lunch and that he'd ring me back later at the hotel. I was calm on the telephone, mind you, but by that time I felt really alarmed. I thought it wouldn't be a bad idea if I told his father about it. I put a call through to his house and his cousin told me the Colonel was in London, staying at his club. So I rang the club and he asked me to come round.

"That was Tuesday. It was early in the afternoon and Colonel Leclerc gave me tea, and I told him I was worried about Julian. I told him that for the last three weeks he'd been very upset and nervy. I told him about my uncle and what he had in mind, and finally I said I was put out because I wanted to discuss details about our wedding with him, and in the circumstances, I couldn't. . . ." Suddenly she looked at me. "Perhaps you think I was in too much of a hurry, because Julian and I had only known each other for six months, but I don't believe in long engagements. Anyhow," she said challengingly, "both my parents and Julian's father agreed with me; at least they didn't disagree."

I nodded, and she went on: "Well, the Colonel was very nice. He said that business of not sharing his worries with other people was Julian all over. Julian wouldn't tell even him about them. In fact, he said, 'I am the last person who would be consulted.' But he laughed and told me not to worry; in any case, he'd be seeing Julian in a day or two. I said, 'For God's sake don't tell Julian anything about my visit and what we've discussed.' He laughed and he said he certainly wouldn't. Then he told me a very amusing story, and asked me about my father and mother. He's a very charming person. . . . I'm very sorry for him. I believe I told you he's had a nervous breakdown now.

"Well, two days later Julian rang me up and asked me to dinner. We went out and that was the last time I saw him. The rest you know."

I was expecting her to cry again, but she didn't. She just looked at me. It was the first time I had noticed the thickness of her eyebrows. Oddly enough, the unfashionable line suited her face. It was definitely an ugly face, but, with its broad forehead, attractive in a slightly masculine way. As I took my eyes off her, I wondered if Julian and I had shared the same tastes after all. I didn't find Ann physically unattractive. "Please go on," I said.

"Well, the next morning . . . this was really strange. I wasn't worried—in fact, I felt relieved. I thought everything with Julian was going to be all right. It was silly really to work myself up and go and see his father. As a matter of fact, early in the morning I tried to ring the Colonel at his club just to tell him that everything was all right; you know. But they told me he'd left for the country the previous day. I thought that was good. It meant he probably hadn't seen Julian. But I knew he wouldn't tell Julian anything I'd said in any case.

"We didn't actually discuss any wedding plans when I had dinner with Julian, but I felt it was all right now, and I went out looking at furniture and things. I had lunch at Debenham's; then I went to a few more shops and drove back to the hotel. There was a telephone message waiting for me. Ring Mr. Mohill. I thought they'd made a mistake. It must have been Julian who'd rung me, and they'd only taken down the firm's name. I asked the porter to put a call through for me, but while I was waiting one of the pages brought Mr. Mohill along. 'I was just ringing Julian,' I said, but I saw his face and I knew at once something dreadful must have happened. Then he told me. He was very nice. He said he wouldn't go back to the office, but would drive me home. I said I didn't want to go home. Then he said: 'Would you like to stay with us for the night?' I thought that was very understanding of him. They lived in Guildford, and I spent the night there. They rang up their doctor and he came out and gave me a sedative and I slept well. . . .

"One awful thing is," she said, "that I can't see the Colonel. He's under medical attention. I rang them up and talked to his cousin, who keeps house for him." She shrugged a shoulder. "But I shouldn't think the Colonel knows anything. I had an impression that Julian didn't really get on well with him and never told him much. I suppose that's our generation. . . ."

I suppressed a smile, not because of what she said but the way she said it. She spoke the moth-eaten platitude like a precocious little girl announcing a piece of supreme and original wisdom. Miss Hewitt was somehow younger than her twenty-five years.

"I don't know," she continued, shaking her head slightly and looking for a moment at my books. "When I had lunch with Julian and he seemed so upset, I thought it might have been some financial worry that was troubling him, but I didn't dare make a suggestion. I was afraid he'd feel insulted. You see, I always felt he didn't like well-to-do people. I mean, he never told me that in as many words. It may be I'm only thinking this because Julian liked working people so much. He knew a lot about them and he said he'd liked them ever since he could remember. While he was up at Oxford he got very interested in a thing called the University Settlement. It was somewhere in the East End of London, and while he was at Oxford he used to work there once a week during the holidays. Then he told me a good deal about the men he knew while he was in the Army." She looked at me as if she were testing my reactions, but I was on my guard. "I must say I'm not what you might call . . . well, democratic. I mean, I don't dislike the lower classes, but they make me sort of shy. Silly, isn't it? Sometimes I feel I'm frightened by them. The point is that I don't really know them. You see, I was rather delicate after I left school. I had typhoid during the war which left me weak for quite a time, and then I did a secretarial course and worked in the brewery. If I hadn't been ill, I'd have been called up and would have met all sorts of people: working girls and so on. As it happened I only met, you know what I mean . . . 'nice' girls. I once asked Julian if he was a Socialist. He said no, and I think he was a bit annoyed. In any case, I felt that even if he didn't actually dislike rich people, they didn't impress him, although he wasn't rich." Here she paused for a second, then quickly added: "I must say I loved him all the better for it, but I just didn't know how to help him."

There was a silence now. I got up and gave her a glass of brandy. She handled the drink like a man. "Tell me about your first meeting," I said.

"That was about six months ago. We live in Hampshire and we have some neighbours called Temple. They asked me over to spend the week-end with them and I met Julian there. He had been in the Army with Roger Temple. I rather liked him from the very first, though I knew absolutely nothing about him, except that he was one of Roger's friends. Mrs. Temple told me that on the telephone when she asked me for the week-end. She said he was good-looking, but I didn't take much notice of that when she said it. You know how it is. I thought she just said it as people do. . . . Then I saw she was more than right. And what was so attractive was that he looked so unhappy."

"A large party?" I said.

"No. Just a small one. They're not rich people." She added as an afterthought: "But very nice. There was Patricia, that's Roger's sister, with her husband. They haven't been married long and they are always chewing each other. Then there was a girl called Audrey something, who was about to be engaged to Roger. So Julian and I were alone quite a lot. Well, there were many things I liked about him. To begin with, as I've told you, he was very good-looking; you knew him, you know I'm not exaggerating. He was so good-looking in fact that my first impression was 'God! He must know it,' but as soon as he began talking I forgot that. He wasn't a bit conceited or anything . . ." Suddenly she became silent.

"Please go on," I said. "I want to get your impressions."

"Well," she said after a short pause, "he was very, very different from anybody else I knew. Really exciting. That may be of course because I hadn't had very much experience and knew few people. . . ."

"May I interrupt?" I said. "What I'd like to ask you is this. Please try to be as spontaneous as possible. Don't criticise yourself. And please remember I didn't know Julian well. So talk as if I didn't know him at all. In fact, I think it'll be better if you lie down on the couch."

She got up and followed my instructions as eagerly as a child anticipating some excitement. In my experience most patients are as impressed by the couch as by the stethescope. I noticed that Ann's legs were thick, but not unshapely.

"Well," I said, "Julian was very, very different from everybody else you knew, really exciting. . . . Go on from there."

"Well," she said, and paused. "I'm sure he made the same impression on other people, too. He had all the experience in the world and he never talked about it. Roger told me later that Julian had a marvellous war record. He was very modest and he had very beautiful manners, and yet, you know, he wasn't a stick. Another thing. You see, I knew he liked me and yet he never tried to kiss me straight away, though there was every opportunity for it. . . ."

"Then?" I said.

"Then, a week later, I had to come up to London. . . ."

Here the pause was so long that I had to ask another question. "Are you sure you *had* to come up?"

"Well, I suppose I wanted to see him again. You see, I had to come up to London sooner or later. I had to see the dentist and do a certain amount of shopping, but they could have waited. I don't know. . . . What actually happened was that a few days after the week-end Mrs. Temple told me that Julian had mentioned me in his letter. It was the usual bread-and-butter letter, and he said he was very glad to have met me. Of course, I never told Julian I knew this. Well, when I came up to Town, I rang him and asked whether he'd like to come to the theatre with me. If he didn't mind the short notice, that was. He said he was free that evening and he'd give me dinner at his club. We had a drink first and I noticed how popular Julian was at the club. He knew everybody. After the play we went back to the hotel and had another drink. He was very sweet. That was the first time I noticed that he could be sort of irresponsible too. I mean, in his talk. So unlike a solicitor. I haven't met many, but they are nearly all dull. Julian was more like a Guardsman, but at the same time he was serious. . . . I don't know how to put it. Well, I suddenly felt a strong desire to see him again while I was in London, but I found out he was going to be busy the next day or two. So I said, 'Would you like to come and stay with us in the country?' and he said he'd love to. A week later he came."

"Sorry to interrupt you," I said. "Can't you tell me a little more about what happened between meeting him in London and when he came to spend the week-end with you?"

"Oh, I don't know. I suppose I was looking forward to seeing him. I wasn't in love with him then, but, to be quite frank, I had nothing much to do. There's so little to do in the country. I've told you already that my parents are elderly people and not what you'd call active. We live in rather a big house—too big, really—and you know how lonely you can be in a big house. We don't give parties or anything, so I know few people, and very few I actually like. . . . For some time I'd been thinking of taking a job in London, but it was very difficult. My mother isn't in the best of health and she doesn't get on well with people. Things would have been very different if there had been no war. I would have been brought out, given a season, presented at Court, all that sort of thing. I might perhaps have gone to a finishing school abroad.

"I once thought of living in London, but my mother wasn't too keen on the idea. I don't know what she really wanted. I suppose really she'd have liked me to stay with her till she died. Only she never said so. Well, we had a little bit of a row—in fact, several. I said there are thousands of girls of my age who have flats in London, living on their own or with other girls, but Mother just wouldn't see that. Well, of course, if one thinks one's ill and never sees anybody—in fact, runs away from them—one wouldn't see the point. Daddy, of course, was on my side. I was certain in any case it wasn't good for me to stay at home."

She raised her head slightly from the cushion. "You see, I'm certain my mother's persuading herself that she's ill. . . . I'm sure you could do a lot for her, but she wouldn't see a psychologist."

"Tell me," I said. "How did your mother react to Julian?"

"Well, on the whole she liked him. I must say, the first time he came it was awkward. Mother was shy as usual. But Father was nice. He liked Julian. But he likes everybody I like. He asked me later how I felt about Julian. Then, I think, Mother found out that Julian might one day become a baronet, and this changed her attitude. Mother's a little bit of a snob, I'm afraid."

I was not absolutely certain that the last sentence was not, in a way, a projection of Ann Hewitt's own sense of guilt. It seemed she was not altogether free from snobbishness herself, but I wasn't certain. I said: "What was the first week-end like?"

"I thought it would be a little awkward with only Mother and Father and Mrs. T. That's Mother's companion, Mrs. Taylor. She's been staying with us some time. Her husband was a canon at Winchester. I tried to make it a party, but the Temples were away, so I asked a girl I knew. She lives quite near. I don't much like her or her friends, and in the end I was glad she didn't come, but I thought it would have been better not to be just the two of us. Well, we drove out. Julian wanted to drive, so I let him. I noticed it gave him enormous pleasure. That was something strange about Julian, strange but attractive. He could often be like a young boy. I mean, driving a car and getting excited about it. We drove to Pinker's Quarry, that's a beauty spot, on Saturday, but we had to drive on to another place, because there were too many people. Then he kissed me . . . Julian . . ."

"Hold on one second. This is very important for me," I said. "There were too many people at the first beauty spot, you said. Who discovered that, Julian or you?"

"Well, we both did, but it was actually I who said so. Julian just drove on. I told him the way."

"Then you came to a second beauty spot?"

"It's called Rowntree's View. It's very pretty. Then when we arrived there he kissed me. . . ."

"Just like that? I'm not trying to embarrass you, but tiny details which you don't consider important are very important for me. Well, he stopped the car. . . ."

"Then he said let's walk over a little further and I said no let's stay in the car or something like that."

"Were you feeling tired?"

"No. I just wanted to stay in the car."

"Was he a little shy?"

"He always was. We were sitting in the car, looking at the view and we didn't speak, then suddenly our hands touched, but he didn't look at me. Then he must have noticed I didn't take my hand away and he turned round towards me. He was doing it very slowly. I suppose it would have been very funny if I hadn't found him so attractive. Finally, he put his face against my neck and his hand was trembling; mine was too, and he kissed me on the neck.

Then he kissed me on the eye. I'd never been kissed on my eye and I wanted to giggle, but I didn't. Then he suddenly kissed me on the mouth. It was very lovely. It was then I knew that I was in love with him."

Again I thought she would cry, but she didn't. And she hardly paused, conscious perhaps that I would prompt her to continue. "Then we got out of the car and walked up the hill. We didn't talk, but I knew Julian was as happy as I was. It was strange; I felt very flattered. Maybe I only thought that much later, several weeks later, I mean about being flattered. You see, the way Julian kissed me, then and later, made me feel that he had a very great experience of love-making. He somehow didn't look it. It wasn't obvious at all. And the idea that such a man, who had all that experience . . . I mean, a terribly romantic past and all that, could be made happy by me, who, well, I suppose I'm plain, let's face it, and I haven't been about much . . . well that was flattering. It was more than flattering, but I'm not very good at talking about it. Do you see my point . . . ?"

". . . Yes," I said. She didn't see my face. I was sitting more or less behind her, as I usually do when patients are lying on the couch. This was fortunate, but I left that "yes" too long, wondering if I could control my emotions sufficiently to make it sound as natural and as noncommittal as I wanted. The trouble is that one is always deaf to one's own voice. There are hundreds of ways to say "yes". I felt I was using it defensively now. Julian had a great experience of love-making. He somehow didn't look it. It wasn't obvious at all. . . . What was obvious was his unhappiness. Beautiful and unhappy. As Ann Hewitt made a pilgrimage into her recent past, I simultaneously made a rapid journey into my own past, and my own reactions to my early experience with Julian were the same as hers.

Suddenly I realised that she was still speaking. "Then, after dinner he talked to my father a bit, then we rolled up the carpet in the drawing-room and danced. He was a good dancer. Then we played backgammon and I said it was a pity he had to go back on Sunday at midday. He had some case on, but he said it could wait and that he'd stay on till Monday morning. Of course, I felt very happy. On Sunday we had to go for cocktails to some people near us. I don't like them much, but Mummy knows them. They had a friend called Barbara, who was in the W.A.A.F.; rather awful. Well during the party she tried to vamp Julian. I told him, in case he hadn't noticed, and we had a good laugh afterwards.

"I think on the whole," Ann said now, "what made me most happy was that I felt I was making Julian happy. I know I'm not imagining things. He changed enormously. He looked very unhappy when I first met him, but a few weeks later he was full of life again and I felt it was me. Then, unfortunately, he changed again, in the last few weeks."

There was a moment's silence, then abruptly she said: "You did make a thorough search of Julian's place?"

"Yes. Why?"

"I'm just wondering." Suddenly she got up from the couch and sat facing me. "You said the letter I found may have been a very old one, but what I didn't tell you—I was so very upset and I still am—is that Julian once asked me a question. I quite forgot it until now. This was some time ago. He asked me whether I had a forgiving nature or was I jealous. I think it was apropos of that girl Barbara whom I've been telling you about. He said there were wives who shared their husbands with another woman. I asked him whether he was joking, and he said yes, it was just a joke, and he laughed. Now the point is, at the time I really thought he was joking, but now I'm not so sure."

III

Was Julian really fond of Ann? I thought about this after she had left. He could have been. When Ann wasn't upset she probably had attractions. She wasn't pretty, but she was young and quite desirable. There was a certain amount of masculinity in her physical features which a bisexual might find attractive. If Julian were just a bit like me, he may have had similar reactions. And I fancied that, normally, she might have been quite a pleasant person, though she was certainly the type in whom reverses brought out the worst. She was also rich and Julian may have wanted to marry for her money, or partly. But what on earth could have happened?

At the last moment, so to speak. Had someone intervened? I felt absolutely certain that Ann wasn't holding out on me, and that precluded an obvious reason for suicide—namely, that she had found him out. Ann, like so many normal people, knew nothing of Julian's secret, even if she thought he led a double life. She suspected a woman, the one who had seemingly written the letter she'd found. And it could quite easily have been the author of that letter; a man. Ginger.

Ann was a girl who had been leading the kind of "sheltered life" which I should have thought was practically impossible in contemporary England. But I was wrong. That old upper-middle-class world is still with us, in places, in isolated pockets off the main stream of life. But in any case, even a girl who had been brought up in different circumstances might have fallen in love with Julian. He had many attractions. And even a young woman who has been around might not have realised that there was anything unusual about him. It has often been said that women's intuition is very sharply developed and that they sense the invert at once, no matter how masculine and normal he may look. This is a piece of contemporary myth, part of the folklore of the twentieth century; an interesting piece of romantic untruth.

Four

I was on my way to dine with John Tidpool at the House of Commons. He was, I thought, the easiest to contact of the four people Bobby had mentioned. I knew them all and they might have known Julian fairly well. For a moment I felt sorry that Bobby couldn't suggest anybody from those social groups with whom Julian was far more likely to have emotional contacts. Then I changed my mind. Perhaps these four people, Tidpool, Harpley, Croodie and Everard, of whose names I had made a note during our conversation, knew more of Julian's past and understood him better than the type of man with whom I had occasionally seen him during the war, who quite likely, I was sure, didn't even know his name.

I had known Tidpool for quite a long time. A few years older than I, he used to come to various parties at my Aunt Christina's before the war. He had, I think, been in journalism and broadcasting and had written a book or two; then he got into Parliament at a by-election just before the war ended.

I didn't really like what little I had known about him before the war. It wasn't perhaps entirely that I found him somewhat pompous, but I didn't care very much for Aunt Christina's friends in general. A well-to-do woman in her own right, she was the widow of my father's only brother and led a busy social life in her house in Hyde Park Square. She was very keen on charity balls, the R.S.P.C.A. and oppressed nations, and she had been trying to be "helpful" to me. She gave me money, occasionally paid for my suits and asked me to her dinner parties. I went because I felt lonely with my father away at sea and my mother dead. She assumed social life would be a good thing for me, for she considered me gawky and without social graces. She didn't think much of my parents, my quiet and—I think—mildly lecherous father, my cultured, emotional, pretty, but dowdy mother, their divorce, and my subsequent education partly in Germany. "If only I'd had my chance earlier," she used to say, "you would now be studying for a diplomatic career. But, of course, Séraphine would insist on you becoming

a 'squirting physician', and Henry didn't seem to mind." Her typi-
cally odd and old-fashioned choice of words sounded strange in
the nineteen-thirties, and I felt "squirting physician" summed her
up. When she died she left me a small legacy, about a fifth of what
went to the R.S.P.C.A.

In the days when I first met Tidpool at Hyde Park Square, I
naturally knew nothing of his emotional life, but in retrospect I
saw that his appearance, behaviour and attitudes were those of the
upper-class invert, a type I had since met quite frequently. Our first
meeting after many years during the war was one of the minor
surprises of my life. It happened that I was talking to someone at
the *Aldebaran* and an Army major walked up to us. I first thought
that perhaps he was after the man I was talking to: a young and
attractive German-American. But he turned to me. "I must say
hullo to you," he said, and the intonation rang a bell. "You may
not remember me, but *you* haven't changed a bit since the days
when I used to see you at Mrs. Page's house. Except that I don't
remember your name. . . . Page? Well, of course. How silly of me.
Mine's Tidpool."

I saw him occasionally in the years that followed. Once we met
by chance at a Soho restaurant; he came over to my table and we
talked psychiatry. He asked me a number of typical layman's questions on inversion, chances of cure, heredity, environment. Finally,
soon after my return from America, he telephoned me to say he
had read a paper of mine on inversion, and I asked him to dinner.

Now that I wanted to see him about Julian, I wondered if he
would remember that he owed me a dinner. Sure enough, he
did. He seemed to have a royal memory, or rather a politician's
memory: for the rewarding of friends and the punishment of
enemies. Would I like to dine with him at the House next Monday?
A comparatively quiet day. No need to send in a green card. He
would be waiting for me in the Central Lobby.

As I walked past the policeman, I saw Tidpool by the entrance
to the Members' Post Office, and he greeted me as if my visit had
made his day. In the indifferent light of that sham Gothic aisle he
looked serene but quite young, although I noticed that his hair was
now almost completely grey. He wore the uniform of his party, but
he compromised to some extent by adopting spongebag trousers,

and the cut of his black jacket seemed to be an acknowledgement of the fact that we were allied to the United States. Probably, however, he just wanted to look young.

"I should like to discuss a legal point with you," I said on the steps as we were on our way to the dining-room, "but it can wait. What do you think of Julian's suicide?"

"Awful business," Tidpool said, and his face and voice at once began to reflect sympathy which I suspected he didn't quite feel. "I haven't seen him for some time, but we were great friends during the war. I didn't realise you knew him. . . ."

"Well, when we were younger. Before the war."

"You never had anything to do with him?"

"No."

"Of course, you developed rather slowly. Extraordinary." He nodded. He seemed to congratulate me for my slow development. "I don't know anything about his youth. You must tell me. I only met him a few months before the war. During the war, of course, he was quite wild. But so were we all."

We reached the dining-room. "You probably didn't see much of him during the war," Tidpool said, "but when he was on leave, he spent most of his time hunting. He was extremely successful. He must have gone through all the available young men, and some of the unavailable too," he chuckled. "He was restless and attractive. Oh, very attractive. But, of course, people like us never had a chance with him. He only cared for roughs. Once, I heard, he was taken for a ride." Tidpool suddenly laughed, just a little bit viciously, I thought. "Did you know Henry Morland? He was killed soon after D-Day. Wigan's eldest son. Well, it happened in the first month of the war. One day Morland, who was then a private, was picked up in a pub by Julian. He pretended to be just an ordinary Tommy. Well, he was an amateur boxer, well built, and I suppose he put on an accent. I couldn't do it, I'm sure. And Julian had a romp with him, not knowing he was Viscount Morland. But, of course, when he found out, that was the end of it. Julian told me he couldn't do anything with people of his own class. Well, I'm the same in a way. I remember just before the war, Julian once or twice took me to the toughest spots in the East End." He finished his soup. "I put on an old suit, but Julian was dressed exactly the same as always. I think he even wore his old school tie. We went to frightfully low pubs, in Canning Town or Limehouse or somewhere, I don't know. There was some music and most of the people were a little drunk and rowdy. I was absolutely trembling at first, but Julian was in his element. He talked to them with the greatest ease. He knew how to, and worked his contacts with great success; you could see it. Today, of course, I've had more experience of talking to workers. I was in the Army for one thing, and one gets used to it in the constituency, but I was very shy about it before the war, even to those I found attractive. . . ."

I heard the tape machine clattering above us. It spelt out the words: "Sir Clarence Pollock, Unionist, continues . . ."

Tidpool cast a brief glance at the tape, then went on: "When he came back from Italy, he was rather more subdued. That was towards the end of the war. I met him while I was on leave a few times, but I was busy myself. I suppose he was getting a little older, but then life in England in general became less exciting, didn't it? In fact, I wasn't surprised when after the war I heard that he'd got himself engaged. I presume he *could* live with a woman; and she was quite rich, I've heard. I remember we once had a talk on politics. I'd just got in at the by-election and I suggested he should stand. Told him I could always introduce him to people in the Central Office. I was keen on him taking up a political career. The Party needs young men, and nowadays money isn't so very important. But Julian said he was very uncertain about his own views and his own plans. Then the thing happened. . . . You've heard the rumours, I take it?"

"I haven't."

"Maybe they aren't true at all." Tidpool paused. "I mean, I heard that somebody had sent an anonymous letter to the girl and she threw him over and told his partner. Mind you, I heard it from that old woman, Tather. He didn't know Julian and the thing's probably not true. But that was exactly what happened to Basil Coolidge. A rich girl fell in love with him and another suitor knew that Basil was queer and arranged for the girl to go to his flat one afternoon, just as Basil was having fun with a sailor. Well, that *could* have happened to Julian too. . . ."

He had hardly finished the sentence when a bell began to ring in the corridor, then a deep, Guinness voice outside barked "Divi-shun" and suddenly the tape moved with a clatter, the word "Divi-sion" appearing in violet letters. Tidpool rose along with several other people at the various tables. "Most unexpected," he said. "Will you forgive me? I'll be back in a minute."

He trooped out and I began to think that our meeting was not likely to bear much fruit. Tidpool knew little about Julian, and practically nothing about him during the war years. He had given me one or two faint leads, of course. If the worst came to the worst, I could always contact Tather, though I wanted to avoid this, if possible. Bobby knew Tather, and I presumed that Croodie did too.

The tape began to clatter again and showed some figures. Tidpool returned. I asked him who Julian's friends were. "I don't really know. I believe for a time he was living with someone and withdrew almost completely. That was the year after the war. Then he began to go to the *Aldebaran*, but one always saw him with people one didn't recognise. Always rather attractive boys on the tall, well-made side. Definitely not our class." He smiled for a second, as if only to himself, then he said: "The point is that they are people who interest me too. Well, I'm not as exclusive as Julian was, but I do like working-class people. How do you explain that?"

"There are various explanations," I said, giving up the main purpose of our conversation as a bad job. "It may be that the work-ing class has been or still is more easily available and, in the past at least, was less troublesome if mistakes were made. My private guess on Freudian lines is that they have fewer anal fears than the upper classes, but what I think more important is that the worker gives us the impression, sometimes quite wrongly, that he's more masculine and virile than the man from the middle class. There's something about manual work that gives him a kind of glamour and sometimes something more real than a glamour. Besides, manual work definitely develops certain muscles. Quite often overdevelops them. You get hypertrophically big hands, fat wrists, a large dorsal, wide shoulders . . ."

". . . and that, of course, fascinates the feminine in us," Tidpool said.

"In rather an unusual way," I continued. "The average woman's reaction wouldn't be quite the same. You show a woman a splendid specimen of a young riveter or stonemason and he leaves her cold. Sometimes, of course, the woman pretends she isn't interested, but I think her attitude is quite often genuine. She wants more refinement. She may even be put off by his masculine appearance. She may think, consciously or unconsciously, that he'd be either clumsy or brutal or both. I've often thought about this: race involves no sex aversion, but class does when it comes to women. Men, of course, are different, even if they're normal. I suppose they are freer. There are thousands and thousands of respectable middle-class men who run after shopgirls and waitresses, but that may be just convenience. I somehow doubt if the fact that the woman is working class acts as an additional stimulus. On the other hand, I'd say that a large proportion of inverts like working men simply because they are working men."

"Even if they're dirty?"

"Sometimes just because they're dirty. Dirt may act as a symbol of physical reality from which the middle-class invert is divorced. Then, they like the apparent simplicity and straightforwardness of the working man. There are also hundreds of working-class fetishes besides body and mind and dialect. Take uniforms, for example. . . ."

"Matelots," Tidpool said and nodded. "I think the British Navy has the most attractive uniform in the whole world, but then the Navy has other attractions. It's an ancient tradition with them. . . ." He smiled wistfully. "I wish I weren't in the Army, or at least that I had no commission. I knew several people who refused commissions simply because they wanted to be among the men. And it wasn't because they were democratic, at least not those I knew."

"Generally speaking," I said, for I could see that he was interested in our conversation, and I felt obliged to sing for my supper, "the primitive, undistinctive, type quite unashamedly goes in for ornamentation. Look at their haircut, for example. Today it's pure Regency, but few people in the middle class would go in for it. I'm talking about the young, of course, the spiv and the millions who imitate him. Sometimes the effect is ludicrous, but occasionally a chap is so physically attractive that he gets away with a sky blue jacket with twelve-inch shoulders and flowery tie. . . ."

"Don't forget the jewellery," Tidpool said. "I knew a boy who wore four rings."

"They're partly weapons," I said. "They use rings to fight with."

"Then, of course," Tidpool said, "they take an interest in their bodies. Go in for weight-lifting, expanders, barbells and the rest, and subscribe to health magazines. Till recently I hadn't realised there were so many of them. Somebody got up the other day and asked the Chancellor who had authorised dollar payments for American health magazines. No one like us would go in for bodybuilding. And in any case it provides a short glory. They usually get very fat and ugly." The satisfaction in Tidpool's voice was unmistakable.

"That's quite true. Working-class good looks, male or female, don't last long."

"No. Inferior background and unhealthy ways." There was a finality in his tone.

"Perhaps," I said. "I'm inclined to think there's another factor. They don't make an effort to stay young."

"Why not?"

"They want to get old quickly. Life's not exactly encouraging for them, or hasn't been in the past, at least."

"That's all changing," Tidpool said with malice in his eyes. "It isn't entirely that people like us have less money now, but the working class no longer respects us as they did before the war. Not to speak of the fact that there's now full employment."

"Boys are more difficult to get," I said.

He didn't realise I was being facetious. He said: "It's an awful thing to confess, but I feel that a certain amount of unemployment would make things easier for us." For a moment I didn't know whether he was speaking on behalf of the Federation of British Industries or the underground. But he continued: "I mean, look at the West End today. The war years were exceptional. What a harvest," he sighed; "but compare the years before the war with the present. You went out on a Saturday and between Leicester Square and Marble Arch you usually found something. Young men from the suburbs, from the provinces. They were yours for the asking. Sometimes it cost money, but not much. Boys accepted us because we were class; and not only that: they liked us because, unlike women, we didn't cost them money. I suppose we made a fuss of them, which their girls didn't. Anyhow, today they can afford women, and if they don't want women they have plenty of money for other amusements. For a time I thought I only felt this way because I was getting older, but that isn't really the case. Not entirely, anyway. For one thing, before the war much older men had a far easier time, and I also know several young men from our own class who aren't having a good time at all. They're good-looking, with all the gentlemanly refinements, and they have some money, but they don't get what we used to get before the war. . . . And what's more tantalising is that the young worker today is so good-looking, so well-built, well-dressed. . . ."

I nodded. What Tidpool didn't tell me, I think, was that he was not allowed to use the only really good card he held, and that was the fact that he was an M.P. The authority of Parliament may or may not have been struggling against the revolution of our time; an M.P. still had a social prestige and some glamour—something between a really well-to-do car-dealer and a film-actor or band-leader, but unlike the band-leader or film-actor, he was not allowed to use his status for emotional purposes.

"The number of inverts is larger today," I said.

"You took the words out of my mouth." He spoke rather loudly, then he immediately lowered his voice again. "Why is it so? You're an expert, after all."

"Because inversion has increased everywhere in the last twenty years, I think, and it's more open today than ever before. That's the other difference. Actual inverts only make up about four or five per cent. of the population; well, over ninety people out of a hundred are still 'normal', but those who aren't are not so worried as they used to be, and not only in the working class. It has something to do with the revolution that has come over the world in the last forty or fifty years. People are less inhibited in all their demands. They can no longer be kept down by private enterprise or semi-public enterprise, by the Church or by the employer. In any case, the masses have always loathed the Puritan, and, for the time being at least, the weapon of unemployment can't be used against them."

"The poor idiots," Tidpool said, "don't realise that in Russia the thing is subject to cruel punishment. I shouldn't think anyone there is safe, not with that supervision and spying."

"I suppose they regard it as a counter-revolutionary, bourgeois activity, if not Fascist." I said. "Somebody once said, rather unkindly, that this was one of the reasons why André Gide gave up Communism. . . ." For some time I had been conscious I knew the face of the man sitting by the window: he had a thin face, greying hair, a long neck. It was the neck, of course, which I had seen in the newspaper cartoons: a former member of the Cabinet. A second later I remembered the name.

"Is that his son sitting with Pintner-Accrington?" I asked, staring hard at the Beaufort arms on the plate in front of me.

"He isn't married. That's his boy friend. I think it's the height of indiscretion to bring him here. I mean, several ministers have younger friends: advisers and all that, who come and have meals with them here, but there's no mistake about their looks. They *look* like advisers to Cabinet ministers. That sap who's sitting with Pintner is in the advertising business. The affair's been going on quite a long time. I'm sure practically everybody must know about it."

"How many people do you know here who belong to the underground?" I said. I was making conversation.

"Well," Tidpool said, "there's Steinmetz, Scudery, Leaf, Minty, Pintner-Accrington, of course, and that old woman, Herbert Nickleby. . . . On our side," he said, much less eagerly, "there's Werners . . . myself. I'm not sure about Plimsoll. . . ."

I *was* sure about Plimsoll. More than sure, in fact. I said "Wedderkopp."

"Oh yes, Wedderkopp."

"What about Ling?"

"Yes; I should say so."

I could have suggested one or two more, but I didn't want to embarrass Tidpool. I said, "There's the legal point I wanted to ask you about. . . . I'm sorry I've left it so late. . . ." This was all bogus. Even though my object in seeing him was Julian, I didn't want Tidpool to know it. I said: "I heard some of you have been thinking about amending the Labouchère Act."

"It's very, very difficult." Tidpool shook his head slowly. He was now looking at me like a statesman at a time of national crisis. "Plimsoll and a group of doctors worked out an amendment to propose that the thing should be illegal only when it concerns people under the age of consent. But they didn't find enough support. I wonder what they're afraid of?"

"Who, the doctors or the politicians?"

"No; I mean everybody in general. Tell me. After all, if *you* don't know, who does?"

"Oh, I suppose, many things," I said. How often had I made this reply. "I'm not talking about the homo-Puritan, because he's in a minority. He thinks that amending the law threatens his own self-restraint, which has already made him half-dead. But there are many people in England who unconsciously feel that the invert is a revolutionary."

"Yes," Tidpool said; he was looking at me sideways like a hen, and now he closed his eyes. I didn't add that there was something in the northern climate, something in the Anglo-American economic set-up, that encouraged sexual deviation of all sorts while at the same time favouring Puritanism. I didn't believe that there was only as much inversion in England and America as elsewhere, but that here it was more open. I believed that it was both more open and more widely practised. And it was in precisely these two countries where the law was as harsh towards the sexual offender as towards the offender against private property. Inversion was largely the price one had to pay for something for which one was not responsible, but I didn't know what that something was.

An usher approached us with a green card for Tidpool. He glanced at it, then put it on the table.

"I must go," I said.

As we were walking upstairs to the Central Hall, I took out my note-case and showed the photograph to Tidpool.

"Who's he?" Tidpool said. He looked round uneasily.

II

Perhaps because my interview with Tidpool had been very unsatisfactory as regards its main object, on my way home I began to think about the pretext for which I had gone to see him. I was, naturally, in favour of altering the law, but I didn't believe that bringing it in line with the current attitude of most other civilised countries would change much. If the law were amended there might be fewer tragedies, fewer people would commit suicide, perhaps the number of inverts would decrease, but public disapproval would remain. The invert would still be in a minority, with a permanent guilt-feeling, and the hostile pressure of society would, to varying degrees, turn him into a neurotic.

Understanding could help, of course, but then understanding was needed for many other things (and was not available), many of them far more important than the happiness of a minority. One should have a sense of proportion.

What was my own attitude towards morals? Like eighty per cent. or so of all inverts, I didn't consider myself an immoral person. I always felt that the invert was one of the least immoral people in a world which was more a-moral than immoral, perhaps because his own guilt feeling often forced him towards scrupulousness in all his dealings. I was not thinking of embittered inverts, of course, whom bitterness had pushed towards crime or just unscrupulousness. Perhaps because I believed in God, I was uneasy having sex with someone I didn't love, but I felt that perhaps the process was capable of reversing itself and I could *afterwards*, in retrospect, fall in love with someone with whom I had had sex. That was precisely how I fell in love with Julian; I might one day fall in love with someone else.

The only moral scruple in my emotional life was against corrupting someone who was normal, especially if he were young. It was a principle against which I never acted, although temptation had at times been strong indeed. For all I knew it may have been an unnecessary scruple and, though respectable, quite a false principle. Stowasser and Hyde in New York and Pollner at St. Gabriel's, all serious experts on inversion and as "normal" as they make them, held the view that in their experience no really normal person could be made into an invert through seduction at an early age. The person who had no predisposition might play, but would revert to normality later, the one, on the other hand, with a predisposition to inversion might well sooner or later become an invert.

I may have been wrong, but I felt I had no right to provide the decisive push towards an anchorage which made life on the whole more miserable than the so-called normal attitude.

The underground contained between a million and a half to two million males, according to the guess of the experts. It is reminiscent of the iceberg the visible shape of which looms so misleadingly small over the waves, the larger part of it being below.

Those inverts the members themselves see, recognise or discover form a small section only. The majority of the underground do not go to the queer pubs, clubs or even parties, do not linger around public lavatories, railway stations or other recognised or obvious places.

There are thousands of young inverts among the millions of normal young men who live with their friends in boarding-houses, small flats, hostels, clubs, associations, sometimes under the roof of the parents of one of them. Secrecy is complete and scandals rare. The underground is everywhere, more conformist and disguised in small, static communities than in large and dynamic ones, but to be found in every district and in every profession. Like Communists, they incline to form cells, but these are small, impromptu and totally unconnected with a higher organisation: the pursuance of individual happiness is hardly a basis for social organisation, however difficult or dangerous to achieve.

Inverts are everywhere. I dare say their proportion is not so great among bricklayers, road-menders or dockers and blacksmiths. These are not congenial occupations and even if born in such families, they do not themselves follow the trade of their fathers or normal brothers. They frequently resist regimentation by family or social-economic circumstances, break away and find congeniality perhaps in becoming a hairdresser or waiter.

But Harry, a Communist airman I met during the war, made me think again. "It is capitalism which is the root cause of homosexuality," he used solemnly to say, and in response to this world-shaking discovery and in hope of ultimate salvation, a number of little poufs in the West End began to sport the badge with the hammer and sickle.

The statement is idiotic, but all the same it reveals one aspect of truth—namely, that poverty encourages a certain amount of inversion among those who have some predisposition towards it.

Besides, in England at least, working-class society has a tremendous basis in male solidarity. This is forced on them by their status, by the nature of their struggle, but in certain cases it leads to strange emotional relations. Friendships among working-class boys are often tremendously strong. This puzzles their girls and irritates the middle-class invert, who finds it impossible to separate them. For many a worker his "mate" is the most important person in the world, inseparable from him; he confides in him and does nothing without consulting him. Marriage for many of them is a necessary evil and sometimes a form of unrealised treachery towards the mate.

Five

Two days had passed. The previous day Ann had been to see me again and told me a good deal of herself and a little about Julian. She asked me to spend the following week-end with her people. Her mother insisted on her return, at least for a week-end, and Ann felt she could face the situation better in my presence.

In the last two days I had been rather worried. Bobby Sillock had already mentioned the possibility of a scandal involving Julian, and Tidpool, in a way, had confirmed it. There was always the chance that blackmail or an impending prosecution was the cause of Julian's suicide. I was fairly sure that Ann knew nothing about Julian's double life, but her people might. I was glad therefore of the invitation. It seemed certain I'd discover a few more, and possibly important, details about Julian's relations with the Hewitts.

Since my meeting with Tidpool my attitude towards the "case" had undergone an important change. For all I knew, I myself might have been involved more than I'd at first imagined, and far more than emotionally. There was the mysterious envelope which had brought Ann to me in the first place.

I decided to ring Digger Sospell, an Australian dentist who lived and practised in South London in a large Victorian house where every now and again he gave parties, which I at one time used to attend. When I dialled his number, I didn't know which was greater, my curiosity or my fear.

"Oh, it's you," Digger said when I got through, and immediately he told me a story in his slightly Cockney accent, as if it was a week and not about a year ago that we had last spoken to each other.

"How is Noel?" I asked.

"He's been ill for a couple of days, but he's all right now. Matter of fact, we're driving out to Southend tonight. Why don't you come with us?"

"Sorry; I can't. But is he with you by any chance? I'd like to speak to him."

"Are you in trouble?" he roared.

"Not yet."

"Well, hold on then. I'll get him for you." A second or two later I was listening to Noel's steady, low-pitched voice.

"Noel," I said, "would you please do me a favour? Would you try to find out something for me? A couple of weeks ago, a solicitor called Julian Leclerc committed suicide. You may have seen it in the papers. I knew him fairly well and knew his family. Nobody knows why he did it, but I've heard rumours that there may have been some scandal." Here I paused. The wartime slogan "careless talk" flashed through my mind. The enemy was everywhere. One never knew. The war between the underground and society never paused for an armistice; it just went on.

I was thinking how I could discreetly disguise what I wanted to say, but Noel knew at once what I meant. He said. "How do you spell his name?"

I told him and gave him my telephone number.

"I'll try to ring you tomorrow afternoon," he said. "Will you be in?"

"Definitely. Then we can meet somewhere afterwards for a drink," I said.

II

Noel was a Scotland Yard detective, a man of twenty-eight or thirty, who for some time had been living with Digger Sospell. He was not perhaps good-looking; just a nice, friendly, reliable English type, who appeared perfectly normal to the outside world. When he was still in uniform he had looked the typical London Bobby who for good reasons endears himself to practically everyone in the country. That is all except the guilty. The guilty. Members of the underground belong to the guilty, and regard policemen in general with the dislike, suspicion and fear of the hunted criminal, or at best with the uneasiness of the poor. The poor have never liked the policeman, and believed and spread malicious rumours about him, about the ambition which had made him stoop low or about his retiring and opening a pub on the bribes he has collected from bookmakers and prostitutes, if not from real criminals.

I had known Noel on and off for a few years, and I realised that members of the underground, especially the poorer ones, were chary of him, if not hostile, when they learnt his profession. Some of this attitude remained with them even after they found out that Noel was a genuine case, an exclusive invert since his childhood, and that he was perfectly straight. There were, of course, some in the underground in whose eyes Noel's attractions grew enormously the moment they found out he was a policeman. There was always the romantic type who liked to indulge in a completely harmless play with danger. I didn't know if Digger was one of these. If asked, he always said why should there be any less inversion among the police than among food inspectors, Customs men, income tax clerks, or postmen. That may have just been a blind.

III

When Noel rang me up the following afternoon he told me there was absolutely no information available, but, finding that he could slip away for half an hour or so, I asked him to meet me for a drink and he suggested a pub near Parliament Square.

He was dressed in a tweed coat and gabardine trousers. I noticed that he looked a little off colour, but his smile was as bright and friendly as ever. I reflected that he was one of the type of new plain-clothes men whose disguise was complete because it was unintentional. Noel looked like an airline steward or a regular N.C.O. out of uniform, and his disguise was his face, which was open and friendly to the point of naïvety. Nobody could suspect any secrets behind those bright eyes and that nice open smile; certainly it was not apparent that he was a policeman or an invert.

"Cheers," he said as he raised his glass. We were sitting in a corner. The pub was fairly empty. "Well, as I told you, there's absolutely nothing known about the man. Of that I'm absolutely sure."

"Would it be indiscreet to ask you why you say that?" I asked.

"Well. As you know, I'm not in the Vice Squad. Actually there was some danger about a year ago that I might have been transferred, but luckily I wasn't. I don't think I could have stuck it for long. I'd have resigned. Just think; one day I'd have been sent out to raid a pub, full of people who knew me. In any case, I'm actually leaving the Yard next year." Here he interrupted himself and slowly felt in his pocket. I was expecting him to show me something, but he only brought out a packet of cigarettes.

"Now," he said after a time, "what was I saying? Oh yes, I have a friend who is actually in the Squad." He had been talking very quietly, but now he spoke in a hush. "I can tell you for certain there were no charges impending against your friend."

"No scandal, blackmail and so on?" I said.

Noel shook his head. "Definitely not. My friend would have known. There are cases when no charges are made out, or when charges are actually dropped on higher authority, but some record always exists. In official language, I can tell you that your friend," he smiled, "is not known to Scotland Yard."

"Not on the List?"

"That I don't know, but it wouldn't matter. Actually, there are very few names on it. Only people who have been involved in scandals, or are known to the police for some special reason. Sometimes there's a raid on one of the queer pubs and the police take all the names, but how can they keep a list of all the queers in London who don't go to pubs, but do their hunting elsewhere, or just live with each other? Anyway, the police aren't interested in hoarding people just for the sake of it.

"I sometimes wonder why the List is actually kept," Noel continued; "I shouldn't be surprised if it is only to frighten people off. At least that's what I imagine is the idea behind the raids on pubs. Just to make people more discreet."

My idea was different. The List had its uses. The police had to know about inverts for many reasons, especially because an element among them was involved with criminals, blackmailers, thieves and deserters. I supposed there was, however, a slight danger that the List could be used for political purposes. The police, after all, could do little if a higher authority pressed them to yield information.

It would be interesting to know what was the official Government policy towards the underground or rather towards the prominent invert. There were many people prominent in various walks of life who were undoubtedly inverts, and there were many others who might well have been. Their number might have surprised the uninitiated, if it was not quite as large as was often believed by those who pretended to know; but it was considerable in any case.

My interview with Noel was over. I was relieved, but I thought it would be a good idea to stay on for a few minutes, just to show him I hadn't really been worried.

"Famous people," I said "are hardly ever prosecuted. Prominent people, inverts or normal, realise, of course, that they have to be discreet in all respects, but they have their moments of madness, or moments of ill luck. Whenever there is a prosecution, two features are usually noticeable: first, that the man is only moderately well-known; second, that an example has to be made. The man who is brought to the dock is not a famous actor, but an understudy; not a university professor, but an elementary schoolteacher; not a captain of industry, but a small business-man. Or else an example has to be made because of the man's position: Service officers involved with their subordinates, clergymen, Scoutmasters, youth club leaders, schoolmasters, people in minor authority abusing their minor authority. Sometimes, of course, there's a flagrant scandal, but this is the result of a man really asking for it.

"On the whole," I said, "I think the police shut an eye to inversion whenever they can or want to."

"Yes," Noel nodded. "But, of course, you know that when it actually comes to prominent people, they are usually warned, as Oscar Wilde was, often by the highest authority. And there are also cases which are hushed up or made light of. I know for certain that if, for example, a clergyman or a high-ranking officer or civil servant is arrested and there is actually no abuse of authority—I mean, if he has actually been caught having fun with an adult who's a total stranger—then the detective is usually ticked off. That's one of the many reasons why most plain-clothes men dislike being transferred to the Vice Squad."

"Who do the authorities want to arrest, then?" I asked.

"I don't really know," Noel said, shaking his head. "Male prostitutes I suppose . . . professionals or people who are blatant about it and advertise the thing. They want to keep it down as much as possible. They know full well it can't be suppressed, but they don't want it to spread through advertising, and they don't want homosexuals to feel too safe. . . ." He drained his glass. "I have to slide," he said.

On my way home I reflected that, even if the police had known nothing about Julian, the possibility of a scandal or blackmail could still not be ruled out entirely, and I was as involved as ever.

Six

The Hewitts lived on the border of Surrey and Hampshire. Ann had told me that the house was named "The Keep", so I expected it to be what is known as "Stockbroker's Tudor", a style much favoured by the new rich of the nineteen-twenties—for very good reasons, I thought: the real Tudors themselves were "new rich" and vulgar to a degree.

The house, I saw, had obviously been "done up" by a reliable firm of interior decorators, everything strictly in period from pewter to leaded windows and from refectory table to Knole settee. But it was a gloomy place even on this lovely summer day, although it looked clean, expensive and reasonably comfortable. The plaster mouldings on the ceilings, picked out in gold and red, reminded me of the Tudor lounges of second-class hotels.

Waiting with Ann in the drawing-room for her mother to come down, I realised that this was the home of a class of people I knew only from novels. Before the war, I would probably have avoided them, but today they had a certain curiosity value for me. It was interesting to see the vulgarity of the mid-nineteen-twenties tempered by illness and the consequences of a social revolution, under bogus half-timber and Tottenham Court Road tapestry. I looked at the life-size portrait of Mrs. Hewitt painted during the First War by a Royal Academician. It was a very exact stock-taking of every detail visible to a man of mediocre competence. She had worn a ball dress of golden yellow, a row of pearls and court shoes. The background was light green; all very dignified.

Then we heard footsteps and I saw that dignity was even now not altogether absent from Mrs. Hewitt, but this impression may have been partly due to her white hair, and the stick she carried, and the slowness of her movements. She had on a hat, and there was just a little powder on her face—no rouge; I fancied that her dressing-table was poorly lit.

She was accompanied by Mrs. T., who looked exactly what she was, the widow of a minor canon who was now companion to a sickly, rich woman. They both talked as if they were understudying Sybil Thorndike.

"It's awfully kind of you"—these were practically the first words Mrs. Hewitt addressed to me—"to take care of Ann. It was a dreadful blow. You know, she's only twenty-five," she added, confirming what Ann had told me, that her mother still regarded her as a little girl.

We talked little during lunch, but I saw that Mrs. Hewitt had confidence in me. She appeared to have an almost religious respect for the medical profession. I also knew for certain that neither of the two women knew anything about Julian.

"Old Colonel Leclerc is such a charming man," Mrs. Hewitt said. "Came to stay with us in March. . . . He must have gone through agonies. My husband too liked him enormously."

Mr. Hewitt was not on view. He was attending a weekend conference of Zion's Messengers, but it was unlikely that he knew anything about Julian either—certainly nothing of great importance. My disappointment was momentary. After all, what was there to know about him as far as these people were concerned? Julian was charming, good-looking, from a good family, in a good job, with good prospects, and Ann had fallen in love with him. What else needed to be known? The really surprising thing, I thought later, was that Mrs. Hewitt didn't seem interested in the possible cause of his suicide. I tried to sound her, but she just shook her head and changed the subject. This may, of course, have been Mrs. T.'s influence: suicide is a crime against faith, no matter what prompts it.

During the afternoon we drove over to the Temples for tennis. I suggested Ann should play, and on second thoughts she brought her racket and shoes.

The Temples were a semi-military family who lived in a largish, neglected house. The paint was flaking off everywhere; in the hall, which contained two grandfather clocks, neither of them working; in the passages; in the large drawing-room with its Edwardian furniture, mixed with everything under the sun—wrought iron and pewter and Georgian silver and imitation Regency. It was an extrovert house, cheerful and slightly down at heel, with several dogs roaring about the place. Major Temple wasn't present, but he must have been deaf, because all the members of the household spoke at the top of their voices. Mrs. Temple was a big, fat woman, the practical joker type. "What really *is* a psychiatrist?" she asked, handing me a cup of tea in a chipped Crown Derby cup.

"The last person you talk to before you begin talking to yourself," I said, and the ancient joke made her shake with laughter. She repeated it at the top of her voice.

"I'll remember that," she announced.

There was not a word about Julian during tea, but afterwards, when Ann began to play tennis with Roger Temple's fiancée, Mrs. Temple and I sat on a bench and she told me about Ann's people. "Poor Mr. Hewitt, of course you know, is dippy. Maybe it's in the family. The elder brother who died had to be bought out of the firm, because he wanted to reorganise it on Christian principles: kneel down and pray before you start work and kneel down and pray after you finish. The grandfather was a market gardener, I believe, somewhere near Southampton. And their money was made during the First War. They complain like mad, but they're really very wealthy. Well, now, Mrs. Hewitt, poor soul, is ill and, bless her heart, fairly mean. Or shall we say parsimonious?" she laughed. "I used to feel sorry for Ann—she went to school with my Patricia, they're the same age—living in that morgue. Roger calls it 'The Tudor Crematorium'."

A little later I had a chance to talk to Roger Temple. Mrs. Temple had said very little about Julian, whom she had only met two or three times. Roger was a pleasant person, but already putting on weight and looking older than his age, which couldn't possibly have been more than thirty. He thought I might have known more about Julian's suicide than most people, because Ann had told everybody that I had been introduced to her by Julian. I upheld the story, which was in any case very convenient for me, but I told Roger I hadn't seen Julian for several months.

"Well," he said, "in that case your surprise must be as big as ours. Mind you," he added—we were slipping away from the party and walking towards the greenhouse, which was empty save for a few geraniums in pots—"mind you, on second thoughts the thing isn't a really great surprise to me. You mustn't tell Ann. You see, I knew Julian fairly well." Here he paused significantly, and I looked up, already on my guard. So he knew, I thought and I was wondering exactly how he'd come out with it. It would be an oblique reference, of course, and at first I would pretend I didn't understand what he meant, the way one always does in a situation of this sort.

"In a way," Roger Temple said, obviously enjoying the dramatic situation he was creating, "old Julian was a dark horse, but I saw through him."

I nodded, with my heart in my mouth. He was watching me.

"You see, he and I were in the same battalion. He was in France first, and came home after Dunkirk. I only met him later in Africa and Italy, but we were together for well over eighteen months. Well, if you're in the Army, if you mess with others, live with others, you can't keep secrets from fellow officers, even if you are tight as an oyster." He paused, then in a low tone he added: "The point is old Julian was a great Tiger in the Taxi."

My surprise was so great that he thought he had to explain the period phrase. "A great womaniser. . . ."

"Amazing," I said.

"I dare say it isn't nice to say that. *De mortuis nil nisi bonum* and all that, but it's the truth. He was discreet, of course, but he didn't always succeed. One day, for example, he was seen coming out of one of the lowest *casinos* in Naples. . . ."

"Gambling?"

"Good God, no. *Casino* means brothel in Italian. There were several in Naples, and the one he went to was out of bounds—a very unhealthy place, always full of native sailors. And he also used to go to low pubs. It's a wonder he never got into trouble: of course, the C.O. never knew; Julian was too popular for that. Everybody liked him. He was a damn good soldier, too." Temple wiped his forehead. "Then every now and then Julian went off for a weekend. He always went to Naples on his own, and it was nobody's business what he did. It was women, of course. Well, he told me so himself, in as many words."

"Did he?" I said.

"Oh, yes. I knew all his secrets. Then, as we moved up, I lost sight of him completely. He was wounded and sent back to England six months before V.E.-Day. Didn't see him for some time, but I suddenly met him about six or seven months ago at the club.

I was up for the day, and there he was at the bar. I spoke to him and we had lunch together. Well, and here comes your story. . . . At first, I didn't notice he was depressed. You know how it is: you haven't seen someone for a long time and you do practically all the talking, but soon enough I realised something was wrong. I'd got to know Julian pretty well in the Army and could see at once he was unhappy in love. I'm quite good at psychology, you know. . . ."

"Oh, yes," I said politely.

"So I tackled him about it, and he as much as admitted it. It *was* some unhappy love affair. Well, of course, one doesn't ask who the girl is and where she lives."

"No," I said.

"Well, to cut the story short, I thought the best thing he could do was to come and spend the week-end with us. He did, and my mother invited Ann. They met for the first time in this house." His expression suddenly changed, "It is a bloody tragic affair." He shook his head. "I was certain he was getting on well with Ann; then this would have to happen! I suppose he couldn't forget the other woman."

"Have you spoken to other people who knew Julian?" I said.

"Well, I was up in Town yesterday, and at lunch at the club three of us were talking about him. We liked him—everybody did in the battalion—but it turned out they didn't know him as well as I did. One of them was actually the Adjutant, an older man, but he was asking *me*. I'm certain it was another woman."

"Another woman," I reflected. Roger Temple apparently couldn't tell me any more, but in a way it was amazing how Julian could have hidden everything from his fellow officers. But was it really amazing? The invert's whole life is spent hiding his real passion from the enemy. A double life becomes second nature to him; he learns the technique in his teens. Besides, if there is no suspicion, there is nothing to bring inversion into normal people's minds.

"Reggie Plummer—that's the Adjutant—said he'd sent a small paragraph to *The Times* about Julian: 'A friend writes'—you know the kind of thing—but I don't think it was published. It was too late. It was Reggie who told us how Julian got his M.C. Julian, of course, was very reticent about it. Well, it was in Palermo. Julian was a very junior officer then. One day in a patrol he carried out an attack against the Jerries practically single-handed. It was such conspicuous bravery that they actually sent him in for the V.C. He *was* very brave, you know."

I quite believed that. Many homosexuals are. I had heard much about the heroic inverts during the war. There were several who were pilots at the time of the Battle of Britain, and oddly enough they didn't crack up in greater numbers than the "normals". Some inverts are brave because they *are* inverts: it's a form of exhibitionism, of self-dramatisation: play-acting in real life. Others want to demonstrate their manliness, because the invert in the average person's mind is usually associated with fear and cowardice. So bravery becomes camouflage. One thing is certain: few inverts are brave through lack of imagination, for most of them have a strongly developed sense of danger. There is also, of course, the romantic, daredevil type, usually of rugged appearance: well-made, tough, hairy and deep-voiced—a type comparatively rare in England, but more frequent in Germany or America. In many respects, Julian was one of these.

It was after six o'clock, but still warm. An ageing spaniel came up to me, smelt my trousers, then ambled away and began to play with his mate the Labrador. Roger Temple and I now joined his fiancée and Ann, who had finished their game. Ann's face was red and in a way attractive. Temple started to tell a story about someone in the neighbourhood. He was apparently fond of telling stories.

Was he the wartime Guards officer? I reflected. And was Julian one? Sartorially they certainly conformed. Temple wore a dark blue blazer with regimental buttons and a scarf round his neck with the Brigade stripes. In Town he would be dressed obviously like the rest—tight suits, stiff collar, narrow shoulders, bowler hat, umbrella. But his manner was not the Guards manner, not even Guards mannerisms. What was it? It was partly the vocabulary, of course, but Temple had a vitality and an exuberance that was slightly vulgar, with a vulgarity one social level lower than a Guards officer's vulgarity.

Seven

I was rather uneasy about contacting Hugh Harpley. I remembered that I had been introduced to him originally by Julian at a dance. His name had then been Saunders. He was the son of a shipping man and his mother had been a peeress in her own right. At one time during the war he used to ring me quite often to ask me to dinner or to see a play. It had been fairly obvious that he was looking for someone, a friend, to whom he could talk about himself and who, in turn, would give him reassurance. There were two reasons why, as politely as I could, I'd refused his invitations. Most of my daily work consisted in doing the very thing he expected of me, the difference being that the people who came to me professionally were not bored and capricious idle, rich young men. The other reason was that his charm and generosity attracted a crowd of sycophants to his house whose company I couldn't bear.

Before I dialled his number, I tried to think of a plausible excuse for phoning him, but nothing came to mind beyond the fact that, since he was extremely capricious, no excuse would be needed if he were in a good mood. On the other hand, if he were in a bad mood, no excuse would be of any avail.

It was the butler who answered the telephone. I remembered the voice, incapable of surprise.

"This is Dr. Anthony Page. May I speak to Lord Harpley?"

I had to wait nearly five minutes. Then I finally heard Hugh's familiar high-pitched voice. "Good-morning. How are you?"

"I've been away," I lied. "Haven't seen you for a long time."

There was a longish pause. Then he said, "I've been away also." As he spoke, I could feel the suspicion in his voice. My task would have been so much easier if I'd seen him somewhere accidentally, and gone up to him. I felt like an idler intruding on a busy man. Then it suddenly occurred to me that he probably thought I was trying to borrow money from him. I said quickly, "Would you like to dine with me one day?" I added: "At the Coquille."

"That's very kind of you," he replied, and I felt I had made it worse, "but I very seldom go out these days. Why don't you come and dine here with me? . . ." Then, as if acting on the principle of let's-get-it-over-quickly, he suggested: "Tonight, if you like. Come at a quarter to eight."

"I'd love to," I said, and, without thinking, I added: "It's an awful thing about Julian."

"Who?"

"Julian Leclerc," I said.

"Oh, yes. Dreadful. . . . You must excuse me. My masseur has just arrived. I'll see you tonight."

II

I had reminded myself on the way not to forget to tell Hugh how young and well he looked, but, as it happened, my statement was quite true. The lights in his room were soft and I noticed his face was made up, but I felt that this made little difference. Even in less favourable circumstances, he would not have been taken for more than twenty-five, whereas one could find out from reference books that his real age was thirty-six.

"I know you never try to flatter people," he said slowly and ambiguously, "and I'm glad to hear you say I look well. It matters enormously to me, coming from someone who hasn't seen me for some time. It probably doesn't bother you much if you look old or ugly, because you hunt. But I like to be hunted, so I have an agonising fear of growing old. It's silly, of course, and one can't do much about it. Soon enough I'll have to fall back on my past, I suppose. But what a past!" He smiled for a second, then he began to rehearse his future.

"I remember once Rodney Croodie and I had a romp in one of the servants' bedrooms upstairs during a dance in Cadogan Square. Then there was the Dudley-Hardies' ball in Venice when I went off with the gondolier." The smile suddenly disappeared from his face. "I used to go to Chatham to pick up sailors—of course, it was usually the other way round and I got picked up instead, and there was actually an occasion when one of them gave me half a crown. Please don't laugh," he said suddenly, but I was not laughing. "Looking back on it, I can't help feeling it was rather beautiful. I was twenty and good-looking, and so was the matelot; he thought I was a little pouf from the 'Dilly, and he gave me a whole day's pay. I suppose he had been brought up in some institution, a training-ship for orphans or something, and as likely as not my father had been one of the founders of the place. I sometimes wonder if that sort of person remembers. . . ."

I didn't reply, but I thought it was unlikely. People of that type are usually primitive. When young they quite often don't discriminate much between men and women, then, as a rule, their early old age and the struggle for existence soon dry up their sex instincts. And they only remember evil things.

"But all that, of course, is finished," Hugh said; "and I feel middle age creeping in in one particular way. You see, it's no longer easy for me to make contacts, to meet new people. I should very much like to, but it's too much strain."

"I suppose so," I said. Hugh Harpley had hardly done a day's work all his life. Delicate as a boy, his education had ended at eighteen. A medical report, on some ground or another, had kept him out of the Services, and apart from driving a Red Cross ambulance for a year or so, he had done nothing else in the war. I had heard that he had an income of about three thousand a year tax free.

"I think you knew Julian Leclerc rather well?" I said during dinner.

"I used to. Who told you?"

"Well, it was he who introduced me to you."

"So he did." Hugh stared at me, then he shook his head. "How time flies. Yes; you came to a party at Grosvenor Square once when my parents were taking a cure at Vichy."

I remembered the party. There were about half a dozen rich, completely uninteresting, tongue-tied young men and a dozen sycophants, and Ray Marsden, the poet who was killed in the war and who had looked as if he were asking himself, "How did I get here?"

"Had you seen Julian much in the last few years?" I said.

"Only now and then. He become drearier and drearier. I've known several people like him. Good-looking and exciting when young; then they lose everything as they grow old."

"Julian was only thirty," I said rather impulsively.

"Well, some people can't keep their youth," he replied, defending his cause. I was sure that very few people would have agreed with him about Julian's appearance, but I said nothing.

"What I mean is, he was pretty wild when he was young," Hugh continued. "I remember a story he once told me. It really is weird. He picked up a young tough somewhere in the East End, and took him to a cinema and tried to play. The man suggested they went to his home. I'd have been frightened out of my wits, but you knew Julian and his bravado. Anyway, he went. The man was actually out of work and lived in some dreadful slum—I don't know . . . Canning Town. It was rather late when they arrived and the young man first showed Julian some snapshots." Hugh suddenly smiled. "Oh, highly respectable ones . . . Southend or Margate with the family. Then Julian tried to play and the man smiled and said no. Then he disappeared for a moment or two. Julian heard him talking in a low voice to someone in the next room. Again I'd have had fits if I'd been in Julian's shoes, imagining the the chap was talking to some accomplice and planning to 'roll' me. Then there were peculiar noises from the room next door that sounded like furniture being pushed around. Then, finally, the man returned and smiled at Julian and in a sort of shy way said: 'Would you like to have the wife?' Well," Hugh said, "that's East End hospitality for you."

The butler came in to serve the main course and Hugh was silent for a time. Then he went on talking about himself, fluently and amusingly, like an uninstructed but well-born and intelligent social hostess.

"Of course," I suddenly heard him saying, "the situation became very difficult when my father and I had a row. He found out about me, you see. It was my fault. I wrote a very indiscreet letter to someone. Well, you know how it is. Sometimes one just can't help it; one has to write something. I thought I was in love with Charles, a very nice boy who was studying to be an accountant. I don't know how his father got hold of the letter. He probably had the same name as his son, but one day my father received a short note from him: 'Dear Sir,—Perhaps you would be interested to know that the enclosed letter was sent by your son to mine' . . .

something like that. My father, of course, was very difficult about
it and very Presbyterian. He told my two sisters. For a whole week
he didn't speak to me; then it was just hell. I had to go to frightful
little hotels near railway stations. D'you know, he's still angry with
me for it. . . ."

"I wonder how many parents know," I said.

"Not as many as one might expect. Do yours know?"

"They're both dead," I replied. "But I don't think they ever
knew."

"You understand a lot about these things," Hugh said. "Tell me,
why is it that working-class parents seldom object if they find out?"

"Perhaps because they care far less on the whole."

"I know for a fact," Hugh interrupted, ignoring my answer,
"that some toughs take a very generous view of bitches. They
actually protect them—and I dare say sometimes the protection
money is paid in kind." He smiled. "Is it because toughs on the
whole have very little feminine element in their make-up?"

"It could be. The reverse is certainly true. The biggest enemy of
the invert is the feminine man who becomes a homo-Puritan. It's
quite safe to say that most of the people who are so vehemently
anti-queer are people with strong feminine streaks. Do you think
Julian's people knew?"

"I shouldn't for a moment. Aren't they dead?"

"The father's alive."

"He's an awful stick. I remember once or twice he came to
lunch. My father was at school with him. Wasn't he an I Zingari?
Just the sort of person to turn his son queer. I say," he continued
in his usual inconsequential way, "do you know any American
soldiers stationed in London? I'm told some of them are madly
queer. I always like their underwear. . . ."

After dinner we had coffee in the sitting-room, all Waterford
glass, white rugs and *directoire* furniture. Like so many people,
Hugh had to "think of his customers", and designed his room to
suit their tastes. He suggested going to the *Aldebaran*. The prospect
was depressing, but I decided to accompany him, as I still had faint
hopes that he might be able to tell me something more about Julian.

Before we got up to leave, I took out my notecase and showed
Hugh the photograph. "What do you think?" I asked.

"One can't really judge people from pictures," he said, a little bored. "The camera cheats. Some people are photogenic. I, for one, am not. . . . ." He suddenly looked up rather guiltily, and put his hand on my arm for a split second. "Please forgive me. He's very nice. Is he your new friend? You must tell me more about him. Where did you find him?"

"Brighton," I said, weakly.

III

The *Aldebaran* hadn't changed much since the war, except that the walls had been repainted. It was one of the half-dozen or so queer clubs in London which those who had been excluded from it generally invested with an aura of elegance and wickedness. In reality, it was neither elegant nor wicked; it differed from the queer pubs only in the fact that its clientele was a little more expensively dressed. There was the same strain, the same expectation and disappointment, the same make-believe, the same lies. It was improper without being naughty.

Hugh was greeted by a few people, most of them anxious to know him, and as we sat down in a corner I knew that someone would sooner or later approach us. I decided to be forceful, and take the plunge: "I keep thinking of Julian's suicide."

"I can see you're interested," Hugh said, looking at me. "Why?"

"Oh, for professional reasons. . . ."

"Of course," he nodded, and I felt he believed me. "I wish I could tell you something. . . . But wait a moment." He had already beckoned to a fat man who was coming towards us. I think I had met him before; he was probably a member of the club's somewhat nebulous committee.

"Good evening, Philip," Hugh said, and stretched out a hand as an Edwardian social hostess might have stretched out a fan. "You know Tony Page, don't you. How are you?"

"Back from my death-bed," the fat man said as he sat down.

"Now here's somebody who can tell you a little more about Julian." Hugh turned to our new companion: "Tony's interested to know what happened to Julian Leclerc."

"It's very tragic and very sad," the man answered. "He got engaged to a rich girl and the girl found out. That sort of thing can happen quite easily. . . ."

It seemed clear I was wasting my time, but the fat man went on: "It's an unkind thing to say, but in a way Julian asked for it. He could be very callous, you know." I noticed that my informant was one of those people who always close their eyes after making a statement.

"Now," he continued, taking me into his confidence, "you and I both know a fair number of people in the queer world who are cruel and callous. They get let down, disappointed, hurt, so they become hardened. I don't know much about Julian's previous life, but some time ago, someone rang me up. A friend of Julian's. He was quite a nice young man whom I'd met a couple of times, and I think he once came to my house to dinner with Julian. Anyhow, he said, 'May I come and see you? It's something important.' I said, 'Yes; by all means.' I didn't quite know what it was all about, but when he came I saw he was almost beyond himself. I gave him a drink and he told me Julian had dropped him and he felt desperate. He said, 'I hope you don't mind, but you're a friend of Julian's, and I don't know anybody else.' I tried to comfort him. Told him it was quite natural he was badly upset, because he was young, but that one gets over that sort of thing. What else could I say? . . ."

"Was it someone I know?" Hugh asked.

"I shouldn't think so," the fat man said. "A young working man from Sheffield. He was a printer, I think. All I remember was that he had an unusual Christian name—Tyrell. . . ."

I almost knocked over my glass, but fortunately nobody noticed. My heart was thumping fast. This was incredible.

It was then, I believe, that the fat man said something to the effect that he wouldn't have been surprised if the young man had committed suicide, instead of Julian. But I was no longer listening. I was waiting for my chance to thank Hugh for the dinner and to run home to look up my file on Dighton, who was coming to see me at six the following afternoon. Tyrell Dighton, my star patient, the man I'd been seeing regularly for months now, the man who had no secrets from me, the man about whom I knew everything—except the fact that he had known Julian.

Eight

The file was large and rather untidy. The notes I'd made during our last meeting, two days earlier, were loose and had not yet been typed out. As I began to sort out the other papers, held together by the spring, a long Manila envelope with a fifteen-cent airmail stamp on it fell out. It contained Stowasser's questionnaire and a carbon copy of my reply. *"Dighton,"* I read, *"T.A., age 26, printer, English. Athletic type. Skin smooth; eyes blue; teeth regular, lateral incisors small. Ears: lower lobe adherent. Hair: wavy lt. brown. No hair on chest. Shaving since 18 dly. Heart: small, rate 78. Bld. Pressure 115/75. No specific change in arteries. Musculature: large-firm. Skeleton: medium. Ht: 5' 10", Wgt: 10 st. 11 lb. Torso-leg ratio 43×86×95. Inter-spinal 11, Biacromial 38.5, Bicristal 23. Carrying angle 161 degr. Skull: male type, Pelvis decid. male. Dimple in chin, dilated capillaries on rib margin."* On the next sheet there were the results of the Ternan-Miles tests, the introvertive response and the masculinity-femininity tests Stowasser was always so keen on.

Then for a moment or two I forgot what I was actually looking for, because I suddenly remember Dighton's first visit. While I was reading the brief letter of introduction from St. Gabriel's, he had given little indication of the struggle which must have been going on in his mind. "Right," I said. "I should like to know a little more about what's bothering you." I suppose I smiled, trying to put him at ease. It was then that he looked at me straight in the eye and said almost loudly, "I want to be cured of homo sexuality." He pronounced it as if it were two words. "I heard from someone that perhaps an operation can help."

"That I don't know," I said. "The surgery of sex, as they call it, is very new and quite experimental and the results are not conclusive. It consists, I think, of the manipulation of certain glands and I should imagine it might cure certain homosexual conditions which are overwhelmingly glandular, but the point is that on the whole very few are. In any case, I'm not a surgeon."

"Psycho-analysis," he said, as if speaking some magic password.

"But it is curable, isn't it?" The diction was boyish, the expression of the face mature and determined.

"I don't yet know anything about your condition, but I can tell you straight away that the fact that you want to be cured is a very promising factor. But, I have to warn you that if it comes to psycho-analysis, cure may take quite a long time."

"How long?"

"Maybe years."

"I don't mind," he said quietly. "I'd do anything to get cured. The only snag's the expense." He looked away from me.

"Don't worry about that."

"I'm a printer," he said, and I noticed there was a momentary relief in his voice. "I earn ten pounds a week. Perhaps I can do some overtime. . . . I have a little money saved up."

"Please don't worry about it. If I find that I can take your case, you can come to see me twice a week and I shall charge you five shillings a session."

"That's very kind of you, Sir," he said.

II

I was looking for some mention of Julian among Dighton's notes and soon enough I found what I wanted. There were many reasons why I hadn't thought of Julian while Dighton had talked about him, the main one being that he had referred to him as Nigel. Inverts in their relations often give false names, but this was unlikely to have been the case with Julian. Nigel was actually Julian's first Christian name, which he never used. Dighton, however, may have had a preference for it. Although it was quite clear now that Julian and Nigel were one and the same, there was no reason for me to have noticed the connection before. Dighton had never told me anything sufficiently explicit to enable me to identify Julian, and what details he had given me could have fitted any number of people.

I read my brief notes of what Dighton had told me: "*In November, he met Nigel, about 28, a former officer, studying for his exams. He took N. home. The next day he felt N. was the man he had been looking for all his life. Soon enough they decided to live together. They were perfectly happy. D. had a premonition the first time that the affair wouldn't last; he forgot this, but remembered it very distinctly after the affair broke up. This happened when N. passed his finals. D. had a 'terrible time'. The first day, partly because he made up his mind to put on a face, wasn't the worst, and he felt he'd get over it. But the second day he felt the full impact. He cried. He had never realised he loved N. so much. And the days after brought no relief. One afternoon he practically collapsed at the works & had to go home. He was away from work the next two days. He went to a pub and picked someone up. It must have been v. embarrassing for the young agricultural student, because D. just couldn't do anything. A few days later he picked someone else up, but all he could feel was disgust. He felt he was on the verge of a nervous breakdown. Finally, he went to see his own panel dr. It was a shameful thing to have to admit all about himself, but the overworked man was quite helpful. He sent D. to the Clinic. The registrar who dealt with him said the waiting list was very long, but finding that he could pay a small fee, he sent him to me with a letter. . . ."*

It was a miracle, I thought, a tiny one, a chance coincidence, but a miracle just the same. Consciously or unconsciously, we wait for miracles all our lives, but life gives us few. Perhaps that is why we have invented the novel: an art form whose real subject, whose most important ingredient, had always been a fictitious miracle. And it isn't silly to wait for miracles, to dream about them, to search for them in novels, for the miracle means no less than freedom and the novel by implication is a revolutionary manifesto. I felt I was *living* a novel now.

Nine

Dighton was wearing his familiar grey demob. suit and his Air Force tie, but I noticed he had on a pair of new shoes: brown box calf with crêpe soles. He smiled as he entered.

"Afternoon," I said. "I don't have to ask how you feel."

"Perhaps because the weather's good," he said, and looked back at me from the doorway.

"Would you like to sit in the chair?" I asked as he made his way towards the couch. I took the seat facing him. "Tell me, what have you been doing lately?"

"Much the same as usual." His expression became serious, as always when he was asked a question. "Tuesday I went to evening class. Colour-printing. It was pretty boring stuff—theoretical, you know. On inks. Thursday I went to the gym. Incidentally"—he looked up—"yesterday I'm afraid I was rather rude to a man at the gym. He comes on the same days as me and he always talks to me. He's queer. I knew it from the first day I saw him. I try to avoid him, but it's difficult. We often have to use the same equipment, like weights, skipping rope or bar-bells, and it's just impossible to avoid speaking. Well, last night I was resting for a minute after a shoulder exercise and he came up and said would I like to go to see the new Humphrey Bogart film. I said I was sorry I was busy. Oh, he said, what about tomorrow. And when he said that, he gave a smile that made me sick. I said I was busy tomorrow too and got up and left him. I know I was rude, but it was the only way to get rid of him. I suppose I was angry because I felt he must have guessed something about me."

"Not necessarily," I said. "An old man?"

"No. About my age. I think he's on the stage. He's got quite a good figure."

"Do people often try to pick you up?" I said. I decided I wouldn't burst Julian on him directly.

"Well." He began to think. "I don't count the gym, because it's full of queers."

"The gym?" I said.

"Yes. Full of them."

For a moment I felt surprised; then I remembered the occasion when Terry had taken me to a swimming pool. This was, I imagined, a new post-war trend in England. A considerable proportion of young homosexuals regularly went to gymnasia and swimming pools, not only to look at, or try to establish contact with, attractive young men, but also to improve their own physique, and thereby their chances of success.

"I have been approached once or twice in the street," Dighton said now, "and on buses. Last time it happened in Coventry Street about a fortnight ago. It was Saturday afternoon. I was looking at some gramophone records in a shop window, and a man came up. I knew at once what he wanted. You can always tell, especially in the West End. But he took quite a long time about it. He'd been looking at me in the window glass. He spoke with an American accent, but he was obviously putting it on. He asked me where Tottenham Court Road was. That's just about the daftest pick-up line I've ever heard. I told him, and walked away. I was in a good mind to be rude to him."

"A natural reaction." I said. "But don't be intolerant. For one thing, it might become suspicious. Really normal people are seldom intolerant towards queers, and if they are, it's usually because they've had some bad experience. Now, Mr. Dighton, where were we?" I pretended to be going through the notes of our last session. "Your brother Len and your mother . . . she died when you were seventeen. Well, now I'd like to interrupt and go a little forward for a time. You remember your whole crisis started with your last, unfortunate love affair. You told me a certain amount; then we went back to your childhood. Now to return. This affair with Nigel," I said. "What I'd really . . ."

Dighton suddenly spoke. For a moment I was taken aback, as I was about to ask him for all the details of the story. Then I saw that he was smiling. "This is very strange," he said. In his excitement his Yorkshire accent became pronounced. "I wanted to tell you this a fortnight ago, boot I tried to concentrate on other things, like you told me. He's dead."

"Really," I said. "How do you know?"

"It was in the paper. He committed suicide. . . . It was very strange." Still smiling, Dighton shook his head. "That's another thing I wanted to tell you. A couple of days before I saw it in the paper, I suddenly thought of him. Without any reason. I was cleaning a block in the works. I remember it was raining. I sooddenly thought of Nigel and I realised I no longer hated him. I mean, you remember I told you I used to hate him; but that day, as I was thinking of him, I was able to forgive him, or, at least he no longer mattered in my life. Well, I mean, if I'd seen him in the street by chance I'd even have spoken to him. But, of course, I could never make it up with him. Then the next minute somebody came up and spoke to me and I forgot all about him. Well! Two days later I read in the evening paper that he was dead. It was probably telepathy, if that's what you call it."

"What was your immediate reaction to the news?" I asked.

"I felt very sorry for him, I suppose, but I was too excited on account of thinking about him just about when he killed himself. Later on, I remember, I thought how lucky I was that I'd decided to give the whole thing up."

Dighton was silent now, and for the second time I thought that my excitement at the *Aldebaran* last night had been rather unnecessary as sooner or later Dighton must have come out with the story and then, although he'd still have referred to Julian by another name, I must surely have realised who Nigel was. But it was a miracle just the same. I said: "Did the suicide surprise you in view of how well you knew him?"

"Definitely," Dighton said. "I never thought he'd do a thing like that. He wasn't soft." He was looking at me as he spoke and he must have seen something in my expression. He said: "I don't know, of course. You never can tell."

"Well, perhaps we can kill two birds with one stone," I said. "I should like you to tell me about Nigel. What you say may reveal some of his motives for suicide. But, of course, that's not the reason I'm asking you to tell me about him."

"No," he said. "I see."

Normally, today, we should have gone on with Dighton's early history. There were questions on a sheet of paper I meant to ask him about his mother. I should have to leave them for the time

being. I presumed it wouldn't do any harm to make him talk about
his relations with Julian. I was at my desk now, with Dighton's file
in front of me. I again saw the sheet of paper I had re-read last
night. Nigel, I told myself, Nigel, Nigel, Nigel. I must, under no
circumstances, refer to him as Julian. Nigel, Nigel. . . . I said: "I see
that you met him at a pub one evening. Nigel, an ex-officer, about
28 . . . I'll tell you what. You'd better lie down as usual and try to
concentrate on your relations with him."

He lay down on the couch. I noticed he was wearing grey-blue
Air Force socks. I switched off the lamp. "Ready?" I said.

"It was a few months after I came out of the Air Force," he
began, and paused. "I went back to my job and I was feeling a little
browned-off with going out nearly every night to pubs. Hunting.
I suppose I was just restless. I wanted sex and adventure; I didn't
really like the pubs even then, but what could one do? There are
lots of people who go to them night after night, just because they
haven't anything better to do. Well, that night I was really fed-up.
I was actually talking to someone. A shipping clerk, called Don.
There was nothing between us. He was older, but quite nice to
talk to. It doesn't do just to stand by yourself in a queer pub. Well,
as we were talking, Nigel came in. I noticed him the moment he
came through the door. We looked at each other for a moment.
He was actually with a friend who knew Don. They came up
and Don introduced me and we got talking. I must say I liked
him from the first moment. . . . There were many reasons. . . ."
Dighton seemed to be thinking, but I couldn't see his face. I tipped
my cigarette into the ash-tray. "First of all," he said, "he was very
good-looking, but he didn't look queer. Then the other thing was
that he had such nice manners. And I knew at once that he was
good-tempered. You can always see that. . . ." There was a slight
pause. "Nigel could be amusing and interesting without being
tatty or camp. That means feminine," he said, trying to familiarise
me with the underground code language I knew as well as he did,
with a few regional variations to boot. "It's very difficult to explain
it," he went on, "but what I really liked about him was that he was
very serious. I'd met several people like him in the Air Force, especially one officer, but they weren't queer. Anyhow, it was nearly
closing time and Nigel's friend said, 'Let's go to the Thirty-two.'

That used to be an all-night café near Covent Garden. I think it's closed down now. It was a dreadful place, dirty and full of spivs and toughs and prostitutes. I saw that Nigel wanted to be with me, so I just didn't mind what Don and the other fellow thought, and I said I wanted to go home. Nigel knew. He said he wanted to go home too. So we said goodbye to the other two. They went towards Covent Garden and we walked up to Oxford Street. When we were alone, Nigel said he was very glad he'd met me and we must meet again. He told me he was studying law and that he was doing his finals and had very little free time. Well, it was a very nice evening, even though it was November, and when I told him I lived in Paddington, he said we ought to walk along Oxford Street to Marble Arch and then he'd take a bus to Kensington. I said all right. I knew that he liked me, but I doubted whether he'd say anything the first time. I wouldn't have minded, but of course I couldn't tell him that. I wouldn't have minded even if he'd spoken to me at the pub without being properly introduced and suggested I went home with him. I mean, many people used to come up to me in pubs, but I just wouldn't play.

"Anyhow when we reached Marble Arch we didn't say goodbye. We walked along Bayswater Road. We were talking. I don't remember what about, but I was getting excited. I wanted him to come home with me, but I didn't like to ask him. Then we got to Lancaster Gate and I got even more excited, because I lived very near and I knew he was miles out of his way. He could easily spend the night with me, because the landlady liked me, and she never minded if I took someone back. I suppose she knew all about me, but she was broad-minded. I always mended things in the house for her, like fuses and taps and locks and the bathroom. But, of course, I couldn't tell Nigel that. I mean about the landlady being broad-minded. So we just walked on, but somehow we were walking a little faster now than before. I don't know quite who was responsible, but by the time we turned into my street I knew he was going to come in. When I let him into the room, he said it was nearly midnight, and he was worried I wouldn't get enough sleep, on account of my having to get up early in the morning. I said it didn't matter."

II

"The next morning," Dighton said later, "I woke up first. It was a quarter to seven. I washed and made breakfast for two and woke Nigel at half-past. We didn't speak much, but I knew I was happy. We said we'd meet two days later in the evening.

"I felt rather funny at work. I was happy to meet Nigel, very happy, but I kept asking myself would it last? Queer people are very fickle, you know; one minute they think they are desperately in love, the next they forget all about you. And he was clearly so different from me. I'd never previously had anything to do with people like him, but I'd often wished I had. Was I good enough for him or was it just a flash in the pan on his side? I knew he was absolutely honest; that I knew straight away; it wasn't that. But would he really become devoted to me? For a moment I thought perhaps I oughtn't to go on; perhaps I should tell him and make a clean breast of it! 'You'll never really love me, Nigel. For a time you'll be attracted while I'm new to you, then you'll drop me because I'm a bore.' Because you see, Doctor, at that time—the morning after—I wasn't yet in love with him. But the more I thought about him—I couldn't get him off my mind the whole day—the more foolish I felt. I was still the little provincial kid from Brightside. That's Sheffield. I'd never get anywhere if I kept to my place. In any case, I thought, what was my place? People were talking about a social revolution, and it wasn't just talk. The workers were doing better now and the middle class weren't doing as well as they used to. Your job was secure, which was something entirely new, and you had a better chance than ever before of getting ahead. A boy I know from back home is at Oxford now. On a scholarship. He used to live next-door to us. His father was a foreman at Hadfield's. We went to the same school. As a matter of fact, I did discuss those things with Nigel as we were walking home the first night we met. He was very much on the workers' side, and it wasn't just talk; he knew a good deal about their problems. It was a big surprise to me. Well, to cut it short, I told myself that my fear about Nigel was daft. Ever since I'd gone into the Air Force I'd wanted to rise out

of the class I was born into, and now I had a first-rate opportunity.
It was very lucky, even from that point of view, that I'd met him.
He could help me. In fact, it looked as if he would." Here Dighton
broke off abruptly. "I may be wrong about that, you know; I mean
the thing I told you about my future plans. Perhaps I just decided
to go on with him because I was attracted by his looks. I don't
know, I'm sure. . . ."

"There may have been several factors," I said. "There usually
are; but don't bother about that. We're getting on fine."

"Yes. . . . Well, in any case by the time I saw Nigel again, two
days later, I'd forgotten all about my doubts. He came round just
as I'd finished having a wash and we went to have dinner at the
Cumberland, then to the pictures afterwards. The Marble Arch
Pavilion. Then we went back to my place."

"Nigel said he was very sorry he couldn't ask me to his room
to spend the night there. He told me he had a room in a boarding-
house in South Kensington, and the landlady would object. In any
case, he was very fed-up with the place and wanted to move. He
had a nice large room, he said, but it was very dear, and he had to
go out for all his meals. I told him how nice it would be if he and I
could share a flat together. He said, yes it would be, but the way he
said it I felt I'd made a fopah. We changed the subject.

"But the third time we met—it was Sunday, and we spent practically the whole day on the river—it was Nigel himself who asked
me if it was possible for him to find a room in the house. In my
house, I mean. It was after we came back. I remember I couldn't
even look at him, I was that flabbergasted. I couldn't speak. It was
stupid, and he asked me whether I thought it was a silly idea. I
said no, it wasn't silly, but I didn't tell him why I was so surprised.
I said I'd love to ask the landlady, but was he sure the place would
be all right for him. I mean, it's just an ordinary house, I told him.
All the people who lived there worked for their living. 'Well, so do
I,' Nigel said, and he slapped me on the back. I told him my rent
was only twenty-five shillings a week, and it included use of the
kitchen. Mind you, I made it comfortable. I bought odds and ends,
such as a reading-lamp and cushions; the wireless was mine and I
made my own bookshelf and hearthrug.

"As a matter of fact, I knew that one of the lodgers, on the second floor, was going back to Ireland. But he had a very little room. It was a pound a week. So I wasn't sure. But Nigel said it would be all right. I thought we could make it attractive, and he was bound to have some furniture of his own. So the next day I asked the landlady, and she said she had a better room than the one upstairs. In fact, the big front room next to mine was going in about a fortnight's time. The Irish couple who had it had found a flat off Harrow Road.

"Well, everything was fine. I was very happy about the way things were working out. A fortnight later Nigel moved in, and after that we lived together. His room was next to mine. I always made breakfast for two before I went to work, and he spent his day reading and studying for his exam, and the evenings with me. Sometimes we went to a cinema or a play, but we were quite happy just to stay indoors talking. Once or twice we went to a pub, but we didn't really care for drinking. We never went to a queer pub or saw other people. Later, I began going to evening classes.

"Well, one evening, several months later, Nigel's father came to see him. Nigel told me his father was very sticky and knew nothing about his life, so he had to be careful. I saw his father from the window as they got out of the taxi. He was tall, just a bit shorter than Nigel, and he had a grey moustache; he was a little lame and walked with a stick.

"I was standing behind the curtain in my room as I watched them getting out of the taxi, and I could see the Colonel didn't like the place at all, the way he looked round. I asked Nigel about it afterwards, but he said his father had nothing to do with where he chose to live. He's very old-fashioned, he said, and just doesn't understand the times we're living in. Of course, I knew that Nigel had no money of his own and had to do as his father said. But I soon stopped worrying. The Colonel never came again, and even if he'd told Nigel to leave the place, we could have found two separate rooms in a better house. I'd often thought of doing that, you know.

"Well that was round March, and in May Nigel got nervy and restless. For days he hardly spoke. He was very nice, mind you, but I could see he was worried about his examinations. It was strange; he calmed down and became quite cool just before he went to sit for them. On the very night before the exams we went to a club. He said he wanted to clear his mind. The place was called the *Aldebaran*, in the West End. It's queer. I'd never been there before and I never realised Nigel knew so many people there. Many of them came up to say hullo—where've you been hiding. I didn't like them much, but of course one has to be nice to people in a club. He introduced me to a few of his friends. They were quite polite and all that, but I noticed that it was just because of Nigel and that they really looked down on me. Most of them, anyhow. You know how it is. They talked about theatres and places abroad and people one didn't know. I thought most of their talk was just showing off. One couldn't talk to them the way one could to Nigel. Besides they looked queer; well-dressed and not tatty and no bright colours, and yet they looked queer, the way they talked and moved about. They were, I suppose, just rich, spoilt people with cars. One, I think, was a lord, very weedy and affected. Anyhow, there was one friend of Nigel's who was nice, Philip, his name was. He had an antique shop somewhere in the West End. He was a big fat man of about forty-five—his voice would make you laugh—but he was really decent. Afterwards we went to his house for a drink; then we took a taxi home. He lived in Chelsea and I'd never seen such a beautiful house. It was all antique furniture and large rooms with the paintings on the walls all lit up. He was very nice to us and said we must come to dinner with him to celebrate Nigel's passing his exam. As a matter of fact, we did go. That was about a week later and he gave us a marvellous meal. He had a cook and a manservant. There was another guest. A painter or something, a foreigner, but he spoke good English. Well, after dinner we went to two night-clubs, both in the West End. I never realised there were so many queer clubs in London. I didn't like the people at all.

"It was soon after Nigel passed his exams that the whole thing started. He went away for a week to stay with his father in the country. He wanted a rest. But when he came back I noticed he was a different man. I really can't tell you in what ways he'd changed, because it's very difficult to say, and as a matter of fact I didn't notice the change at once. He was still very nice to me, but he began to spend his evenings outdoors. First he used to tell me where he was going. He had to see people about a job. His father was putting up the money for him to buy a partnership, I think. Then he went away again for a week-end. He said he was going to stay with his family, but I wasn't sure. He was still nice to me, but. . . ."

"Were you still on affectionate terms then?" I said as tactfully as possible.

"Not after he came back from the week-end. That's exactly why I thought he hadn't gone home. He must have been with someone else. A few people rang up from time to time, but nobody ever came to see him, except one evening a man in an expensive car. Nigel said he was a solicitor. They went out to have dinner. Then one evening he didn't come home at all, and wasn't in his room when I got up. I felt awful. You see, Nigel and I had been talking about our plans for the future. I was doing two night classes a week, one for English and the other on printing. I wanted to get on, and I was pretty sure I could. We thought we could share a flat later.

"Well, after he came back from the week-end, I naturally didn't say anything to him—just asked him how things were—but I knew something was wrong. When he spent the night away, I cried for about the first time since I was a kid. I saw him the following evening, when I came back from work, and I talked to him about it. . . ."

"What did you say?"

"I just told him he was making me very unhappy. And I asked him what I'd done that was wrong. He said it was all his fault. He said he owed me a confession. I could see it was very difficult for him, but he got up and said, 'Look, Tyrell, I thought I was in love with you, but I wasn't. It's an awful thing to admit, but you asked me to be honest about it, and I can't lie, in any case.'

"He was very silent after that, but I just couldn't speak. I'm not the type of man to make a scene, even though I was in love with him and badly hurt. Then he said in any case he was now a solicitor and was starting work almost immediately, and he'd have to spend a good deal of his time getting business and working late and going out with people; so he'd have to take a flat somewhere else. He told me, of course, we must stay friends. Well, I knew exactly what that meant: that's the brush-off. I'd never said that to anyone in my life, but I know what it means."

"Did you actually find out who the other man was?" I said.

"Never. Nigel seldom talked about his past, so I don't even know what type attracted him. . . . If there was a type. There are lots and lots of queers who have no type."

"Didn't Nigel talk about his past at all?" I said.

"Well, he did, but not much about his love affairs. Once I asked him. I suppose that was a mistake. He tried to laugh it off. He said, 'Why do you ask?' I said I just wanted to know, but I noticed he didn't like the question. He told me when people are very young, they get mad, but later they usually settle down and look more and more for friendship and understanding as well as love. And he said that since he'd found me he hadn't thought of anybody else; he never liked looking back. I said I felt the same way about it. But, of course, I'd already told him all about myself. . . ."

"So you think Nigel did love you?" I said.

"I think he did for a time, or he found me attractive. I don't know. We lived together for nine months, you see, and up to the time of his exam he hardly ever went out in the evening without me. In fact, I remember one day in the winter I had a bad cold and stayed away from work the whole day. Well, in the evening he was going out to dine with one of his lawyer friends—I know that was on the level—but he rang his friend and put him off. I told him he was silly. Well, he stayed indoors with me and we played pontoon. . . . As a matter of fact he caught my cold, although I told him not to come near me. He had to stay in bed for two days himself."

Dighton was silent now. For a time, for quite a time, I wasn't conscious of the surroundings.

"Why do you think he gave you up?" I said eventually.

"I don't know." His voice was very matter-of-fact and unexcited. I noticed that all the time. He was no longer trying to be objective. He was succeeding. But I was not at all certain how far that objectivity went yet. This was more interesting than the things he had told me about Julian. Had I really been successful in reshaping his emotional pattern towards normality? For nearly a year, three times a week I had been working on him, digging out his early past, combining superficial and deep analysis as Weblen had suggested, and this was the first occasion on which he'd given me a sign of some definite response to treatment. I was very pleased, but had to get back to Julian. "Won't be a second," I said, and in the semi-darkness I made a few hurried notes for further reference on a sheet of paper. Then I continued the discussion.

"How did your other affairs end?" I said.

"Well, usually because of the war. After a time we were posted somewhere else and separated. You know how it is. One makes friendships and almost at once either you or your friend is posted away. I'm certain that's why everyone became so . . ."

"Promiscuous," I said.

"Promiscuous," Dighton repeated, trying to memorise the word. ". . . I know I was that way after the war, when I came back to England. I went to pubs and picked up boys. Sometimes I took somebody home without thinking whether it would work. But, of course, I was really looking for a permanent affair. . . ." Suddenly he stirred on the couch. "You asked me why I think Nigel gave me up. Well, now that you've made me think about him, I believe it was because he lost interest in me for some reason. Now that I've got over it, and it doesn't really matter any more, I can see that quite clearly. My first thoughts were right. I wasn't good enough for him, you see. As long as he was busy studying, it was all right to live with me, because he didn't want to go out. I suppose it was convenient for him to settle down for a while. Then when he qualified he wanted something better than me."

"In what way better?" I said.

"I don't know. Somebody better-looking, maybe younger. Somebody from a different class. His own class, like the people I met at those queer clubs, you know. He always said he liked me as I was, but I knew it wasn't true. And I wanted so to be like him. Not only because I was in love with him, but—— Oh, I don't know. . . . I just always did. I tried to talk the same language, dress the same way, act the same way. . . ."

So that was it, I thought. Dighton's mistake was obvious. I already guessed as much, but now I was certain that the real reason Julian had lost interest in him was that while consciously he may have approved of Dighton's attempt at bettering himself and may even have encouraged it, underneath he resented it and hated it. I said: "You lived with Nigel for over nine months. Did you feel that under his influence you changed your attitudes much?"

"Definitely," he said. "You wouldn't have recognised me if you'd seen me two years ago. I mean, I know you are very frank with me." He suddenly sat up. He was now facing me. "Would you believe that I left school at fourteen?"

"No," I replied, and that was more or less true. The invert, or rather a type of invert, sometimes has a feminine elasticity which can turn him into more than a successful social climber. It enables him to adopt the culture of a higher group in all senses, including the moral. Dighton was one of these.

"Did you begin to dress like him?" I asked.

"Well, yes. I mean, before I met him I seldom wore suits as I do now. And I never wore blazers. Now I always wear dark grey flannel trousers with a blazer. I also took to wearing Air Force ties, and I went to Nigel's barber."

No wonder, I thought. I said: "And your speech?"

"Well, I asked him to correct me if I made a mistake. But when I went to English night classes, I occasionally took speech training, you know. The instructor took an interest in me. She said I was the best in the whole class."

Little by little the picture became clearer and clearer. I don't know if, owing to the conscious efforts at improving himself, Dighton had actually lost some of that masculinity which originally may have sprung partly from his working-class background and culture, but it was clear that he had lost something that Nigel, and people like him, especially cherished. It is not only inverts who become attracted by that "something", but a fair number of normal middle-class people who romanticise the worker and sometimes invest him with virtues he doesn't really possess. Thousands of young middle-class leftists did think—and still do—that the proletariat has some particular virtue which makes it alone capable of salvation from the evils of bourgeois civilisation. With the invert, this belief can become a passion and is strongly fused with sexual attraction. One has only to read the novels of the younger university men of the 'thirties to see how powerful this passion was.

I was wondering whether Julian had seen that the transformation he noticed to his dismay in Dighton was typical of the whole working class. The workers, it is true, have some particular virtues—vitality, tolerance, loyalty, simplicity, generosity, sincerity, a deeper feeling about life than the middle class, and above all a seriousness about life. If I were asked to offer a brutal generalisation between the working class and the middle class, I would venture to say that the working class take *life* seriously, whereas the middle class take *themselves* seriously. But the moment a worker has a chance to improve his economic or cultural situation, he assumes the mantle of the middle class. His particular virtues are largely created by circumstance, and they mostly change with circumstance. Dighton, for example, often gave me the impression of looking down on the working class, without being ashamed of his own origin. He was probably using me not only to be cured, but also as a means of social improvement. One of the reasons he wished so ardently to be cured was that he felt that inversion was interfering with his career. He was right, of course. Because he wanted to rise out of his class, he couldn't help taking himself very seriously, although he had retained a sense of humour. I rather fancied that one of his strongest attractions for Nigel must have been his Yorkshire accent, and this was now almost gone.

BOOK TWO

Ten

All Gordon's drawings had one theme in common: falling down. This time the design was on the Humpty Dumpty theme, and as usual there was the symbol of the new moon in the background. I thought the time had come when I could ask him the question that had been puzzling me for some time.

"Gordon," I said, leaning over the armchair, "did you hurt yourself when you had the fall?"

He looked up, but as usual he avoided my glance. After a time he shook his head.

"Are you sure?"

He didn't reply. I saw that he was blushing. Stubbornly, he looked at the sketch-book, then very suddenly he wrenched out the page and tore it to pieces.

"Why did you do that?" I said.

Instead of an answer, he began to cry. This was more or less what I'd expected. The bolt had gone home. There *had* been a fall. And at *night*, too. "All right, Gordon," I said. "Have you got a handkerchief?"

He nodded. I reflected that when he'd finished crying I'd ask him to draw another picture. Then we should see. Perhaps a little music might help.

As I turned towards the radio, the front-door bell went. It was half-past ten and Terry was out shopping. My next patient wasn't due till eleven. I asked Gordon whether he'd like to play the radio. "I'll be back in a second," I said as I went to answer the door.

It was Ann.

"May I come in?" she said.

"I have a patient with me," I replied. "What is it?"

"I tried to ring you yesterday afternoon, but the first time your telephone was engaged, and the second time there was no reply."

There was a slight reproach in her voice and I realised she was uneasy.

"I was expecting you tomorrow morning," I told her.

"I'm sorry," she said. "Could I sort of wait?"

"It's very difficult," I said. "I have two more patients before lunch and several this afternoon. You just happened to have picked on my busiest day."

"Could you lunch with me?" she asked.

"I'm afraid not. I have to be back rather early. I'll tell you what. Can you come back at ten past one and have something to eat here? It'll have to be sandwiches and coffee; I don't eat much for lunch. But I'll give you nearly an hour. How about it?"

II

"I had lunch with Julian's partner yesterday," Ann said later, when we were having our coffee. "He was extremely nice to me. I spent the first night with them at Guildford, you remember, after that dreadful day. Well, he didn't talk about Julian at all. It was I who brought the subject up. But I'm sure he knows. I mean he knows more about Julian than he wanted to tell me. But he was obviously trying to spare my feelings."

"Why do you think that?" I said. "Did he make any specific reference to Julian?"

"Not really." Ann's face was almost angry. "But the way he talked, or, rather, the way he changed the subject . . . I have a premonition."

"You've told me your premonitions are usually false."

She shrugged a shoulder slightly. "I don't know. This time I feel sure."

"Did you discuss anything about the other woman with Mohill?" I asked.

"I wanted to," she said, "and I had the opportunity, but I just didn't. You know how shy I am. Besides"—she shook her head—"I can't just bring up the subject like that with a man who's almost a total stranger. Could you please go and see him?"

"Mr. Mohill?"

"Yes." She hesitated, looking at the floor. "The point is you're a man and I'm sure he may be willing to talk to another man. You can quite easily ask him questions, and you know how to. You can read a man's mind. I know you're busy, but it would be awfully kind of you to sort of try to find out. . . ."

"Yes," I said. "But I can't just ring him up and ask him to see me. He doesn't know me from Adam."

"Well, actually he does. I told him you were my doctor. That you were treating me, and that you're a famous specialist." She was blushing, "I say, I hope you don't mind. I did something quite rash." She suddenly raised her head and looked me straight in the eye. "When I couldn't get you yesterday afternoon, I rang him up and asked him to see you. He was very nice, and said he'd be delighted if you'd care to ring him. I hope you'll forgive me, going behind your back. . . ." She made a move to open her handbag, obviously to give me the telephone number. Her face was anxious; then a shadow of a smile began to soften the lines around her mouth when she saw that I wasn't annoyed.

"Here it is," she said quickly, like an excited child. "Let me get him for you." She was already on her feet. She lifted the receiver on my desk and began to dial the number.

"He's sure to be out," I said. I tried to disguise my excitement. I'd never thought about Julian's partner in connection with the case.

III

As I was on my way to see Mohill the following afternoon, the idea that he was perhaps a member of the underground again crossed my mind. If this were so, my job would be fairly easy. He would either recognise me or I would make my membership obvious. But it was amazing that I hadn't already thought of this possibility, that I had in fact thought of everything except the obvious in pursuing my investigations. The most inexperienced policeman or the seediest private detective, not to speak of the merest reader of detective stories, would have contacted Mohill at once. For all I knew, I might have met him somewhere. I was feeling excited as

I got off the bus in High Holborn and walked down a devastated street towards his office.

It was really idiotic not to have thought of him in the first place and instead to have wasted my time with Tidpool. I felt in my pocket for my notecase. It was there, and Ginger's photograph inside it. If Mohill was queer, he was sure to know.

The office was on the first floor of an early Victorian building with a blue medallion outside: *Philip Whitaker, historian, lived here 1843–1881.* A woman secretary let me into the large front room, saying that Mr. Mohill would be with me in a matter of minutes.

The walls were panelled in late Victorian oak, which clashed with the reproduction Chippendale furniture and the old framed maps and engravings on the walls. The room had a pretentious air, a certain Tottenham Court Road staginess. There was just a suggestion in the glass chandelier, in the pearl grey Axminster carpet, in the glass vase and the flowers on the desk, that my suspicions about Mohill might be justified, but the moment he came in I knew at once that I was wrong.

"I hope," he said as he shook hands with me, "you don't mind coming here, and so late, but this was about the only time I could fit you in."

He was a plump man of forty, already half-bald and with an air of marriage and children about him. There was also an air of "ruthless normalcy", of lack of culture, and of greed; he struck me as what is known as an astute businessman, but also as a snob. "A glass of sherry?" he suggested: but he had already crossed towards the bookcase and pulled out his keys before awaiting my reply. "As it happens," he said, "I'm going to the Law Society's dinner tonight, so my time till then is entirely yours."

As I suspected, the sherry was South African. "So Miss Hewitt's your patient," he said. It seemed we had each already weighed the other up. He was as sexually normal as they come. It wasn't the psychiatrist, but the invert in me who instinctively knew this, from the way he came in, shook hands, held himself, looked at me and from his voice and diction. Most inverts are practised at spotting others, whether obvious or not, in all countries in general and in their own country in particular. It is partly experience, partly intuition. I suppose I was a little quicker than the average, and fairly good at spotting the middle-class "respectable" homosexual who tries to hide the thing, but who gives himself away by his anxiety to appear normal; he is usually over-restrained and disapproving and tries to project his guilt complex on others. But the "male impersonator" is equally obvious, because he overdoes things.

"I am," I told Mohill, "in a difficult position. For obvious reasons, Miss Hewitt wants to talk about her fiancée, but I have to try to make her forget him. We're at cross purposes. . . ."

"Well, she told me she has the greatest faith in you. I suppose I'm not breaking a confidence in telling you this. . . ." He smiled. "Probably she told you herself. You know her family of course. . . ."

"I've met them."

"They are very charming people," he said with deep conviction. "At least, so Julian told me. I never had the pleasure of actually meeting them. . . ." he added, and I began to wonder to what extent Julian had confided in Mohill.

"What do you think was behind your partner's death?" I asked boldly.

"It's one of the biggest mysteries I've ever come across," Mohill said, and nodded twice over his slight paunch. "You didn't know him well. He was, I should say, a level-headed man, but then one never knows, does one? He had a distinguished Army record, Military Cross, mentioned in despatches, and all that. Mind you"—he suddenly raised his head and dropped his voice slightly, taking me into his confidence—"mind you, he was highly strung. . . . But for that matter I'm highly strung too." This was another confidence, but made with an eye on business. "It's the strain of modern life . . . the struggle. But then a man of your professional standing and experience knows far more about that. . . ." He smiled.

"That's very kind of you," I said. I decided to play into his hands and assumed an air of Scholarly Humility. "But the hideous truth is that we know so little about the mind. A good deal is just guesswork. . . . I suppose you knew Leclerc a long time?"

"A couple of years. I met him through a mutual friend, just before he passed his finals. Then my father—he was still alive then—decided to offer him a partnership in the firm. I was keen on it too, because I liked him from the start. His father put up the money and he came along to work here. That was his desk."

Mohill pointed to a small mahogany affair facing the other window. "One of the reasons we liked him so much was that he . . . how shall I put it . . . brought something that was lacking to the legal profession. I suppose you have to know a little more about solicitors to understand that. We're rather a closed profession, like you doctors, with traditional attitudes and ways. Well, some of us, of course, become dry and inhuman. Therefore, if you know what I mean, a solicitor who is every bit an efficient lawyer, but doesn't look like one, is an advantage."

It would have been simpler to have said that it was a good thing for a solicitor at least to look like a gentleman. Now I understood the fake Chippendale, the mezzotints, the Air Force tie, the glass of sherry.

"He had great charm. At the same time he was very conscientious and hard-working. I don't know whether his heart was in it. It was too early to tell, but our business in any case is seldom exciting. We don't deal with criminal cases and only handle divorce in connection with old clients. I sometimes thought that Julian would have made a good barrister. I don't mean it unkindly, but he had something of the actor in him. And that's a decided advantage at the Bar. As a matter of fact, when he began to study law, the Bar was his first intention. Then he changed his mind and decided to be a solicitor." Mohill nodded. "Nobody could blame him. Like most solicitors, we're overworked, but if you knew the number of briefless barristers in my acquaintance alone . . ." He left the sentence eloquently unfinished.

"I may have to look for a solicitor myself one day," I said, hoping to give him some small encouragement, "but mustn't waste your time now. I think you know why I came. When you're dealing with a patient suffering from a nervous shock, it always helps to find out something about the circumstances that caused the shock. It's not absolutely essential, but it helps. Miss Hewitt knows nothing about the cause of Mr. Leclerc's death. Do tell me, was there anything unusual in his behaviour just before the end?"

"Well, yes and no. He had his ups and downs. About six months ago, he seemed rather upset about something. In the end he said he didn't feel well and he took a couple of days off. I quite forgot about it, because he was perfectly all right after he came back. Then just

about three weeks before he died, he became a little more temperamental than usual, but he tried not to show it, and I *of course* didn't
say anything; one doesn't. Looking back on it, being wise after the
event, Julian must have been putting up a tremendous fight. The
last day I saw him alive, a Tuesday, he left the office a little earlier
than usual; then the next morning he telephoned to say he wasn't
feeling well and wouldn't come in. That was Wednesday. The following morning the charwoman found him dead. It was almost
unbelievable." Mohill shook his head. "It was the biggest blow I've
had in my whole life. He was young and absolutely healthy. He was
wounded during the war, but he'd completely recovered; I'm sure
he wasn't ill."

"Financial worries?" I said.

"I very strongly doubt it. I dare say he was living on a small
income, but that was entirely his idea. He was paying the premium
back to his father. I don't know why. I suppose he did it out of pride.
But in any case that was only something temporary. We'd been
doing very well and in a couple of years' time he'd have been comfortably off." Mohill suddenly looked straight at me. "Incidentally,
do you realise that Julian, if he'd been alive, would have ended up
as a baronet? The present one, Sir Redmond Leclerc, is his father's
elder brother; an old man with no children. Actually he's a clergyman in Northern Ireland. Penniless, I should imagine. . . ."

"Miss Hewitt thinks there may have been some emotional
disturbance. . . ." I suggested.

"Well"—Mohill looked at me sideways, hesitated just long
enough to arouse my expectations—"as a matter of fact, that's
what my wife said. I disagreed with her at the time. As it happens,
she is not a good judge of human nature." He smiled indulgently.
"Well, Julian came to dine with us occasionally. Once he came for
the week-end and my wife told me afterwards that she thought
he was unhappy. I wouldn't like to admit it to her face, but now
I somehow feel she may have been right, after all. But, of course,
one can't even guess what the trouble may have been. He was in
love with Ann. I actually knew of his engagement before it was
announced in *The Times*. I was an intimate friend of his, after
all. . . ."

Another "intimate friend", I thought. And Mohill firmly believed that, yet he had never suspected that Julian was an invert, which was the most important single factor governing his life. For the thousandth time I realised how difficult it was for the normal world to recognise an invert, unless he happened to be screamingly obvious. And now I felt more than ever certain that even Julian's father, in spite of that intent gaze and the surly silences, knew nothing of his son's private life.

"One couldn't help liking Julian," Mohill said wistfully. "He was charming to absolutely everybody, in the best tradition of the English gentry. You don't find that in any other country." He shook his head sadly. "Unfortunately, it's on the wane today, but Julian was a splendid case in point. As a matter of fact, I've just received a letter, obviously from one of his Army comrades, that was forwarded along with Julian's letter to me. The chap was a working man, but do you know they were actually on Christian name terms. The former officer and the former man in the ranks! I was terribly impressed. . . ." He shook his head. "You know, I could never have done that. I was in the Air Force for four years; I served in the ranks for a time and I suppose I'm what's called a democrat; but I just couldn't have got on like that with the men. It would have embarrassed me to call anybody by his Christian name unless he came from the same background as myself. Well, wouldn't it you?"

"Most certainly," I lied fluently and enthusiastically. But I felt sure my voice was a little hoarse as I said, "What's actually in the letter?"

"I was just going to show it to you," Mohill said as he began to pull a sheet of paper from under some others on his desk. My heart began to thump. It was the same thick, yellow, ruled paper that Ann had found on Julian's desk. "There, read it," he said, as he pushed the paper over to me.

"21 Palm St. Bedfd.

"Dear Jul,

"Here is the great news, but I reckon you already noticed from the adress. We have just moved into a brand new council house having been on the waiting list for three bloody years. The rent is only eighteen shillings and the kitchen is large and comfortable the reason why I couldn't come to London or write you was this, and Artie has been

down with broncitis. I hear the O.B. is having a rally at the Albert Hall
in September. We shall definitely come up for the day, but why don't
you ever come over to see us, now we can put you up?
    "*Your most sincere friend*

                                                        "*Ging.*"

"It's pathetic," Mohill said, as I looked up. "The man doesn't
know. And I certainly don't want to send his letter on to Julian's
father, who's ill in the country. The old man's badly shaken. He
couldn't even attend the inquest. Julian was his only child. He
divorced his wife quite a long time ago, you know, and his second
wife died during the war. He's had blow after blow." Mohill shook
his head. "There's a lot I shall have to discuss with him. Legal matters, the partnership, and so on. Julian left no will. But all that'll
have to wait. Well"—he reached for the letter still in my hands; I
had already memorised the address—"well, I suppose I shall have
to send the man a reply. It's the sort of thing I hate doing. I feel I
ought to make it warm and friendly; I can't just send him a solicitor's letter. But I haven't got the touch. Besides, I shall have to ask
someone to find out the man's name. I can't just address a letter to
Ginger"—he glanced at the notepaper—"Twenty-one Palm Street,
Bedford."

Tomorrow afternoon, I thought. It means, of course that I shall
have to postpone Dighton's visit.

                              IV

I took the two-twenty train to Bedford the following afternoon.
There was no need for me to rush, because I felt sure that Mohill
wouldn't be writing to "Ginger" for several days, but I was anxious
to follow up my lead. I had already sent an express letter, addressed
to "Ginger, 21 Palm Street, Bedford", saying I was a friend of Julian's
and that I was coming to see him in the afternoon. All being well,
he should have received it a couple of hours before my arrival.

The possibility that Ginger might refuse to speak only crossed
my mind when I was already somewhere near Luton. The two
letters on the yellow lined paper came from an open minded, ami-

able person: a good mixer, natural, generous, slightly exuberant. The photograph, however, suggested somebody entirely different. There was—I was examining it now—a slight sullenness around the mouth, a stubbornness, a certain vanity, perhaps even a suggestion of fear. If anything, it gave the impression of an attractive misfit. I felt convinced he'd be reserved.

I saw only two things in common between the letters and the photograph: Ginger appeared to have a decidedly masculine personality and he seemed generous, the type of man who would do anything and everything for someone he liked. Dighton, although rather better educated, must have been like that when Julian had first met him, except that he was not quite as physically attractive as Ginger. I felt sure, however, that Julian had not deserted Dighton for better looks. I knew I was right in my theory that Dighton had embarrassed him with his ambition to climb out of the class whose ways and mystique were an immense attraction to Julian. Dighton, for example, had almost managed to suppress his accent, whereas Ginger had almost certainly had a fairly broad one, not to speak of other native attractions. In any case—and here I suddenly thought there was a third identity between the letters and the photograph— Ginger was adventurous and unconventional; perhaps something of a "sport". Dighton now was almost a tame conformist, who was only revolting against one thing—his past nonconformity.

As the train approached Bedford the doubts left me. The chances of getting some information suddenly outweighed the chances of a rebuff. The feeling that in some way I was directly or indirectly connected with Julian's death was still there, even though by now it had changed from fear into a minor uneasiness.

But there was still also the call of adventure, so unusual in my uneventful life. I found myself actually enjoying my uneasiness. I was *living* a novel. All my life I had been attracted by the romantic figure of the private detective. Conan Doyle and Edgar Wallace had exercised as powerful an impression on my childhood as Proust, Gide or Dostoievsky on my young manhood. But how much more absorbing it was to *be* the private detective than just to read about his doings—actively to live not just some of his doings, but every small detail of his investigation.

The detective story takes one to the edge of the abyss, but only for a brief moment, thanks to the author's care. Now I was living a real-life detective story, and I remembered Nietzsche's saying that the abyss looks back on the man who looks at it too long. But to such danger I was immune. I had already faced the abyss a few times in my life and I'd got away safely, because I knew the tricks. I was a "pro", seasoned, highly trained, almost tough.

But was there any justification for talking about the "abyss" in connection with Ginger? There was not the slightest question about my *bona fides*; if the worst came to the worst, I was going to see him on behalf of a patient of mine, who happened also to have been a friend. The abyss was elsewhere.

It was easy enough to find Palm Street, and I arrived sooner than I'd expected. It was only half-past four and it seemed unlikely that Ginger would be at home. I was rather alarmed when I remembered that he was living in a new council house, possibly one of those large blocks that are being built nowadays, with many tenants at each number. To look for a man called "Ginger" in such a place probably meant asking several people.

But as it happened, Palm Street was a row of recently built red brick cottages of the traditional type that are so much a part of the English landscape that they could be anywhere in the country.

As I rang the bell, the door was opened by a woman in a flower-patterned overall, trying her best to keep back a little boy of about three.

"Good afternoon," I said, but an idea had already crossed my mind. "Hullo, Artie." I turned to the boy, who began to stare at me. "Sorry to trouble you," I said to the mother. "I'm looking for Ginger."

"Oh," the smile on her face widened into a grin. "Are you the Captain?" She showed a row of plastic teeth of crude perfection.

"You mean Captain Leclerc, don't you? I'm a friend of his. Page is my name. I sent Ginger an express letter."

"We just got it, not ten minutes ago, but Stan is still at work. I had to laugh. It was just addressed to 'Ginger'."

"To be quite frank, I forgot his surname." I looked at the sky. "What on earth is it?"

"Well," she said flirtatiously, "think of the Army."

"I'm thinking hard." I was completely at ease now. This was

better than I'd expected. A nice, friendly woman with peroxided hair and a lullaby bosom, about twenty-eight or so. "I'm still thinking hard of the Army," I said.

"Well. Atkins," she said.

"Of course," I said. "Stan Atkins." I shook my head. "I'm getting dafter and dafter. What time do you expect him back?"

"Not before six. It's a shame, isn't it?" Her face was now serious. "Would you like a cup of tea? It won't take a minute." She had already turned towards the hallway.

"No, thank you. I've had tea on the train and I'd like to get back to Town soon. I'd better see him at work straight away. Is the place far from here?"

"Quarter of an hour by bus. It's in Coronation Street. Just past the Bridge Hotel—on the left-hand side. Mimram's Garage it's called. It's a fourpenny ride. Ask the conductor to put you down at Coronation Street."

"Well, thanks, Mrs. Atkins," I said. "I hope to see you later."

"Cheeriby."

I walked away. If all went as well as that, the thing would be easy. In any case, it was clear she knew nothing about her husband's past. And I was sure he had one.

I didn't have to wait long for the bus and it took less than a quarter of an hour to get there. The place seemed quite small and a little out of the way. Three petrol pumps stood in line with the pavement like a surrealist trinity; behind them were the office and an old-fashioned gateway of what must have been a former smithy. I saw a young man in a dark blue overall standing by the office door. "Mr. Atkins," I said.

"He's in the back, sir," he answered eagerly—too eagerly, I felt —as he showed me the way. My heart was beating fast as I walked through the yard, and I told myself I must be calm, comforting, easy, social.

Then I suddenly saw him. He must have heard us coming and straightened himself up from leaning over the engine of a van, a tall, broad-shouldered man in a greasy, blue overall, a red, cheerful Army face and curly ginger hair.

"Yes, sir?" he said, in a half-friendly, half-deferential manner. I heard the footsteps of the young man walking back to the pumps.

"Mr. Atkins?" I said. It was broad daylight and I must have looked stupid. Only God knows what would have happened if we had not been alone in the garage, if there had been other people staring at me watching my confusion.

The man facing me was not the one whose photograph I carried in my pocket like a passport. This was not the youth whose facial details I knew by heart like a policeman. This was a man at least thirty, maybe more, and his features were not even remotely similar. He had a broad, friendly face, a long, generous mouth, and eyes that were almost always smiling under the whitish eyebrows.

"That's me," he said. He didn't see my embarrassment. He was watching me in a good-humoured, friendly way, entirely without suspicion, in the manner of an exclusively normal person.

"I'm sorry to trouble you," I said, feeling rather more sure of myself by now. "My name is Dr. Page—I sent you a letter from London. It's already arrived at Palm Street; I saw your wife. . . . I came to see you in connection with a former friend of ours, Julian Leclerc. . . ."

"I'm pleased to meet you, sir." He made a fast, friendly gesture, indicating that his hands were greasy. His lips opened in a broad smile; like his wife, he had false teeth, a trifle too large and mercilessly white. But a second later he must have seen my face, my expression must have told him what my words had obviously not conveyed. I said nothing and my silence was apparently eloquent, for somehow he knew the truth; perhaps my use of the word "former" had just struck home. My eyes were on a large Chinese serpent tattooed on his naked forearm, which was broad and hairless and free of the blue grease that covered both his hands. The arm moved now, slowly, very slowly, downwards. "You don't mean to say, sir, he's dead . . . ?"

"I'm very sorry," I murmured. I still didn't look him in the face.

For a few seconds he said nothing and I was beginning to fear he might keep silent indefinitely. But soon enough our eyes met. Quietly he said: "How did you know my name, sir?"

"Please don't call me sir," I said. "Your last letter . . . the one in which you gave your new address, was passed on to Julian's partner. He'll be writing to you in a few days. . . . I say, can't we go somewhere to talk?"

"Might as well," he said slowly. I saw that he'd been keeping a sparking plug in his hand all the time, as if holding on to something. Slowly he placed it on the running board of the car. "I'll just wash my hands and tell Ernie. Won't be long." He made his way towards a passage on the left. A big man; he must have weighed fourteen stone.

V

Ten minutes later we were sitting in a deserted café overlooking the Ouse. Ginger was reading the newspaper clipping I'd given him. It took him some time; he must have read it again and again. Finally, he looked up, then gently he pushed the piece of paper towards me across the glass tabletop.

"Why did he do it?" he asked.

"That's precisely what I'd like to find out, and why I came to see you. As I've already told you, your first letter, with no date on it, was found on Julian's desk. That was the only clue I had." I took the letter out of my breast pocket and handed it to him.

"I wrote that about six months ago," he said after he'd read it. "Must 'ave been." He seemed to reflect for a few seconds. "It was like this. I went to London on me own to get some spares and wrote and told him I was coming. It was a Friday. That was the last time I saw Jul."

"How was he then?" I said.

"He'd changed a bit. We all change when we come back to civvy street, but he was very nice. Told me he was courtin', getting married soon. We went to the Hippodrome, then to a pub, then I took the late train back. We had a very nice time."

"Did you get a reply to that letter?"

He tried to think. He was the type of man who looks older when he thinks. "I don't rightly know," he said. "I had a letter from him before like. That was after we got back from Italy."

"You were in the same outfit as Julian, I suppose?"

"No. It was like this. I was in the Armoured Corps, and me an' Jul met in Naples. We were both of us on week-end leave and met on the train. I liked him from the first moment. He was one of the nicest blokes I ever met, not one of them lahdidah officers. Mind you, we had some smashing officers too; you must have heard about Captain Park, V.C.; well, he was in my own mob, but it was different. It would've been nice if me and Jul were in the same mob. . . . Well," he continued, "we were standing in the corridor. He said what would you be doing like in Naples, and I said I expect I'll go round. I've only been to Naples once previous, I said, and I'm on me own. He said he was too, so we spent the day together. We had a look-round, had dinner at one of them Italian places, went to the pictures, then we went to one of those big arcades. I don't know if you know Naples, but it's got this Galleria as they call it. Everybody knows it there. It's full of shops and people walking up and down and boozers. Well, we did some of the places. . . ."

Here Ginger became silent for a moment. I felt for my cigarettes and offered him one. "Ta," he said. "Then next day we went out bathing, and we made a date to meet again. On our next leave, like. That was three weeks later. We always joined up whenever we could get a spot of leave. Sometimes we only met for the day. Once, I remember, I forgot my A.B. Six-Four—that's the book you had to carry in the Army. I was waiting for Jul in the arcade and the redcaps tried to pick me up. It was just luck he turned up in time and got me out of it. Then he was posted away from Naples. . . . You know, I shall never forget those nine months. . . ."

He may have noticed something in my face. I don't know how I looked.

"You were a friend of his too?" he said quietly.

"Yes," I nodded. "And I knew *everything* about him." This was a rash statement and only partly true, but it didn't register. Apparently I hadn't sufficiently emphasised the operative word.

"What do you think made him do it? Do himself in?" he asked.

"I think his suicide was connected with the fact that he was a different sort of person from you. And that made him unhappy. Mind you, that's only a theory."

"You're a doctor, you said?"

"I am. A psychiatrist."

Ginger nodded silently. "When did you see him last?"

"Some time ago. I've been away from England. . . . But we'd known each other since we were quite young." Here we go, then

I thought. I added slowly and with emphasis: "We were in love once." This was an enormous risk to take, an insane risk, but it was now or never, and I felt Ginger was easy to trust.

I was right. The arrow hit its target. He was looking at me in his friendly way. There was far more sympathy in his expression than curiosity or even surprise. Quietly he said, "I reckon I loved him too."

"You see, Ginger," I said—my relief was immense—"he was a very different man from you inside. You are in a way lucky. You suffer, we all do, but you don't get really hurt. . . . D'you mind if I ask you a very personal question?"

"No," he said.

"It's very personal. It's this: Were you married when you met him in Italy?"

He nodded. "I know what you mean. I was, but it was different."

"Yes; that's the point. It was different. With you it was different. That's why many people would envy you."

"Envy?" His lower lip suddenly dropped. "Why?"

"Because you don't realise how good the stuff is you're made of. I'd say you've got a marvellous balance of mind, if you get my meaning."

"Go on," Ginger said, meaning that I should continue.

"I have to be personal again."

"That's all right."

"You see, you're a happily married man. I met your wife and saw your kid. They're both very sweet. She's nice-looking too. And at the same time . . ." I didn't mean to leave the sentence unfinished, but I just couldn't express myself satisfactorily. I said, "I knew several people like you and I envied them as I envy you."

He smiled. Slowly he spoke: "It's like this. I couldn't put it the way you would. I'm only a working bloke. I left school when I was thirteen like, but what I mean to say is this: if a working man likes someone, he'd do anything for him, wouldn't he?"

The question at the end of the sentence suggested that Ginger half-realised that what he'd said was a fairly blatant generalisation, but we both felt, there was some truth in it. I said, "I suppose so."

"Do you know anybody who knew Julian?" I asked. "Any of his friends?"

"No. I can't say I do."

"No," I said. I looked at my watch. "I shall have to go back soon."

"I wish you wouldn't."

"I'd like to stay, but I have a lot to do in Town. And I start work early tomorrow morning. I'm sorry I had to bring you sad news, but it's perhaps better this way than getting a letter in a few days' time from Julian's partner. Incidentally, if you write to him or see him by any chance, please don't say you saw me."

"I won't." He looked at me warmly. "You sure you won't have tea with us. I'm sure the wife's expecting you."

"Sorry, Ginger. It can't be done."

"Well, I'd better walk you to the station." He fastened the zip on his leather jacket.

VI

There were two people talking in the compartment, so I walked out on to the corridor and stood by one of the windows. There was a little breeze and it looked as though it might rain any moment. If a working man likes someone, he'd do anything for him. That's what Ginger had said, and I couldn't get the thought from my mind. Perhaps the proportion of people who wouldn't think twice before following a natural impulse was higher among the working class than elsewhere, but I wasn't certain. It may have been that they didn't take sex or an affair with a man as seriously as they did with a woman. But in a way they did. Possibly Ginger represented that primitive type of man which, like our ancestors, made no rigid distinction between the two sexes, but followed his instincts of lust and affection.

We passed Luton. I was still alone in the corridor. Julian had met Ginger abroad, I thought, and the foreign surroundings had probably acted as an aphrodisiac. Then, of course, the war was another factor . . . Julian was good-looking—even men realised that, and a gentleman, an officer in fact; the personification of authority and power, but human and with a spontaneous charm. But even then . . . I knew a lot about the particular situation that was exercising my mind; I'd had personal experiences with people like Ginger. But their make-up was still a mystery to me. A mystery beyond the fact that every human being has something of the opposite sex in him. That was in the textbooks. But this was life.

VII

Since I'd told Terry I mightn't be back until quite late, I had some food in Soho. Then I took a bus home. It was about half-past nine when I returned. As soon as I entered the consulting-room to look for any letters or messages that might have arrived, Terry came in.

"Hullo," I said. "I've just got back. I hope you've had dinner. I've eaten already. Any messages?"

"None." He walked up to me. "I owe you a confession and an apology."

"What is it?"

"The china horse on the mantelpiece."

I turned round and saw it was missing from its place. "Did it fall off?" I said.

"Well, I'm afraid it was my fault. While you were out I thought I'd give the room a good do and I took it to the bathroom to wash it. It slipped from my hand. I'm ever so sorry, I just don't know how it could have happened. Luckily, only the top part broke off. I took it to the little shop near the station. It was still open, and they said it would be practically invisible, but still . . . I'm ever so sorry."

"That's perfectly all right," I said. "You couldn't help it. Besides, they said it's easy to mend. I'd forget all about it."

Eleven

Three days had passed, and I was typing some notes when Terry entered. "You haven't forgotten we're going to the theatre tonight?" he reminded me.

"No," I said, although it had slipped my mind. I looked at my watch; it was twenty to six. The morning following my trip to Bedford, Terry had suggested seeing a play called *Music at Night*. I'd agreed, and he'd booked and paid for the seats. It crossed my mind that this might have been his attempt to make up for a china figure he'd broken, and about which he'd been unnecessarily upset.

"Dinner'll be ready in less than half an hour," he said and returned to the kitchen. I was feeling sticky, and decided to take a bath. There was plenty of time.

Lying in the warm water, I began to think about Terry, for the first time in three or four weeks. It suddenly dawned on me that I'd taken him too much for granted, especially lately since Ann's first visit. It was only now that the broken china figure assumed a significance. He had taken it to a shop and was told the join would be more or less invisible. I decided I must insist on paying for the repair. The problem was that he thought the china figure used to belong to my "dead mother" and that it had a sentimental value. This was untrue, and I don't know how he got that impression. Actually, I'd bought the thing during the war in a junk-shop off Wigmore Street because it was attractive and a bargain.

As a matter of fact, a couple of days earlier he'd broken a large, glass casserole dish, not valuable, but a little difficult to replace. He'd spent the best part of an afternoon trying to buy a new one and finally managed to get an order accepted for one. I remember being surprised when he told me he'd smashed it, rather shame-facedly, because he's always been so careful. He was extremely efficient and reliable as a rule.

I now knew that it was only because I'd been so absorbed with the "case" and its implications that I'd attributed no importance to these two minor breakages, which meant only one thing, as anyone with the slightest acquaintance with the subconscious would have realised at once. Terry was jealous, or at least he resented my neglect of him.

It was true that I seldom discussed patients with him—only very occasionally, when I tried out his response, which was usually intelligent. But since Ann had appeared on the scene, he must have noticed that I'd changed: become secretive, and in any case spent quite a lot of what otherwise would have been my free time away from him without telling him what I was doing. Before this, even when I just went out to dinner, I usually told him where I was going, partly in case somebody telephoned, but partly also because our association was far more intimate than that of doctor and receptionist. And the beauty of it was that neither he nor I ever made any reference to our relationship. From time to time I'd felt that he instinctively understood me and most of my actions. Now I knew I was not quite right in my assumptions.

In a way we were very fond of each other, but until recently I'd thought the devotion was stronger on my part—in fact, so strong that once or twice I had to take a grip of myself.

For one thing, he was a delightful freak of Nature. He loved housework as much as any woman. In that respect he was decidedly feminine, but attractively and touchingly so—not a bit like those tragic parodies of women: the little, tripping pansies with high-pitched voices, whom I understood, but detested all the same. He was about five foot eight but his bones were large, and constant exercise had brought out a nice, harmonious muscle development on his body. I had a suspicion that sooner or later the over-exercised muscles might attract fatty tissue. I dare say in ten or twenty years' time he might look bloated, but, at least when I saw his naked forearms, his impressive biceps and deltoid, I was conscious of his present attraction.

I confess that the attraction was much stronger when I saw him doing the sort of work I would never have dreamed of asking him to do. When my charwoman left, he insisted on scrubbing the kitchen floor, kneeling on the rubber mat, bending over the mop in his singlet. One saw the servant's humility in the attitude. But one also saw the broad shoulders, the arched back with the freckled skin under the rebellious hair, and he would look up as I entered and give me a beautiful smile of his brown dog eyes and white teeth.

Terry, in dungarees and rubber boots, cleaning my car; sometimes under it, whistling as he polished the undercarriage the way he'd been taught in the Army. Terry sometimes after dinner when I helped him with the washing up, telling me about his childhood, the poor home in Stockton-on-Tees, the death of his parents, his years in the Army, one or two unfortunate love affairs, which strangely enough left no mark on him. He remained sweet, unspoilt and gentle.

I contrasted all this gentleness of mind and character with the somewhat harsh, masculine dialect of his native city, which was still with him, with his cheerful, manly appearance and the things he wore. Sartorially he was typical of at least one section of his generation all over the Western world. He had one suit, a single-breasted gabardine affair, for uneasy, representative occasions. He was more at home in blue jeans, lumber-jackets, moccasins and loafers, windcheaters, cowboy shirts, in essentially masculine, revolutionary, anti-traditional, almost anti-capitalist garments. All of which, oddly enough, emanate from the most demonstratively and aggressively capitalist state in the world.

I was careful to avoid being tempted by Terry's attractions. For one thing, I'd decided to leave sex alone for a time; for another, I didn't wish to risk losing a really first-rate employee, to put it bluntly. Furthermore, an affair with Terry would have been almost too easy. He had never given me the slightest conscious indication, but I felt—I knew, in fact—that he'd have jumped at the slightest approach on my part, and I was sure he'd have been extremely affectionate. And how easy an affair would have been as regards the outside world; far easier than for a normal doctor to have an affair with his female resident housekeeper or receptionist. Danger of scandal in my case would have been practically nil and, unlike a woman, Terry could not have sued me for breach of promise. That was a cold, brutal, legal fact, almost shameful even to think of, but there it was. Nor was he the sort of person to tell anyone about me, even his closest friends, however badly I treated him. On the contrary, it was perhaps his very subservience and devotion to me that provided the strongest argument against having an affair with him. I was very uncertain of my own affections, if it came to an affair, and I felt I had to take care of him, protect him if need be. I knew I must never, under any circumstances, hurt him.

That explains my side of our complicated relationship, but the two broken objects suggested that, even if Terry were not in love with me, he was more devoted than I thought and he was feeling jealous. This was, in retrospect, not altogether unexpected, yet all the same I was rather surprised. Terry, no doubt, liked the job; he was obviously contented. He was adequately paid, and had as much free time as he needed. Relations with his "employer" were as friendly as possible. I smiled as I remembered how well and how instinctively he knew how to conform to social patterns and traditions. If ever he had to address me in front of people, he always said "Doctor"; when we were alone I was always "you" and, once in a blue moon, "Tony".

The devoted servant can at times fall in love with his master or mistress, but how much stronger are the chances when both happen to be inverts. And, for all I knew, Terry may have found me attractive. He always liked people slightly older than himself.

Ought I to tell him about the "case"? Not the whole of it, of course. It involved me too much. Just explain to him that I'd been worried and excited, inspired and tantalised by it, and that that was why I'd been so reserved, withdrawn and preoccupied lately. But by the time I'd got out of the bath, I'd decided—I don't quite know why—to keep Julian's death to myself. But I felt I had to tell Terry something. That I'd been rather overworked the last few weeks with problems that I couldn't properly resolve. Something like that.

II

Music at Night was Allen Everard's first serious play and, perhaps because one associated him with light comedies dealing with a mythical upper class, it was a slight disappointment. The fact that it had been playing to packed houses for more than a year was, I thought, due to various factors. It appealed to the middle-class employee working for a boss, and at the same time it represented a vague protest against the totalitarian tendencies inherent in a planned economy. Furthermore, what to me was one of the weaknesses of the play may have been an additional reason for its success: there was hardly any motivation for the actions. Everard realised that the theatre-goer was frankly bored by analysis or philosophy, and carefully excluded them, although, in view of his first-rate sense of dialogue and action as well as a cast-iron construction, a few intelligent lines would not have been amiss.

As we left the theatre and walked across Shaftesbury Avenue towards Piccadilly Circus, Terry asked me if I knew Everard.

"I met him once or twice during the war," I said.

"What's he like?"

"About thirty-five or so, normal-looking, quite pleasant."

Terry was a great theatre-goer and kept a notebook of all the plays he'd seen and a collection of theatre programmes.

"I dare say he must have been comfortably off when he started," Terry said. "I read somewhere he comes from an old City banking family."

I suddenly remembered that Everard had known Julian.

"Shall we go to the Lily Pond?" Terry asked.

"Yes, let's. I'm quite hungry."

This was about the first time in four or five years that I'd gone to the large place in the heart of the West End known to the underground as the Lily Pond. On Sunday afternoons and on weekdays after the pubs had closed, it was full of the less well-off section of London homosexuals, but there were usually one or two fleeting visitors from among the higher income groups also.

We were lucky, for Terry's eagle eye discovered a small table for two by the wall. One seat was empty and the other was vacated by a man just as we arrived. He cast an avid glance at Terry, then smiled a greeting at me, seeing that we were together. I knew him almost too well, from the war years. He was a regular Air Force officer whom I had met repeatedly at the *Aldebaran* and other places, but I had found contact with him impossible. For one thing he was completely unscrupulous; he cut you when he saw you were alone, and butted in when you were with someone he fancied. For another, he was incapable of intelligent conversation even about the one single pursuit to which he devoted all his free time. He was one of a type of invert whose facial expression is frozen or paralysed into a smile, into a sort of half-mask. The upper part of his face grinned, but the lower, with the weak chin and the peevish, shopgirl lips, betrayed the fear, the uneasiness, the many rebuffs against which education at a cheap public school was inadequate armour, and eight hundred a year no compensation.

"Why don't you like him?" Terry asked.

"Because he's a menace," I said. "I suppose I ought to feel sorry for him, but it's difficult. He gets my goat. It can't be fun running round night after night for one-time adventures."

"Why are they so oversexed? I mean, so many of them?"

"Probably because they're incapable of love. Some early disappointment, or bitterness may have killed it, or else they put up a guard against it for some reason. You can kill your own love. If the heart becomes stunted, sex can and does become very important; a miserable substitute, but a substitute. You find they are usually stupid people who quite often have an agonising fear of old age because they feel that once youth is gone, all their attractiveness is finished. I suppose it's true that one can't always get away with the things one did when one was young. So they try to make hay while the sun shines. Besides, the homo is more inclined to use sex as a means of escape from the adversity of life than a normal person, who is likely instead to escape into something else: religion, drink, or sport and so on."

"Why are they so fickle?" Terry said after we'd given our orders. "Is it because so many of them are neurotic?"

"Partly," I agreed. "The homosexual Don Juan who must have sex at least three times a week and with three different men—he can't possibly use the same person twice—is definitely a neurotic, but there are many who just drop people because homosexual relations are as a rule sterile. Marriage, for one thing, is impossible. Living together isn't exactly marriage. I'm not suggesting that something which is solemnised by Church or State is marriage either, but the fact that it is solemnised has an enormous effect on a man and woman living together. They have legal obligations and legal advantages, divorce isn't really easy, and then the children, if there are any, keep them together."

"Is that why so many queers can't get on in the world?"

"Perhaps. A neurotic is handicapped, no matter what the cause of his neurosis, but I'm equally certain that for a number of people inversion is an advantage."

"You mean, on the stage?" Terry said, and the way he looked made me feel that he doubted my statement.

"I wasn't thinking of the stage in particular, although it is one field in which the invert has certain advantages in much the same way as a pretty girl, if he wants to use them. What I had in mind was that certain people, by virtue of being homosexual, can profit enormously through having affairs with people in a position really to give them something. Not money and presents, because that's just prostitution, but something spiritual and emotional. The classic example, of course, is Plato and Socrates, but you don't have to look for examples at such a high level."

I was actually thinking of Dean Emmerling, one of the greatest American psychiatrists, who had taken a great interest in me and helped me considerably. He would have enriched my knowledge of life enormously if only I could have put up with the physical side of it. But that would have been unbearable; he was, for one thing, twenty years older than I. But others didn't find it so, and the young Polish refugee doctor whom Emmerling took up after I left him was making great headway.

"What I wanted to ask you," Terry said a little abruptly, just when I was anxious to change the subject, "is why all plays and novels dealing with queers have an inevitably tragic end. I mean, there's always murder, suicide, insanity or imprisonment. I mean, that's not so in real life, is it? I don't say all queers are happy, but the vast majority aren't unhappy, anyway, and even if they are they don't go round cutting their throats or killing each other."

"The answer to that is that the only way normal society at present accepts the homosexual in literature is with a compulsory tragic end. To be a homo is a crime, and crime mustn't go unpunished; not in books at least. Besides, I think the author himself, by giving you a tragic end, is trying to engage your sympathy: 'Pity us poor buggers.' Which explains the tear-jerker title, the frequent Biblical quotations, the lugubrious tone, the underlining of the tragic element. Besides, happiness—normal or abnormal—is uninteresting."

Terry smiled; I wondered if he was really listening. He said slowly: "If ever I could write a book on the subject, I'd try to tell the truth. I'd write about the majority for whom it isn't really tragic." He raised a soda-red hand. "I suppose disaster is always there, well . . . a sort of threat, in the background, but the real trouble is that most of them are afraid of love. That's what makes them so miserable. One should never be afraid of it, even if one gets jilted. It's the only thing in life, isn't it? I mean love. That's the message." The brown dog eyes were not looking at me. He was talking to himself.

"Do you know, sometimes you find a bottle floating on the sea. It's come a long way and someone finds it and there's a message in the bottle. A piece of paper. Not an S.O.S.; nothing really important; just a couple of lines. As a rule, it isn't even signed, but it cheers you up. . . ."

III

It was not Everard's play that kept me awake, but probably the coffee we'd drunk at the Lily Pond and the heat. For a time I tried to read one of Céline's wartime novels, until I suddenly recalled, for the second time, that Bobby Sillock had mentioned Everard's name in connection with Julian. In fact, Dighton had done so also. He had apparently refused to accompany Julian to one of Everard's parties.

I got out of bed, went to the consulting-room and brought the file to the bedroom. My recollection was correct. Everard's was the first name on the sheet of paper, but I'd crossed it out, probably when I'd decided to call first on Tidpool. I'd been full of confidence then, and I'd wanted if possible to avoid contacting Everard, since our relations were somewhat strained. I'd first met him during the war at a party to which I was taken by an American actor named Gene. Everard was in the Navy, but stationed permanently, so it seemed, in London. He was extremely charming to me. He asked me to his house and gave me a copy of one of his plays. Then he came to a small party I gave, and for about six months after that we saw one another quite frequently. When Gene left England, however, Everard cooled off towards me. He may have been under the impression that Gene and I had had an affair. The last time I'd seen Everard was at the *Aldebaran* just before the end of the war. "We must meet again," he'd said with a completely unmeaning air. For some reason, I was angry, and I replied in as offhanded a manner as I could assume, "Yes, we must."

Was Everard likely to have forgotten the incident? And what if he hadn't? In any case, he was sure to think it rather unusual if I tried to contact him after so long a silence. I shrugged my shoulders and decided to sleep on it, if I could.

As I placed the file on my bedside table, the photograph fell out. I picked it up and looked at it once more. I told myself petulantly that this was no sign or omen, but I couldn't convince myself. It was all very well, but all my efforts so far had come to nothing. The photograph was my only lead, and I knew instinctively that it was all-important. In the disappointments of the last few days the likeness of the unknown young man had grown in mystery and attractiveness. It had crossed my mind before, but I now felt more than ever sure that it was he for whom Julian had died.

L'homme fatal. I examined the photograph again. I think Julian and I had similar tastes and were attracted on the whole by similar "types", but there was more to it than that. I was very curious and just a little uneasy. My life lacked something, and that something wasn't sex, though sex, like alcohol for some—offered a substitute. I didn't want to read novels and I didn't want to write novels, I wanted to *live* novels. The fact that the novel I wished to *live* at this particular moment was a penny-dreadful, mystery story, was significant, because I always felt the penny-dreadful was the *real* novel. As a species it was immortal.

I managed at last to fall asleep, but the passage of seven or eight hours of unconsciousness made no difference. I thought of Everard as soon as I opened my eyes, and I knew I had to see him.

At ten o'clock I telephoned. As I expected, his secretary, a man, answered.

"Dr. Anthony Page speaking," I said. "Could I speak to Mr. Everard?"

"May I know in what connection? I mean, does Mr. Everard know you?"

"Yes," I said. I felt I was blushing with shame.

"Will you hold on, please?"

Perhaps his tone wasn't as abrupt as I'd thought at first. I shouldn't feel so touchy. There was no reason why the man should have known my name. Besides, a famous playwright is always besieged, not so much by admirers as by success snobs and by people who want something out of him. Especially a man whose reputation as a homosexual was almost as well established as his reputation as a playwright. Everard, I had always been led to believe, had an almost overwhelming supply of young men in the same way that a normal successful playwright may have a supply of young women. I had been discussing this with Terry last night, but it had been put to me that young actors and actresses simply could not find jobs unless they were prepared to pop into bed with someone, normal or abnormal. Then, others, more bitter, said the case was worse than that. Popping into bed was the inevitable minimum, which did not necessarily lead to an engagement.

I had heard many stories about him. He was said to be spoilt and mean—particularly to those with whom he had affairs.

"Are you there?" I suddenly heard the secretary's voice. This time it sounded slightly less perfunctory.

"Yes," I said.

"Mr. Everard is very sorry he cannot come to the telephone, but he would be pleased if you would like to come to his house-warming party. It's next Saturday, a week today. At about six. The address is . . ."

Twelve

In the afternoon post there was a note on crested hotel writing-paper. "*Coming to see you Friday. Love, Ann.*" There was also a cheque for fifty pounds. This was the first time I'd seen her large and rather messy handwriting. It suddenly occurred to me that she had an appointment with me for Friday, actually the next day. We had a standing arrangement that she would come every Monday and Friday. Why on earth had she bothered to remind me? And why the cheque? I had certainly not asked her for money.

I had seen her in all five times, I think, not counting the weekend, and I had given her little "treatment" as such, beyond talking to her and trying to relieve her mind. Five visits at ten pounds each; no psychiatrist, even in America, ever charged that sum. No; the letter could only mean one thing: "It is Wednesday morning and I'm sitting in the hotel doing nothing. I should like to see you and talk to you, but you'd get annoyed if I rang or called. I can hardly wait to see you the day after tomorrow. I think I'm in love with you, but please don't make any reference to this letter when I come to see you—in fact, burn it. I'm enclosing a cheque; take it as an advance, a present, a love token, anything you like. Love. Ann."

It was transference, a mild case, but an unexpected one. Now, in retrospect, I seemed to remember the way she had said goodbye last Monday, giving me her hand and not withdrawing immediately. I also recalled that she had been less abrupt and self-assertive than before.

This was all too sudden, although transference was by no means unusual even after only a couple of meetings. With Miss Wilkins it had come fairly quickly; with Mrs. Redfern not until after a few months. But with Ann, in any case I had never done any of the usual stuff, such as free association. I'd just asked direct questions. The whole thing was surprising and not very pleasant. Perhaps I was wrong; perhaps there was another explanation. I would know on Friday.

I felt like having another cup of tea. After a couple of gloomy, rainy days, it was hot again, and the sunless, damp heat made its insidious way inside my body. It found its way under my skin; it interfered with my stomach and made me listless. Terry—not subject to climatic changes—cooked simple, invalid food for me and got in a supply of Coca-Cola. Originally I had not intended to go on holiday till the middle of August, but the urge to leave England as soon as possible suddenly began to assail me.

It would, of course, need arranging. I had nine patients, not counting Ann, and Mrs. Redfern was a difficult case. I must ask someone at St. Gabriel's to look after her while I was away. The South of France or Italy, I reflected, and should I take Terry? He certainly deserved a holiday, but I couldn't make up my mind.

It was now a quarter to six and I looked through my engagement book. It seemed unlikely I could leave before the end of the month. As I turned a page, I saw Everard's name and the new address in Kensington. I must have been in a bad mood, because I suddenly felt despondent. What was the use of seeing him? It was to be a party. A crowd of irritating, uninteresting people. The odds were I should have only about two to three minutes to talk to him, but even if he gave me two to three hours, or two to three days, for that matter, what were the chances of my getting a lead on Julian? If Everard knew something he would probably tell me, but he most likely knew nothing.

That the normal world knew nothing about Julian was understandable. He took care on one hand, and was lucky on the other. But the fact that his own world, the underground, should know so little about him exasperated me, although I supposed really that I must have made the wrong contacts. Many people must have known; it was just that I hadn't found them.

An unsolved case, I thought. But how different it was from the officially unsolved cases, or, rather, how different was my own position from that of the police! They were professionals with many cases on their hands. They could always shelve one problem or transfer their activities to another. Perhaps later a solution might present itself in the normal course of events. This might even be true of my own case; my first, and probably my last as well.

I was merely an amateur with clues which at first looked really promising, but which had turned out useless. The great advantage the police enjoy is that they can publicise a crime, and thereby obtain popular support in their enquiries. It is, in fact, the public that more often than not solves the mystery. In six or seven cases out of ten it is that sense of revenge which is known as "sense of justice" and that envy which is known as "public spirit" that confounds the criminal. England is the home of the anonymous letter, without which the police or other authorities would be very baffled indeed.

Unfortunately, I couldn't stick photographs on placards inviting people who had recently seen Captain Nigel Julian Leclerc to come forward and assist me. I wondered perhaps whether a real private detective would have discovered more than I had, even with a knowledge of the underground. With better experience in detection, he might have looked for other clues. Not perhaps in Julian's flat, because I felt certain that my search had been adequate and that Julian had kept no "compromising documents" under the carpet or inside the legs of his armchair. The man would perhaps have looked for clues elsewhere, in places of which I never dreamed. But where?

The photograph? Yes; what would have been his attitude towards that? I reasoned that, judging by the haircut and the clothes, it had been taken since the war, and Julian's relations to the original of the photograph were therefore comparatively recent. But this was as far as I got. An intelligent private detective, seeing that there was no print or trade-mark on the photograph, would have taken it to an expert. That, I had also done. I took it to Adrian Berger, the photographer in Compton Street, whom I had met once in a pub and who had a great respect for me. He kept turning it in his hand. "Couldn't have been taken more than a year ago," he said with the finality of a police witness, "but the man didn't know his business. Look at the lighting; look at his camerawork." There came a dissertation not so much on the photograph as on how Adrian Berger would have taken it. "I think it was done by a cheap jack or just one of those boys who stop you in the street."

Now I could put the picture back into the file without the slightest hope of finding out who he was. For all I knew, he might be a merchant seaman, at present on his way to Buenos Aires or Port Elizabeth or on his way back to England. He may for that matter have jumped his ship in Galveston or New York. He may have been a soldier, an airman, a stevedore, a bricklayer, a barrow-boy. Maybe he was in jail. Or maybe he was in London, and living a couple of minutes away from me, a perfectly respectable married man with a son of two. Maybe I should come across him by some chance ten years later, only to find out that he was as relevant to Julian's tragic end as Ginger had been. I must have a cup of tea, I reflected again, but I had a little whisky instead. The moment I'd swallowed it, the bell went. I put the glass back and went to the hall. It was Dighton.

"Well, how are we?" somebody said in my voice and through my lips. I must take a shower after he'd gone, go to a cinema, get drunk. It was only when we were both in the consulting-room that I noticed he hadn't replied.

"I wanted to ring you yesterday," he suddenly said. "I was very excited, but it would've been stupid." He looked into my eyes with a serious expression. "I think I'm in love." He added with unmistakable triumph: "with a woman."

Sometimes we try to humour people in order to hide our real emotions. I felt my heart thumping and I knew it wasn't the whisky. I said, "You must tell me about it. But perhaps you'd like to sit down?"

I looked at him with a smile, which I meant to be rather sceptical; a little authoritative, a little doubting, and a little tender; the kind of smile with which one reacts to a slightly exuberant statement of a child. I had no spontaneous desire to smile and I didn't know how my facial muscles obeyed my intentions. But Dighton didn't even look at me. He took my words literally and deadly seriously. He seated himself in the armchair and began to speak before I had time to take my seat at the other side of the desk.

"I don't know," he said, "if I told you a few weeks ago that there's a girl in the office where I work. There are about twelve all together. This girl works on the switchboard; her name's Pat. She's been there some time and once or twice I've talked to her. She's a little shy and I think a year or two older than the others. Twenty-four. Sometimes we sat together in the canteen at dinnertime. Well, the other day there was hardly anyone about and we got talking again. I knew she was interested in films. Well, she said there was a very good foreign picture at the Studio cinema

and she was going to see it. I said I wanted to see it too. I didn't
want to ask her to come with me, she mightn't have liked it if I
offered to pay, you know, but she said why not go together. So, the
day before yesterday we went. It was a good film. French. As we
were sitting together I felt her hand touching mine and after a time
I took it and she didn't mind. Then when the big picture was over
and they put on another one, after the news I mean, we kissed. It
was very exciting. It was the first time I'd kissed a woman since I
was a boy. . . ."

"What happened afterwards?"

"We had a cup of tea at a café and talked. About the film. We
didn't say anything about holding hands and kissing. Naturally. . . ."

"No," I said. Dighton was a changed man. His whole outlook,
behaviour, diction, everything, was different from that tragic young
man who had come to see me a year ago. He looked younger, happier, triumphant, excited. As a matter of fact, for some time I had
been conscious of the change in him, but now I was taken aback. If
only one could photograph a patient's mind before treatment and
after. The person sitting opposite me was a man younger than his
years, boyish, and even a little silly. At least that was the impression
he would have given to someone not familiar with his case history.

"Then I saw her home on the bus," he was saying. "She lives
in Kennington, quite a long way from me. I had to walk home
afterwards, but I didn't mind. . . . When we came to a street near
where she lives, we kissed again. . . ."

"Did you want her very much?"

"You mean, did I want to sleep with her? Yes, very much. Do
you think I'm cured?"

I was silent for a moment. The struggle, the embarrassment,
was terrific, but I knew Dighton did not notice. "Cure," I said, "is
a big word. But I'd say you are definitely on your way. Have you
seen her since?"

"Yes. Yesterday I saw her home again and today we had lunch
in the canteen. I feel that I love her. In the same way as I liked
men. . . . Perhaps more. . . ."

Love her and *liked* men, I thought. Perhaps *more*. Had Dighton
said that consciously? Was he trying to delude himself?

"How does she feel about you?" I asked.

"Oh, I think she likes me all right."

"The most important thing is for you to forget your previous life somehow," I said. I had to say something. "Memories are dangerous."

"I know," he said, rather like a reprieved schoolboy, "I shall have to continue treatment."

"I ought, I think, to keep you under observation. But there are other very important things. I meant to tell you later. Please remember that women are very different from homosexual men. And their responses are different too. For one thing, you mustn't expect this girl to hop in to bed with you like a man who takes a fancy to you. But that you already know. Now let me give you a few words of advice. . . ."

II

When Dighton had gone, I returned to the consulting-room feeling as if I were slightly drunk. I had to sit down. Had the miracle really happened, or did Dighton just believe that he was in love? But a second later I saw that the question was meaningless. It was a big thing—for him a tremendous thing under the circumstances—even to believe that he was in love with a woman. Even to be as much interested in a woman as he was. I didn't know whether I was more alarmed than pleased. While he was with me I could keep control of my feelings to some extent at least, although I knew that I hadn't asked him quite the right questions. But now I gave way to an excitement I had seldom felt throughout my professional career. I had little experience with people like Dighton; on the whole, few psychiatrists had. You cannot save people who resist salvation, and most inverts do.

From time to time I had talked to Weblen about Dighton, and he was interested in my "progress reports", but we had not discussed him for at least four months. Weblen had originally said it was most important to do deep analysis to see what was inside, but he had later agreed with me that a "short-cut" would do just as well.

Dighton's sudden interest in a woman was almost unbelievable. I remembered telling him once or twice, almost in casual asides, that he should find female company: some "nice" girl. In his social group, the meeting place was usually the ballroom, the place where he worked, occasionally even the streets. Offhand, I couldn't remember if he had ever referred to the fact that he was acting on my advice, and I hadn't questioned him on the subject. After all, that was something that could wait. The analysis was more important. Week after week, month after month, he had come to see me and we succeeded in delving deeper and deeper into his past. He had been one of my most frequent visitors. Even then the thing was too rapid. But sometimes the short-cut method brought results every bit as good as a long-term analysis. I must see Weblen and ask for his views.

But, thinking again of consulting Weblen, I knew there was something more important I wanted to discuss with him, something I could repress while Dighton was sitting in my room, but which I could keep back no longer—and that something was myself.

I remembered often, especially in the first weeks after Dighton had come to see me, I was a little uneasy about transference, a very common occurrence between patient and psychiatrist. The patient became involved. But in this case I felt it was the psychiatrist who was more involved. It wasn't Dighton's attractive physical appearance. He wasn't quite my type; besides, there was my self-discipline. It was more his personality, that steady masculine determination to fight his way through, that appealed to me. Then I suppose I sublimated it somewhere, somehow, and Dighton became my favourite patient and nothing else.

But now I felt I was losing my control. I was in love with Dighton's achievement, and the achievement was very difficult to separate from the man. And now I knew there was only one thing to do: I myself must change, must fall in love with a woman. The implications flashed through my mind with a bewildering rapidity. I must change; I must be normal. There was no way out. I felt, if I didn't change, I might fall in love with Dighton.

I got up and dialled Weblen's number, but the housekeeper said he had gone out. Just as my luck would have it. In my disappointment, I left no message for him.

It was half-past seven. I decided I wouldn't have dinner at home.

It would be too much of an effort to try to talk about other things or try to listen to Terry's conversation. I clearly couldn't tell him a word about it.

I went to the kitchen and practically bumped into him, obviously on his way to tell me dinner was ready. "I have to go out at once," I told him and, before he could say anything, added: "Should anyone call me, you can try to ring Dr. Weblen, but only if it's really very urgent. . . . No, perhaps you'd better not . . ." I said. "Just take a message . . ."

III

Wars often have results which are entirely unconnected with the aims and purposes for which they have been fought. When I accepted Dighton as a patient, there seemed to be only two ultimate alternatives: I would either succeed in curing him or I would fail, but the chances of success seemed good. Once or twice I began actually to wonder how I would feel if I succeeded. The personal triumph would be great, no doubt. Wilbur Stowasser would have asked me to publish the case in *Sex Variants* and there would have been the usual correspondence about it. For me, of course, there was always the blind-leading-the-blind principle which would have added to my glory; the triumph of the operatic coach who cannot sing, the athletic trainer who cannot run.

But the fact that Dighton's success would make me jealous and bring me to a crisis never entered my mind. It was true that when he first came to see me I didn't realise that, in Julian, there was a connecting link between us, that in fact both of us had, so to speak, been jilted by Julian. But even if I had understood about Dighton and Julian from the start, it might not have made all the difference. There was a very good reason for this: Julian was then alive and I felt more or less indifferent towards him, but now that he was dead, young, tragically, suddenly, he had assumed a new significance and I felt involved. All the more because he had wanted to contact me just before his death.

Both Dighton and I had been in love with Julian, but his death affected us very differently. Dighton was almost relieved by it, even

if he didn't think about the Mills of God. In fact, I was certain
that Julian's death was one of the many contributory causes which
resulted in Dighton's falling in love with a woman.

While I was thinking about all this, I had been walking in the
park. I crossed the bridge over the Serpentine. It was still quite
warm under the dusty trees and the couples were ambling along
slowly, waiting for darkness to fall. I looked at them nostalgically
as seldom before. Pick up a woman, the thought flashed through
my mind, and it made me feel bitter. Technically it may not have
been difficult, but emotionally it seemed as impossible as to pick
up a man. I realised that it must have been eighteen months since
I'd picked up anyone. Errol, I thought. Yes, he must have been the
last, a hitch-hiker between Poughkeepsie and Concord to whom
I'd given a lift in Stowasser's car. He had freckles on the back of
his shoulders. Errol was a college boy who was working during
the vacation, and a congenital case. "It's a nuisance I guess," he
said in the hotel room, "but what can one do?" Suddenly, the once
attractive memory became foul and shameful.

There was no doubt that what had attracted me about affairs
with men had been the ease, especially during the war. There was
no fuss, the minimum of preliminaries, no reserve; the partner was
as independent as I was, a complete equal. He was usually matter
of fact and urgent at the same time, awe-inspiring and irresistible.
I had then felt that somewhere at the deepest level of existence this
must be, must have been, the equivalent of real freedom.

Because he was a man, our world, our interests, had more in
common than would have been the case between a man and a
woman. There are millions of perfectly normal—in fact, happily
married—men, who only use their wives as sex instruments and
the home for little else than a place to retire for bed and breakfast.
Their best friend, their only friend, still remains another man.
True, of course, they don't usually realise the homosexual implications, if any. If any . . .

During the war the fact that one sometimes never again saw a
man with whom one had slept once was little cause for dismay.
One soon found another. But that lack of permanence became
tiresome after the sensation of novelty had worn off, and coupled
with a few other factors, was instrumental in my retirement.

There was the moral issue. The battle in my conscience had caused me to decide that freedom had to be sacrificed for virtue; my new moral code said that it was immoral and foul to have sex without love. I meant it at the time in relation to men, but it was the same with women.

It was amazing how little I had thought—consciously at least—of conventional morality. Sex relations with men, whether you loved them or not, were against conventional morality, and many people, therefore, had they known about me, would have regarded me as a moral criminal. The fact that some four, five, maybe six per cent. of doctors were probably homosexual didn't alter the case, any more than the fact that the number of male inverts in England must have been over the million mark. One was alone.

Nor had I been thinking much about the prospect of age, except in a few brief, bitter moments. There was little reason to think about it when one was young and the climate of the age revolutionary. Now the prospect came back and it was not the ripe wisdom and Apollonian serenity of the old Greco-Roman priest or philosopher, towards whom young men were respectful and affectionate, but the prospect of a seedy, old homosexual doctor haunting the twilight in twentieth-century England. Chances of success would be reduced to money, perhaps to a few rare young men with gerontophile tendencies or with a devastating sense of pity. It was true that ardour might weaken with age, but one had seen almost too many elderly inverts whom the passage of time merely drove into satyriasis.

Thirteen

I usually feel better in the morning. Even when I've drunk a lot and taken sleeping pills the previous night, I always feel rested when I awake.

Punctually at ten the next day Ann arrived. She wore a rather striking new dress of dark grey silky fabric; she oozed a scent which gave the impression of camphor, but which I imagined was fashionable and expensive. She wore no hat.

She smiled as she sat down. "I've been thinking about that letter in Julian's room. I wanted to ring you up. What a fool I was to be worried by it. But then you think of such wild things when you're in a fix, don't you? It serves me right for prying. Haven't we always been told not to read other people's letters?" She smiled again, and I nodded. She had either changed or she had an unexpected side to her character. Crisis apparently brought out the worst in her, contentment the best. Where was the arrogance now, the nasty, old-world purse-proudness, the heavy underlining of synthetic county?

"Some time ago," she said suddenly after a moment's hesitation, "when I first came to you, you said I ought to go abroad. You do remember, don't you? Well, when you told me that, I just wouldn't hear of it, but now I think you were right. I ought to go, even though the weather's been good lately. As a matter of fact, I've already made up my mind. . . . Or nearly, anyhow." I had the impression her little speech had been carefully rehearsed.

"The point is," she went on, "I'm wondering if I could, so to speak, continue treatment abroad. I know for a fact that change of air and atmosphere and all that will help, but it won't be enough. Well, I thought you might like to take your holiday at the same time. You did mention something about going to France last time, didn't you?"

She was looking at me quite calmly. No doubt this had been rehearsed too. I said: "As an idea, it's very good, but it needs careful thinking over on my part." Here I gave a secret sigh of relief. I had managed to collect myself sufficiently to bring out this sentence. I was now thinking hard what to say, how to hedge, how to hide.

"You don't have to decide at once," she explained, and I saw the disappointment.

"No, no," I said. "In any case, I couldn't. Not straight away. You're free to move. I'm not. I have a number of patients and I have to arrange my holiday accordingly. . . . Besides, it isn't an easy matter. Your parents . . ."

"Oh, they don't come into it at all." For one single second there was almost anger in the bushy eyebrows, then her face assumed a quiet determination. "I've quite made up my mind. It's time I led my own life." She shrugged a shoulder as if in resignation instead of defiance, and a whiff of her scent came towards me. "I'm old enough."

We were silent now. She was feeling in her handbag and took out a packet of cigarettes. It was stupid on my part to have mentioned her parents, but her suggestion had taken me so much by surprise that I hadn't thought of the obvious thing first; a doctor going away on holiday with one of his women patients. And to the outside world, Ann was one of my patients, even if I returned her cheque, even if I myself paid her a fee to come to see me. But that wasn't the real problem. Nor was it transference. This was going to be difficult, I told myself, but a moment later I already knew what I must do. I must send her away after a few minutes. Then I could think.

"Well," I said, "I shall certainly consider it." I was looking at her without seeing her. "Tell me, how are you getting on?"

"Oh, much better." Her voice came out brightly. She shook her head. "I was a fool about that letter business, but I think I've got over it." She paused for a second, then added: "I suppose we shall never know why Julian killed himself."

"I suppose not," I answered, but there was so much detachment in the way she had spoken that I became startled. Did she have a far greater balance, resilience, buoyancy—call it what you will— than I had expected? Or was her attitude due to me or simply to treatment?

She must have noticed something in my voice, something of which I was quite oblivious. Suddenly she said: "You're not thinking of giving me up?" She spoke loudly now and almost imploringly; a moment and she would cry.

"Of course not," I said. "Why should I? You can come and see me as long as you need to."

"I'm still ill," she said.

"Well, perhaps. But in any case you mustn't admit to yourself that you're ill. Particularly since you've certainly made very rapid progress. Haven't you?"

"Thanks to you." Her voice was quiet now, almost subservient.

"That's quite beside the point," I said. "The important thing is that you're getting on well. You're thinking much less about Julian nowadays."

"Well, he's dead," she countered just a little argumentatively, but a split second later we both burst out laughing.

"There you are," I said. "Your reactions are getting more and more normal." I pulled up my left sleeve cuff, but I didn't see the face of my watch. "Goodness," I said, "I have a consultation and I haven't seen the notes yet. Well, Ann, you're coming to see me on Monday."

I realised that I had called her by her Christian name. It wasn't a conscious act on my part, but what really was a conscious act?

"I shall be waiting to hear from you," she said as she rose. Again I smelled her perfume.

II

Miss Mayhew was not coming for another hour or so, but I felt relieved when I'd closed the door after Ann. What I really would have liked to do was to put my patient off, switch the telephone into Terry's bedroom and sit down and think. But what I actually did was to go to the telephone and dial Weblen's number. There was no reply. Apparently he had already left and his housekeeper was out shopping. I looked at my watch and dialled St. Gabriel's. It was Friday; he would be there. If I was lucky, I could get him before he started his rounds. But I was told that he had not yet arrived.

"It's Dr. Page," I said. "Would you kindly tell him I phoned?" I gave the man my number.

No, it wasn't about transference that I was worried. That aspect didn't bother me, because experience in the past had taught me how to handle it. The real problem was the one that had popped up last night and driven me from home. This morning I had felt better. I had at least thought I should be all right until Dighton's next visit, but now, after Ann's suggestion about a holiday, the situation was as bad as it had ever been—in fact, worse.

The desire to show—not to Dighton, who must never know about it, but to myself—that I could do what he had done to fight for my personal happiness and succeed, became violent. And the desire to turn normal was now far stronger than it had been the previous night now that there seemed actually to be a possible solution for me. Here was a woman who thought she was in love with me—what had induced her love was immaterial—who could in the end perhaps love me, who in any case would be quite willing to marry me. Ann was the right age, and in a way, physically at least, she was acceptable to me. Though her occasional helplessness was feminine—it may only have been upbringing—she looked just a little masculine. There was no question about it, I did not find her unattractive.

But would there be much emotional stimulus? Ann was not highly educated; that was a good point; but she was not uneducated, like the men I had liked in the past. With her, there was no working-class folklore and mystery, and she lacked a masculine independence. These things were missing, but my liking for them, for regional accents and other fetishes, was something I needed to get rid of, or at least to guide away from the sexual channel.

It was no use thinking about those inverts who lived in polygamy, because the arrangement would suit neither of us. There were a few who told their wives all about it and if the wife was exceptionally understanding and felt that it was always she who came first, the complicated arrangement sometimes worked. The others, who kept it a secret from their wives and carried on furtively, made me shudder. I thought of Allen Lepage. He had started life as a normal-looking and in fact fairly normal person who had received in his young manhood a strong homosexual stimulus. I don't know what happened later, but he married a rich girl and tried to run away from his past. The normality of his appearance increased—in fact, it became a parody. Once somebody had called him a "male impersonator" and the crack was fully justified. He assumed an unnecessarily deep voice and adopted gestures that were too big and too heavy for his five feet ten inches and his thirty-eight chest. Bred in London, he also became a caricature of a country gentleman, with his tweeds, a concealing moustache and his new vocabulary with the dropped "g's". It didn't need a trained psychologist to see that he was a failure. He tried desperately to love his wife, rather a stupid little woman with money, who was in love with him and whom he tried to rope closer to himself by giving her two children. But he still wished for men to make a tremendous fuss of him, to love him romantically, hopelessly. Eventually dissatisfaction brought out the frustrated bitch in him with a vengeance. He was now thirty-eight, still tolerable-looking, for women at least, but touchy and nasty and feminine under the disguise.

It was Lepage's wife who reminded me of the fact that Ann was rich. If I married her I would be far more independent than I was now. I could move to Harley Street, or, if I wanted to, give up most of my patients and concentrate on research or teaching. But I didn't feel that Ann's wealth was an important consideration. If I wanted to look at it from the material aspect, it was the steadiness a good marriage usually brought that was the real attraction. Because, when all was said and done, I was still unsteady, even though for the past year or two I had behaved well, kept to a routine, worked hard and in a way got on in the world.

No, that wasn't the material factor; it was this: would marriage for me—with Ann or with any other woman—work? That was the question. Since the end of the war I had wanted to settle down—I presumed I had never been basically promiscuous, even though circumstances had driven me to it—but I could never find the right man. Perhaps that was the reason that the one-night adventures lost their romance for me.

"Marriage is an adventure": the phrase leapt into my mind. Yes, but the man who coined the phrase had entirely different problems in mind from my own. To a man like myself about half the maxims and wisdom of the world don't apply; I'd learnt that early in life. In my case marriage was more an experiment than an adventure. But had one the right to involve a woman in an experiment, of which she was to be left in ignorance? And, besides, Ann was a patient. It would, of course, be tragi-comic if I were struck off the register for having an affair with a *woman* patient.

Ann, apparently, had been Julian's *femme fatale*, in more than one sense. But why shouldn't I succeed where he had failed? I lit a fresh cigarette. I found that for every single sober argument that occurred to me, there was sharp counter-argument equally sober. In the end I tried to leave Ann out of my thoughts, and succeeded. But nevertheless the problem remained. What was I going to do with myself? Try to struggle to be normal? Move about and find another woman? Or return to men? Because now it seemed obvious that the attitude I had maintained for the past year, of not having any relations with anybody, was unlikely to continue. It would just drive me mad. To be a psychiatrist was not the same thing as to be a priest, and even a priest had his difficult moments.

I had been alone, but now I was more alone than ever before. And this time I knew that, far from sympathy, I would get nothing but derision if I explained my situation to most members of the underground. If there is anything the average exclusive homo loathes, anything that gets his goat, anything that makes his blood boil, it's the bisexual—who provokes all his pathological spite, envy and malice. The normal world is an enemy with which the invert may come to terms, but the man who tries to struggle out of inversion by having affairs with women and getting married is a traitor who ought to be exposed. There is a nasty arrogance about him, a triumph of the hypocrite who bettered himself, knows all the secrets and probably exposes them; the thief who turns detective, in short, a monster.

I felt desolate and miserable. And even the "case", which I realised now was a temporary outlet for me—some sort of substitute—even the case seemed at an end.

III

I had difficulty in contacting Weblen. When I rang him at the hospital after Miss Mayhew had gone, I was told he was on his rounds. Then I tried again later at his home, but he wasn't in. I finally caught him at home after dinner.

"Pity you didn't ring up before," Weblen said. "I had *chicken à la reine*, artichokes and a *crêpe suzette*. . . . No; I never had your messages. You rang *three* times? How infuriating. . . . Why don't you come over and have coffee?"

Weblen lived off Cavendish Square in an Edwardian block of flats amid the comforts of Turkey carpets, shining brass and heavy mahogany panelling. I was shown into his large study, which had all the opulence of the nineteen-tens, except that a Philpot drawing of a small girl's head hung over the mantelpiece.

I didn't sit down. I was too impatient and perhaps a little afraid. I looked at his books. Facing the windows there was "shop"; possibly the best private collection of technical books on psycho-therapy I had ever seen. Almost nervously I turned away from them. There was fiction, history and art on the rest of the shelves, which lined the whole room. I walked to the window and looked out, then almost immediately drew back. I must calm myself. Weblen was sure to be able to help me. I stopped on my way to the settee, because among the old book backs I caught sight of the spine of a brand new dust jacket. It was glossy, large and pink: the portfolio of Lewis Carroll's photographs. I put my finger on the shiny surface, and I saw there was quite a collection of Carolliana. There were his mathematical treatises, his letters, his poems, four or five books on Carroll and, of course the two volumes of *Alice*. There was no need to pull them out. They were obviously first editions.

Then Weblen came in, followed by his housekeeper with a large coffee tray. "You never took to cigar-smoking in America?" he said when we were drinking the strong French coffee. He was about sixty with beautiful white hair and a misleadingly wistful expression. Half the time he never seemed to be listening to you, but he could, with the greatest ease, recapitulate all your conversations a year later, practically word for word.

"Well," he said.

"It's a consultation, sir, in a way. That is if you don't mind shop. . . ."

Weblen looked at me for a moment. His face was anxious, but he must have noticed my concern and he suddenly began to smile.

"I never mind shop, Page; and you know it."

"It's about two people. . . ."

"The more the better. The night's young." He had fine teeth and the hands of a sculptor. Modelling was his hobby.

"First of all about my star patient . . ." I said.

"Dighton," he nodded. "I was expecting a progress report from you. How is it going?"

"He's in love with a woman. It looks serious. And I've barely finished the analysis. I'm wondering if he'll remain pretty normal or revert later."

"You can't tell in advance. If I remember his case history correctly, he had been interested in women in his early youth. Isn't that so? Then he'd drifted towards men and had a shock through an unhappy love affair. He came to us and we sent him to you. You did a short-cut analysis and also tried to reawaken his early heterosexual memories."

"Yes, but only very sketchily."

"It may have been enough. For the time being, all I'd do would be to keep him under observation and go on increasing his heterosexuality, if you can."

There was a long silence. Finally, I just managed "Thank you, sir," and that was all.

I felt my hand shaking. What was this? I was a man whom life had taught to be bold when necessary. Upbringing had given me social ease and perhaps a certain faculty for expressing myself. I was usually good at "difficult situations", but now I was as tongue-tied as the small boy I had once been whose father had questioned him about something he was ashamed to discuss. I felt I was blushing. I must change the subject, talk about something else. I must go home. Yes; I must go home.

But it wasn't I who moved. Slowly, as if he had been timing it, Weblen turned towards me. "You said there was another patient"; he nodded, and then took his eyes off me. "I think I know *that* particular case history very well." This was a father talking to his son, only my own father was never so gentle, so good, so understanding; he never knew me. Weblen knew that I was the other patient.

He spoke again. His voice was soft, caressing, intimate: "You're in love with Dighton, aren't you?"

"With . . . his success," I stammered. "With the fact that he is being cured. . . ."

"And that it was you who cured him. I should have been surprised if this hadn't happened. But then I knew you'd cope with it. . . ."

"Will I?"

"Oh yes."

"I'd be a happier man if I were normal. This is the first time I've really felt that intensely. . . ."

His left hand moved. "You want me to tell you what your chances are, I suppose?"

"Yes, sir."

"Well, it depends on what branch of medicine you intend to take up in the future. You're still a young man; you have private means; you're intelligent, adaptable, conscientious. Patients have great confidence in you because they know they can trust you. . . . Well, there's internal medicine, chest, heart, stomach. . . . Wilson-Hemingrove was thirty-five or more when he gave up cardiology to become the best dermatologist there is. . . ."

"You mean if I change I'd be useless as a psychiatrist?"

"Well," Weblen nodded. "You might be."

How petulant my voice must have sounded. "In other words," I said, "you approve of Dighton being cured, but not of *me*."

"It sounds awful, doesn't it? But that's more or less how I feel. Dighton is a very different case from you. He's a printer and you're a psycho-analyst. Being a far less complicated person than you and doing a far less complicated job, he can only gain by being cured. Whereas you . . ."

Two beautiful hands rose slowly, simultaneously, with fingers slightly bent. "You're upset, I think, not only by the fact that Dighton is being cured, but by the fact that it's *you* who've been instrumental in curing him. Let's look at it this way," he said. "You haven't completely cured him yet, have you? The chances are that you will, and I hope you do. But hasn't it occurred to you that you weren't entirely responsible for what happened, though you worked hard and I'm sure, extremely well." He nodded. "Dighton was a bisexual, a borderline case, who had been attracted by women before and who made up his mind to return to women after an unfortunate adventure. Now for all we know, there may be hundreds of people like Dighton, who cure themselves on their own with some degree of success. It all depends on the man, his circumstances and personality. You surely realise that. You may not have thought about it because you were enthusiastic and, of course, the case was very interesting. Mind you, I'm not trying to depreciate your work in order to help you. You did a first-rate job. I'm sure I couldn't have done better. You definitely facilitated what Dighton himself was trying to do. . . . Perhaps he couldn't have succeeded on his own. Who knows?"

"For the past year or so," I said, almost as if talking to myself, "I've had absolutely no real contact with anyone, emotionally or physically. . . ."

"Didn't you feel the need? Or, rather, would you have had relations if you'd had the chance?"

"Perhaps. I suppose ever since I returned from America I've tried to rationalise things. Once or twice in the beginning I went out in the evenings, looked round, but I saw there was nothing—nothing available, that is. But I suppose that may not have been the real reason I've just refrained from everything."

Quietly Weblen said, "I must ask you a question."

I guessed in advance what he was going to say. I was no longer embarrassed. In fact I replied almost before he could continue.

"The answer is yes," I said.

He nodded. "And your erotic image is masculine?"

"Yes."

"There you are." He turned his hand palm upwards.

"I suppose," I said, "it's unnecessary to go over all the arguments for and against my being cured?" I probably sounded a little bitter. "I mean, I'm certain I can be as good a therapist in trying to cure heterosexual patients if I am heterosexual myself. . . . I should probably be better. I mean, the vast majority of the patients of *any* psychiatrist, after all, are heterosexual, suffering from various neuroses, nervous insomnia, bed-wetting, night fears, claustrophobia. You're not suggesting that I shall be a worse doctor if I turn normal?"

"Of course not. In fact, you may be better for all I know. The point is that you are a good doctor whether you're a homo or not, if you want a compliment. But that's not the point. You know what the point is, only you want me to tell you in my own words. All right. Years ago I tried to assess you on your homo-hetero rating scale. I came to the conclusion that on points you're more homo than hetero because . . ."

Here it comes, I felt. Suddenly I closed my eyes like a frightened child. My heart froze. "Because of your unresolved narcissistic components. . . ."

"Because of your unresolved narcissistic components," Weblen said, slowly as if he were dictating to his secretary. "You know as well as I do that it takes years and years of deep analysis before narcissism can be resolved. . . ."

"It rarely happens in any case," I said. What a good thing it was that my tear glands no longer functioned.

"I don't know," Weblen said, "but I can't see you at this stage benefitting from further analysis. Even if you did submit to analysis, your emotions would be so fluid that you'd become useless in your job. Of course, I'm only theorising, but I'm afraid there's another and very important reason for advising you against change. I know absolutely no one in London for whom you could develop a sufficiently strong positive transference."

My answer came like a shot. Was this a rope I saw in the twilight on the surface of the water for just one tenth of a second? "What about you, sir?" I said.

It wasn't a rope. Weblen was smiling charmingly, enigmatically and somewhat sadly. Gently he shook his head. Quietly he said: "This mood will pass. I said *mood*, not crisis. You'll cope with it. Your balance, on the whole, is first-rate. You do your best for Dighton, and his cure may be permanent. But you yourself will have to stay as you are. In a few days' time you'll forget all this upheaval. I dare say it may be a little difficult, especially tonight—or you'll think it is—because you're still young. . . ."

I didn't answer.

"You're feeling depressed, of course."

"Well . . ." I said.

Weblen was silent now. He wasn't looking at me. Then slowly he spoke: "This sort of situation, this particular mood—crisis, if you insist—has come to many psychiatrists before you, homos and heteros." Slowly he got up and walked to the mantelpiece. He took down a little bronze bust.

"Have I ever shown you this?" he said. His smile was no longer enigmatic. It was beautiful and sad.

It was a good but conventional work, such as might have been seen in the Royal Academy of the 'twenties—a greenish bronze bust of a small girl. I was suddenly aware of her overwhelming innocence and sweetness. I wasn't looking at Weblen. I wanted to, but I felt it would be wrong. I had heard rumours about him, but attributed no importance to them, perhaps because of my immense respect for him as a really great teacher and the kindest of men. Besides, his problem was so very different from my own. Now I thought I understood his interest in Lewis Carroll.

But I was wrong about my tear glands.

BOOK THREE

Fourteen

It was a few minutes before six when I left home to drive over to Everard's house.

It was, in a way, amazing how my interview with Weblen the previous evening had relieved me. I felt, the next morning, that a psychiatrist was as much a human being as anyone else; as any of his patients for that matter: weak, vacillating, irrational and helpless when it came to his own private life. I had a good cry, but all the same I felt as if I'd suddenly grown up. That I happened to be the way I was might well be a professional asset; in any case, it was no real handicap. Weblen's charm, wisdom and gentle goodness had done me a power of good. His silent confession, his admission in as many words that he himself was not normal, and that, like Carroll, he sublimated his desires in various ways, I thought beautiful and relieving.

I knew that now I would regard Dighton with pride and satisfaction and not with semi-hysterical envy. And I knew it was a good thing that I'd said nothing to Weblen about Ann. I could now look at her as I looked at other patients. I should have to do something about her transference. That was always a delicate operation, but I felt I should take pride in curing her. Then she could go abroad alone.

As for my own holiday, I decided to go away as soon as circumstances permitted. I was quite calm now. It would take me at least three weeks to settle my affairs. I hoped in that time to deal with all matters of outstanding importance concerning my patients, including Ann.

It was natural that in my recent turmoil I had forgotten all about Everard's invitation. In my mood of the previous day I would almost certainly have ignored it. But now I saw Everard and the reason I wished to contact him in a different light. I was back where I had been in the first instance and my interest in the case had revived. I realised that solution was improbable, but since I was to stay in England for a few weeks anyhow, and having invested so much time and energy, I decided that I might as well go on with it, at least until my holiday began.

Everard was unlikely to know what had really happened to Julian. But of all the people I had contacted so far, I was sure it was he who knew Julian best. He might be able to make some helpful suggestion; at least he would probably know someone who could help. I made a mental note to go early and catch him before most of his guests arrived.

As it happened, I was not early enough. There was already a number of cars in front of the house when I reached him just after six. I knew the neighbourhood. It was a part of Kensington that still remained prosperous, if not select, where the well-to-do concentrated themselves in a tiny corner around a Victorian Gothic church that had been so much damaged during the war that it looked three hundred years older than it really was.

The house was Victorian, but an ingenious architect had turned it into as Hollywood a version of an Italian villa as London's climate and the Ministry of Town and Country Planning would allow. I saw that the large garden at the back was full of pergolas, fountains and Roman statues, and I guessed that the rooms were Italian too, and as highly dramatic as stage sets. Like Rodney Croodie or Hugh Harpley, Everard had to "think of his customers".

A tall young man with wavy fair hair, wearing a tweed jacket and an expensive wool-crepe shirt, and looking like some knock-kneed Apollo, let me in. A fellow guest, a servant, a general hanger-on, a pimp? It was not easy to guess his function in the house. He told me in a Rada voice that Everard was not yet back.

The man who came up to me as we entered the large room was obviously the secretary. Like his voice, his movements suggested nervous efficiency and a semi-hysterical energy. "Mr. Everard has been called away to a conference, but he is on his way back. What would you like to drink?" he said with the speed of an express train about to leave the rails. And before I could reply he bolted away on legs like stilts towards a chest-of-drawers made of mirror-glass, on which there were about a dozen bottles.

He gave me a drink and introduced me to the one man in the room whom I had actually met before, during the war. I didn't catch his name, but I think he was a South American. I remembered that Bobby Sillock had called him *Don Juan des Lavabos*.

He told me he had just been to Paris for a few weeks. He spoke more or less standard English with an occasional trace of foreign accent. Now that I saw him close up it was clear why his features had always looked to me so strange. The face to an extent was artificial, and he suddenly reminded me of an airman whose facial wounds had been patched up by a plastic surgeon. The wounds which Don Juan had received in his battle with time had been eliminated with a skill for which American surgeons are famous. His face had been lifted and the pouches under his eyes ironed out; I had suspicions about his forehead too. Consequently, it was embarrassing to watch him smile, although his teeth were good. He wore a dark grey suit with a discreet, embroidered overstripe, a cream silk shirt and a plain, ribbed, silk tie. Everything about him had the simplicity of a Rolls Royce.

"After Paris, London is most depressing in every way," he said. "The French were occupied, and yet they've completely recovered. England cannot recover because in their despair they decided to penalise enterprise, talent, intelligence. I came back a fortnight ago and haven't got over it yet." He closed his eyes in agony. "And the queer world in Paris is so different. You don't have to go to St. Germain or the Étoile. . . . You find it everywhere. In a way this is new in France," he added reminiscently. "The first evening I spoke to a young student at a café terrace near the Batignolles. He couldn't have been more charming. I asked him afterwards to my hotel to have a drink and tried to find out whether he was willing to play. Do you know what happened? The young man actually *apologised* for being normal, but he said he knew a fellow student who was queer. First I thought he was a kind of pimp, but he wasn't. He was just a civilised man. As for his friend . . . well, he was a perfectly charming young man, quite nice-looking, but unfortunately not my cup of tea.

"What happens in London is that ageing Guardsmen with pencilled moustaches and bad teeth come up to you in pubs and cringe drinks from you, if they are not anxious to peddle themselves.

Well last night, I was in a West End pub—as they say. I was with a friend, and a man made overtures to us. He may have been about thirty-five, but he looked more. I tried to cut him a few times, but he was insistent. Finally, he came up. And do you know what he said? I can't imitate his accent. 'It was put to me that you're an iron.' Well, I am told this in gutter English means pouf. Iron hoof, you see. . . . And he sniggered, in a nasty, miserable sort of way. I got very angry. I said: 'Yes, my friend. I'm an *iron* all right, but I draw the line and you are fifteen years outside that line. Now will you just excuse us.' I turned my back on him. Probably on Coronation night in 1937 a drunken old pansy took him home and gave him five bob and the man is still intoxicated with success."

I was now watching the guests. There were three women who looked like actresses and pretended hard that there was nothing unusual about the party. All the others were men. There were about twenty standing in small groups, by the mantelpiece, by the bookshelves, leaning against the backs of the two settees. With the exception of a couple of sailors, both young, earnest, good-looking, semi-normal and "haveable", all were inverts. But they were a mixed lot and, despite two social revolutions within thirty years, class stood out sharp as if its frontiers were cut by razors. I'd always known that sex, normal or abnormal, was not the great social unifier that the wishful often claim, but here in this room I was more than ever certain. Like work and pleasure and national emergency, it only brings people together temporarily. Contacts are made, but they seldom deepen into friendships. Sex—not to speak of love—knows no frontiers, social or political, but in nine cases out of ten the stranger must return, after the brief visit, to his own environment, however much he wants to stay.

One could so easily classify each of these people, even though, generally speaking, with the exception of the two sailors, they all came from some middle-class group. I couldn't hear their voices individually and there was very little difference in dress, little even in stature or appearance, but their background was obvious. There was not the slightest doubt that the three talking to the sailors and the other three in isolation by the mantelpiece had been to public schools. The rest were clerks, shop assistants, small-part actors. They betrayed themselves in their gait, in their posture, in the way they held their glasses. They were none of them well off, and they were all putting on an act, pretending that the house, the room, the surroundings were their natural habitat. But the public school groups pretended with greater ease, the rest with perceptible strain. There was little mixing as yet. After a time the frontiers might be crossed, then swiftly recrossed. At present the inferiors watched the superiors with an ill-disguised mixture of curiosity, hostility and fascination.

They all tried their best to appear hard-boiled, sure, unruffled, incapable of surprise, but they failed to make it look authentic. They lacked the background. Experience and faith in their skill, feminine elasticity and an ability easily to assimilate were not satisfactory substitutes. One could pick out the boys from the lesser residential suburbs who were trying desperately to run away from it all. They were ashamed of the semi-detached, the fumed oak, the thwarted aspirations, the lower middle-class tyranny or sheepishness of their parents, the dropped aitches, the boredom. They stood there, talking, listening with a frozen smile, in their one good suit. They had gathered a smattering of culture, pretentious and second-hand, at the price of round shoulders, knock-knees, ill-calcified teeth and chicken legs. They had read a few fashionable books and managed to bring into their conversation an occasional mispronounced French word. They were losing and they knew it. The fixed smile was a form of self-defence.

It was partly something to do with their generation. These people were in their early thirties. There is a tendency for the younger, post-war generation of inverts to be tougher in both mind and body. They know that tolerable biceps and a good pair of shoulders are better selling points today than an acquaintance with books by Sartre and Maugham or cracks by Gingold or Coward.

I had moved across to the window with Don Juan. He put his large gold cigarette case back into its chamois cover, then suddenly announced: "Our host is back." I turned towards the window, but saw nothing.

A minute later Everard entered the room. Everybody looked up. There was almost a hush and for a moment the classes were united as if it were an air raid or a royal visit. The entrance was dramatic. Everard seemed to have a good sense of the theatre even in his private life. He wore his usual dark grey flannels, overpolished tan shoes, a silk shirt and the O.E. tie. His movements suggested a masculine energy that was slightly American, but one could see the strain in his eyes and round the lips, and the veins of his forehead stood out like whipcords. He didn't look young, but he might have been described as 'young for his age', which was about thirty-five.

As I expected, he greeted the uppers first. Above the now slightly subdued conversation one could hear his voice. He talked loudly, like a country gentleman, but the speed was out of tradition and suggested neurasthenia.

He was now approaching us. "Pedro," he said to Don Juan, while his right hand rested for a second on my shoulder, "tell me all about Michele Duval. They're trying to get her to do Sarah in *The Eye of the Needle* in Paris."

"Well, what I heard, she used to work for a dry-cleaning place in the Faubourg St. Honoré; then she lived with a man who took part in the Resistance, or something, and became a heroine. At least that was the build-up. She had a small part in an Anouilh play and she was such a success that she was made at once. You know how it is in France. She's about twenty-eight . . . *jolielaide* . . . frightful ankles . . ."

"Must hear more," Everard roared. "I'm going over in a fortnight's time. Give you a ring Monday." Suddenly he turned to me. "I'm so glad you rang up. Haven't seen you for such a long time. You've been away, haven't you? Now let's see, who would you like to meet? There's a very charming boy from Italy coming later, a medical student. Wants to be a psychiatrist. I'm sure you . . ." But he was already smiling at someone else.

I said: "May I keep you for just a moment? I remember you were a friend of Julian Leclerc. What on earth happened to him?"

His face suddenly became serious. "I can't tell you much, though I have my suspicions, of course. The last affair Julian had was with a young tough called Ron Ackroyd, about twenty-three or so. Very beautiful and very butch. Your height, well-made, curly dark hair, spiv haircut—well, the cockney glamour boy." He suddenly smiled. "He actually came from Everard Street in Islington. We built the place. My cousin Tim sold it some time ago. It's a dreadful slum.

"Anyhow, Julian told me he was in love at last. 'I've been looking for a man like Ron all my life,' he said, 'and luckily, I've found him.' I said, 'Knowing you, he's a tough.' 'Yes, I suppose he is, and that's one of his attractions, the contrast between his appearance and that wonderful tenderness and sweetness he has inside. I know he'd do anything for me.'

"Then," Everard said, "I *saw* Ron. He was nice, but frankly he frightened me. Julian brought him to my place. There was something of the triumph of the lion-tamer about the whole affair. They seemed to be in love, and people in love are so dull. Then I don't know what happened. He left Julian or Julian left him; I was in Bermuda at the time. Julian was half-mad, and the silly ass decided to get married. I saw the thing in *The Times*. Then the man went after him, I suppose. It must have been blackmail, although I shouldn't be surprised if Ron murdered him, he was that tough.

"In any case, I hear he can always be found in one of the queer pubs, sitting alone; I don't know which, but someone told me he's always there, drinking and becoming very rude if anyone tries to pick him up. Well," Everard said, "now let me introduce you to a very charming young man."

"Thank you," I said. "But just a second." My hands were trembling as I took out my wallet. "Is this Ron?" I said.

The briefest glance was enough. "Yes," Everard almost shouted. He looked hard at me. "Where did you find it? Do you know him?"

"I don't, but I've got to find him."

"I wish I could help you," he said. "But for God's sake don't tell anybody what I told you."

"Well, of course not," I said. "But now I really mustn't keep you."

"But how did you find the photograph?"

"I'll tell you all about that one day. It's a promise."

"Come to dinner." Everard offered me social promotion.

"I will. Well, I really must go now."

"But the party's only beginning."

"I always have to miss good things," I said.

"Why?" Everard said. His voice was warm. He suddenly became a human being.

"To find a needle in a haystack."

Fifteen

I enjoyed the mystified expression on Everard's face, and felt that my reference to a needle in a haystack made a good exit line. But on second thoughts it was all wrong. I had snubbed Everard instead of thanking him, and there was neither needle nor haystack.

I knew the boy's name was Ron Ackroyd; I knew roughly what he looked like; I knew the name of the street where he lived.

As I drove up to the Angel, it never for a moment occurred to me that I might perhaps draw another blank, as in the case of Ginger. Perhaps this was because Ron lived in Islington, which had for me a special significance. It was a district that had always spelt mystery and magic for me ever since I'd walked through it one summer evening when I was very young, years before I met Julian, when London was still new to me. I never really came to know the place well, but in my imagination I had invested it with a strange sense of romance. It certainly had life and a good deal of colour. There were secrets about Islington, some of which in the ensuing years I had solved, but many of which I dared not touch for fear that the magic would vanish. For one thing it had a past, and its past, as in the case of many poor districts in London, was exciting and noble. In the early nineteenth century it was still smart and some of its good architecture had survived; Regency grandeur mixed with the gaudy vitality of working-class life in the twentieth century was an exciting contrast.

People south of the river were different. They still had the warmth and naïvety of provincials. The men of Islington were metropolitan, tough and seasoned, in contrast to their environment of gentle squares, quiet parks, old cemeteries, deserted railway stations and vistas of a canal which could look incredibly romantic. But perhaps I was investing the place with a glamour that didn't really exist outside my imagination.

A smoky sun was setting behind King's Cross as I arrived at the Angel and parked the car in a quiet alleyway behind a cinema. On enquiry I learnt that Everard Street was quite some way from where I was, but I walked there past chapels, disused railway yards and a brand new block of flats. It was a long street that must once have been smart. It was what an expert might call provincial Regency: not perhaps the best, but still quite good. The proportions of doors and windows were first-rate, the ironwork of the balconies and area railings pretty and the fanlights over the doors most attractive. But today, of course, it was entirely proletarian and neglected.

During the day places like Everard Street are deserted and deadly quiet, as if the district were haunted, and one's footsteps echo on the pavements; but now, in the early evening, it was busy with children playing ball games all over the place, mothers gossiping in doorways, young couples arm in arm on their way to the cinema.

At the corner of the street I saw a small group of young men; they were talking in deep voices about girls, jobs, money, dogs, pictures. Two of them were dressed to kill in expensive suits of delicate grey and all four wore their hair in fashions almost as elaborate and decorative as women. There was about them that coarse and rugged attractiveness so much favoured by some inverts, who would probably avoid them, however, for fear of the danger. In any case, the greatest problem for inverts is that young men of this sort are never found alone. They invade the West End, the former haunt of the middle classes, but always in groups. By themselves, separated from their mates, they are usually tongue-tied and frightened. Having never been alone, they dread solitude, need their friends and are afraid and jealous of them.

I decided not to ask this particular group where I could find the Ackroyds, and I walked past them almost unnoticed. I wanted if possible to find an old man or woman who might be less inquisitive, but it was surprisingly difficult to come across the right person. The first one I asked didn't know. "We're new here," she announced cheerfully. "Better ask those boys."

There was nothing else to do. The woman was watching me, and I could see that the boys had overheard her remark.

"Excuse me, please," I said as casually and "normally" as possible to one of them, who wore a bright, jazz tie. "D'you know where the Ackroyds live?"

"Who?" He frowned.

"The Ackroyds."

He repeated the words twice, then as he began to shake his head, the youngest of the four, with red hair, interrupted. "Oh, you mean the *Ackroyds?*" He made a sudden movement towards my arm, a touch of provincial intimacy. But he stopped halfway; he was halfway out of the provinces. "I don't know the number, mate, but they live over there." He pointed. "D'you see the house past the corner? Well, it isn't that one, but two along, the third one you come to. Anyhow, I'm going that way meself; I'll show you." He turned to one of his pals, in a fawn gabardine suit. "Look, Eric, I'll take the old bike to Club Row tomorrow like I told you. I'm going, any case. Just leave it out for me first thing. Four quid you want? Well, cheerio all."

We were on our way now, but I didn't want to discuss Ron Ackroyd with him, so I quickly said: "Can you still pick up good bargains at Club Row?"

"Well, it's all accordin'," he said, and now we were walking much more slowly after the initial quick march. "You have to go every Sunday an' know all abaht it. Lot of stuff's no good. Sometimes you see the same things week after week. But if you know the ropes, you can pick up a bargain once in a while. Bloke I know bought a racing bike the other day for seven quid. Almost new. The frime alone's worth fifteen. It's alloy tubing see. They mike 'em at a plice in Stoke Newington. Smashing job." He went on talking with fascinating speed. He had a broad Cockney accent, which was becoming rare among the twenty-year-olds, and a pleasantly deep voice. I became so interested that it gave me a jolt when he suddenly interrupted his monologue and, raising his voice, turned to a woman standing in a doorway.

"Evening, Mrs. Ackroyd. Gentleman to see ya." He gave me a friendly glance and one of the briefest nods and was already on his way.

I had suddenly been pushed into the river, fully clothed. My original plan was to find out the address and write to Ron. But now I had to swim. The shock of the cold water was soon gone, however. I was well used to dealing with situations like this. The sense of danger or just the sense of unpleasantness was inspiring.

A second later I was already in command, acting with my voice, my face, my hands and feet, body and mind.

"Good evening, Mrs. Ackroyd," I said. The woman was about forty-five, or just over, well made, but already running to fat; an Islington mother, looking at me without a word, with fear and defiance in her eyes, lips severely tight, nostrils wide with suspicion. "My name is Page," I said. "Dr. Page. I came to see Ron."

Her lower lip twitched slightly. She gave me a brief glance which plainly said, "That's what I thought," and looked round for a moment. "You better come in," she beckoned and like lightning retreated into the house. My heart missed a beat, but I already had my cue.

As I followed her through the dark passage smelling rancidly of food, which the warm, undisturbed air made more intense, I already knew what to do.

"I'm from the Ministry," I said. We were now in the kitchen. There were the remains of dirty dishes on the table facing the range with the two black gas mantles at each side. The Ministry; just the Ministry. It didn't matter which. This was the surest excuse in our time to obtain entry to almost any house. I was the new meaning of the word "they"—a representative, albeit a humble one, of the State, all powerful but benevolent, rewarding the faithful and punishing the infidel. "Evening, Ron," I rehearsed quickly, "sorry to trouble you. Could I see you alone for a moment?" Yes, that was the line, then later we could invent a plausible explanation of my visit for the benefit of his mother.

"Trouble; nothing but trouble," she said, looking at me with hostility. There came a pause almost as long as the day. "Is he in 'ospital?" she said suddenly, more in anger than anxiety.

I suddenly felt warmth all over me. So Ron was not living with her. She hadn't even heard me mention the Ministry. Apparently the most important thing in her mind was that I was a doctor. I laughed aloud in relief. "Nothing so bad," I said. "For all I know, Ron is as fit as a fiddle. It's just some simple, red-tape affair. National Health. I hope I didn't frighten you."

"Takes a lot to frighten me, it does," the woman said. She spoke with relief, but a fresh outburst of anger spread across her features, perhaps on account of her own gullibility and my laughter. "Well, 'e doesn't live 'ere and I don't know where 'e lives. . . ." I knew she wanted to add, "And I don't bloody well care," but she checked herself, perhaps because of my appearance or her own self-respect. A little more quietly she added: "Per'aps you people find out an' let me know."

"Oh, it's like that, is it, Mrs. Ackroyd?" I said. I was now talking to the mother of a patient in hospital, trying to put her at ease. "Do have a cigarette." I pulled out my packet and offered it to her. Slowly, very slowly, she took one, and after I'd given her a light, she began to smoke a little more sociably, but inexpertly. "I am a doctor, after all," I said, reckless with relief and success. I shook my head. "Nothing ever surprises me."

"I really don't care what he does," she almost shouted, but it was clear she felt I was already on her side and ready to condemn Ron.

"'E walked out on me three months ago, 'e did. 'Aven't seen him since. The whole street knows it. I took in a lodger a fortnight ago; 'ad to. It's very hard. I'm a widder. Ron's father died two years ago; it's hard with three children. . . . 'E needn't think I want 'im to come back and start all over again. Well"—she suddenly looked at me—"you better take a seat. 'Ere, lemme get them things out of the chair."

She removed a coloured overall from the armchair facing the fireplace. "Like a cup o' tea? It's still 'ot."

The brown, earthenware teapot was on the table and it looked cold and thoroughly stewed. Flies were buzzing round the messy sugar-bowl.

"I'd do anything for a cup of tea," I said recklessly.

She poured some hot water from the kettle into the pot, then she took a cup from the dresser and looked into it; then she took another and poured out a cup of tea.

The kitchen had a low ceiling. My gaze wandered from object to object: the worn lino, the row of socks and stockings drying on the line, the large, old-fashioned radio in the corner, the cheap, gaudy gold-and-black marble clock on the mantelpiece and the grocer's calendar behind it. Opposite the fireplace, out of the range of the gas-jets, was a watery photograph of the father, a very young man, in some uniform of the 1914 War.

I suddenly realised that Mrs. Ackroyd was talking to me. " 'E was courtin' a girl," she said. "In Burton Street. That's the next turning before you get to Liverpool Road. She was a nice girl, Valerie. Don't much care for her people, though; stuck-up. Ron had quite a good job. 'E was a welder. 'E earned quite a bit with overtime. When 'e was demobbed, I expected he'd settle dahn. It's difficult with the 'ousing shortage, but I wouldn't 'ave minded 'is girl coming here or Ron goin' over to live with them. Their 'ouse's bigger, anyway. It was all goin' so well; then one day they 'ad a tiff. Mind you, it was the second time, but 'e walked out on 'er, an' me too. Gave me ten quid, 'e did. That's all he'd got saved up like. 'E spent a lot of money on clothes. Just a fortnight previous he had a new suit made, cost 'im *thirty* quid! Give you some more later, 'e said. But I 'aven't seen 'im since." She pushed a chair back violently. "I know 'e's still working for Malcolmson's—that's the big engineering place at Holloway. I saw a man the other day that works with 'im."

The dirty crockery was now piled on a tray and I got up to hand her my own empty cup. The shrill whistle of a train came from some goods-yard. "I'm sure 'e's up to no good," Mrs. Ackroyd said. "God only knows, I used to love Ron; 'e was my eldest, see. I don't know, per'aps that's what's wrong with 'im. 'E was all right when he was young. Nice-lookin', strong, too. Used to win all the boxing competitions. I still 'ave the cup and the medals upstairs."

A car hummed past and Mrs. Ackroyd sat down in a rickety Windsor chair. "Thank the Lord, I used to say, he didn't take after his father. Well, Dad used to drink 'eavy; 'e was a good worker and a good 'usband too, seldom a cross word, but he drank 'eavy." She got up suddenly to adjust the gas-cock, but it went on fizzing. "I'm sure it was the war that did it. When 'e was demobbed Ron used to go with the Miller boys. They were a bad lot. Used to live next door, only they moved to a Council 'ouse, one of the new ones in Seven Sisters Road, central 'eating an' all. Well, Tommy, that's the younger one, got three years' Borstal for thieving an' the older one Harry's been in and out of jail ever since 'e came out of the Army. Their old man used to send them to school barefoot, though 'e 'ad plenty of money. Kept a stall at Chapel Street Market. 'Ad an 'orse and cart too."

She came to a sudden halt and I had a great desire to ask her a few questions. I was sure that unwittingly she'd have revealed a lot. But I resisted the temptation. It wasn't quite safe. I said: "Your other children are all right?"

"Well," she said, her hands in her lap, "I used to think Ernie wasn't much good. That's the second one. He's very quiet; you wouldn't believe Ron and 'im were brothers, if you saw them. But 'e turned out all right. You never can tell, can you? 'E's on the Borough Council. Maureen's working in a shop in High Holborn. Wholesale tobacconists. She's eighteen, and Bob's still at school, but leavin' next year."

She was silent for a moment. I heard someone open the front door.

"That'll be Mr. Redpath. 'E's the lodger I took in. Works on the Water Board."

But it was a young boy around fourteen who entered, his hair tousled and a scowl on his face. He looked dirty, but not unpleasant. I remembered having seen him playing in the street.

"Oh, it's you," Mrs. Ackroyd said frowning. "Look at his clothes." But I was looking at his eyes. They were the same as Ron's on the photograph, but the younger brother was not attractive, wasn't even promising; one can generally tell.

"Where 'ave you been? I've been looking for you all the time," his mother said.

The boy said nothing, and just looked sullen. I got up. "Well, thank you, Mrs. Ackroyd. I'd better be getting along. If I see Ron, I'll let you know."

"Ta," she said. I walked out. I had hardly closed the door behind me before I heard her voice shrill and sharp.

As I walked down the road into the Islington night, warm, mysterious and exciting, I reflected that she obviously knew little or nothing about Ron. She had carried him in her body, brought him up and lived with him for over twenty years, but it was I, who had never met him, who knew the most important single factor about his life.

It would have been interesting to see what Mrs. Ackroyd's attitude would have been if she had known. She was perhaps not the harpy she seemed and, in spite of her sharp tongue, there may have been in her personality a strong streak of tolerance, a virtue which often flowered in slums, whose inhabitants the world over seem fairly benevolent towards everything; race, colour and sometimes even emotional unorthodoxy—perhaps because they have to be.

As I passed the terraces of Liverpool Road, lonely and noble under the silver light of the moon, like some stage-set for a Regency drama, I wondered whether Julian had shared my nostalgia for an atmosphere like this.

II

It was now a quarter past eight and I was in the West End. Since I didn't know where Ron was living now, I thought the best thing to do was to try to contact him at one of the pubs where, according to Everard, he was now a frequent visitor. I looked in the *Treble Bob* and the *Beehive*. There was no sign of Ron in either. These pubs had always been very crowded during the war and quite notorious, but they were now practically empty. A few from the underground still came in: provincials, people who had been away from England, one or two who sauntered back for old times' sake, perhaps hoping the place would have a revival. I walked over to the *Great George*, a large pub which had been raided several times. Somebody told me once that on the site there had formerly been a hotel known to the notorious Vere Street Coterie of Regency fame and mentioned in *The Phœnix of Sodom*; and later it had often been frequented by Wilde and his friends.

As I got my drink and looked around, I saw the manager approach three somewhat feminine young men standing quite near me. I overheard him saying, "Will you finish your drinks, please, and leave?" They soon cleared out without as much as a shrug; and their acceptance was frightening.

I waited a few minutes, then I walked over to the *Red Dragon*. It was a large, cheerful place and, unlike the *Great George*, clean. It was Tudor and had leaded windows and oak and shiny brass, the ideal place to celebrate a Cup Final. It was fairly full. I had heard that it had been raided once and was now apparently making a come-back. Ron was definitely not there. Just as I was leaving, somebody touched me on the sleeve and I saw the beaming face of

Percy, a builder's foreman from Liverpool whom I used to know. I stood him a drink, realising that was the easiest way to get rid of him. He was as enthusiastic and friendly as ever. He told me he still went fairly regularly to a Turkish bath on the other side of the river, where he was lucky sometimes, but he'd given up the room at the naval depot in Kent where he used to spend an occasional week-end. "It's as gewd as ever," he said. "You can't go wrong there, but it was a little too mooch."

I liked Percy's company. He was genial, well-balanced and perfectly happy. But now I had to hurry; time was getting on. I went back to the *Treble Bob*. It was rather fuller: there were young men with their women, a few soldiers and one or two queers, in small groups, talking quietly. I thought I'd get a drink and sit down at a corner table where there was plenty of room, spend about half an hour there, then make another tour of the other places. It was only nine o'clock. I saw there was a stack of cigarettes on the shelves and I had none.

Then as I moved towards the bar, I suddenly saw him.

Sixteen

I had little doubt it was he. Although at first I saw only his profile, I knew by instinct. With my heart in my throat, I walked past the bar to get a better look at him. Now I saw his full face. He was staring at the drink in front of him, smoking a cigarette, seeing nothing, meeting nobody's eye.

I recognised the haircut, the forehead, the lines of the mouth, the hollow cheeks, the slightly square chin—the eyebrows which met above the broad nose. I had examined his picture so often in the past few days that, with the additional clues Everard had given me, I would even have picked him out in the street. But I hadn't realised his shoulders were so wide, though doubtless the blue pinstripe suit was padded.

I waited for a second or two, no longer looking at him and knowing full well that the single barman was busy with the many customers standing by the long counter. Then I pretended suddenly just to have noticed the two empty stools next to Ron, and I walked over, slowly, casually. I took the stool next to him, but ignored him almost rudely, looking in the direction of the barman as if I had a train to catch and was dying for a quick drink. I knew what I was doing. I had played this part so often before. I knew that nobody had noticed me, except perhaps Ron. Carefully, I removed the notecase from my pocket, then placed it "impatiently" on the counter as near his glass as possible, opened so that he couldn't fail to see his own photograph. I searched my other pockets, as though looking for something else, but my eyes were still on the barman. I couldn't see Ron's face, though he was only ten inches from me. A whole minute passed and the barman was now serving people at our end of the counter. I gave him my order. I began to get anxious wondering whether perhaps Ron had not seen his picture, but I realised that he must have done.

So, reaching out for my notecase, I spoke to him. "Mr. Ackroyd," I said. There was no need to raise my voice.

A slight flush of anger covered his face; he seemed confused and surprised. I saw that he really was most attractive. Before he could speak, I continued:

"My name is Dr. Page. Please forgive me for speaking to you like this. I was a friend of Julian Leclerc."

He remained speechless and unsmiling, and his face reflected four or five vivid emotions in incredibly fast succession. The barman approached with my drink. I waited till he'd gone. Then, turning again towards Ron, "Please forgive me," I repeated. "I've been looking for you for some time. I'd very much like to have a word with you if I may."

"Not here," he said. These were the first words he had spoken. He had a quiet, deep voice, but slightly commanding, almost brusque.

"Anywhere you like," I told him.

"I'll see you outside," he said almost menacingly. "You go first." He turned the other way.

As I finished my drink, I saw that only three people had noticed us talking: three quiet, hostile, anxious queers sitting at a table by the wall half-facing us. Slowly, I put down my empty glass, and got up and made my way out. Few normal persons would have understood Ron's behaviour, but it was obvious to me why he hadn't wanted to talk in the pub.

It was now half-past nine and the air felt cool all of a sudden after the warmth of the day, but maybe my face was hot. I lit a cigarette and walked past a pin-table saloon and a crowded milk-bar. I knew he'd wait at least three minutes before leaving, so as not to give the impression that he was following me outside. But soon I walked back towards the pub and took up a position where I couldn't possibly miss him as he came out.

I threw away my cigarette. There was no reason to believe he wouldn't come; so far everything was perfect, couldn't be better. But now that I was alone, waiting and thinking about him, I didn't feel absolutely certain how I was going to approach him. And would he come to my place tonight? That was another problem. I somehow felt that in my consulting-room he would be at ease; most people were. At any rate, we must be alone. He was apparently a person who had crossed the frontier of his slum without help. He had not struck me as shy or uneasy, and it was obvious he could do without the company of a friend, unlike most boys from his class. But even if he were an invert—and I now had pretty strong doubts—would he come at night to my flat? Perhaps I could suggest going to his place. He must live somewhere on his own now.

Several people came out of the *Treble Bob*, but Ron was not among them. I lit another cigarette and moved slightly nearer the entrance. The crowd outside now seemed larger. They were mostly young people: little Greek waiters off-duty, looking for the girls that the tall Americans off-duty had already found; young men from Stoke Newington and Bermondsey, dressed like last year's New York gangsters; and a few girls trying hard to look like gangster's molls. There was also a group of Americans in T-shirts and blue jeans, their jaws masticating, their hair closely cropped. I looked round under the heat of the neon lights. The very air felt second-hand and sordid. Then a drop of rain fell on my forehead and I suddenly saw Ron in the doorway of the pub. He stood there for one single second, tall, debonair, almost statuesque. Then he saw me and slowly approached. He was quite my height, but broader in the shoulders. Seeing him now, it was difficult to associate him with the meanness of his mother's house, the rancid smell of food in the passage, the nagging, the brother in rags.

His face was now serious and calm. I felt much more at ease.

"My car's in the next street," I said. "We can drive anywhere you'd like. The places around here are crowded and I don't belong to any clubs. It's got to be either my house or yours. Unless you have a better suggestion."

"We can't go to my place," he said. His tone still a little brusque, but I knew he was already warming up.

"Then it's got to be mine," I decided aloud. "I'll give you a lift back home afterwards."

He spoke suddenly. I expected he would hesitate, then refuse. But he didn't. "You said your name was Page?" he asked significantly, as if demanding some sort of guarantee.

"Yes," I replied. "Anthony Page." I added my only claim to prestige: "I'm a doctor."

"All right," he nodded. It took me a few seconds to understand what he meant.

We crossed the busy roadway, made our way through the crowds and reached the side-street where I'd parked my car. He had heard the correct password and had seen my credentials.

"I live in Kensington," I said a little later as we were waiting for a traffic light to change.

He just grunted. I was most anxious to get back as quickly as possible, for now that he was sitting beside me after all the false trails and frustrated hopes, I could hardly believe I wasn't dreaming. The whole thing seemed slightly improbable.

He was probably somewhat bemused—and this had nothing to do with alcohol—because he didn't ask a single question. There must have been any number of things that puzzled him: "How did you know I'd be in that pub? Who told you my name? Who gave you the photograph? Who told you I knew Julian? Who are you, anyway?"

He said nothing. There was, no doubt, an element of surprise in the fact that he was riding in the night in the car of a stranger. But there may have been some wish-fulfilment too. He was probably content just to let events take control of him. It may even be that he'd been waiting for a stranger to turn up and take him to some far-away place, where he would hear something "to his advantage". I had had something of the same vague longing myself when I was a child. Perhaps it was for a miracle like this he had been waiting in that pub, night after night—drinking slowly, seeing nothing. I also thought that all his toughness, the hardness around his lips and the disapproving tone of his voice was largely camouflage. They were by now second nature and had in any case been bred into him.

We drove up at last to the house. "Here we are." I felt I had to say something to ease the tension. When I opened the front door it was force of habit to let him go ahead of me, but at the staircase I took over. From now on I was leading.

I switched on the light in the consulting-room and he came in after me, looking round slowly as he did do. There was hardly any bounce left in him. Perhaps the bookshelves, the sober desk, the steel filing cabinet and the couch and the restful colours were the last links in the chain. It was not by accident that, in this room, people sometimes told their greatest and most shameful secrets. Perhaps it promised them relief even if it couldn't offer absolution.

"Sit anywhere," I said. "I should take that armchair if I were you." I walked over to the fireplace. How often I had already rehearsed this scene in my mind, but the frustration of not finding Ron had shattered my plan. I only remembered that I'd decided to stand by the fireplace.

"It was," I said, "very kind of you to come here. I'm very grateful. I don't know whether I can be of any help to you, whether, in fact, you need any help. But you can help me enormously."

Here I paused for a second, and I could see that he was no longer hiding his excitement. He looked anxious and just a little ill at ease, like a poor patient at a hospital listening to the doctor. I thought he was about to speak, but he changed his mind. I said: "As I told you before, I was a friend of Julian's. We knew each other for years, ever since we were students, but you know how it is—we lost contact. An envelope addressed to me was found on his desk, but there was no letter inside. Apparently he'd tried to contact me just before he died. I don't know why. I found your photograph in his room and took it before anyone else had a chance of seeing it. So I began to look for you." I hesitated for a second; then I added, "That's all."

It was only now that I saw that his eyes were brown; I had known for some time they were unusually large. And I noticed how flat his nose was, the only coarse feature in a semi-classical face, but the contrast was not uninteresting. I took my eyes off him.

There was a longish silence between us. I knew that under the circumstances he would need some time to take in what I'd said and I wasn't sure how intelligent he was, but I felt in my bones he was as straight as they come.

The moment I looked at him again, he suddenly spoke. "How did you find out about me? I mean . . ." This time the voice was quiet, a little anxious perhaps, but not suspicious. The curiosity was in the slight movement of his left hand, which rose for a second.

"Sorry," I said. "I ought to have told you to start with. It was almost by chance. One of Julian's friends whom I know personally saw you in the pub twice running. He mentioned it to one of my friends, who told me." I felt I had to make this lie a little more plausible. "I can always find out what the man's name is, if you want to know. He's a friend of a friend of mine. Previously I'd contacted all the people I knew who had known Julian. I'd been looking for you all over the place. You see, I'm absolutely certain Julian wanted me to help him, but I don't know in what way. I don't know what his trouble was, and I don't know why he didn't write the letter he wanted to send me. He must have known I'd have helped him. . . . I may as well tell you that I loved him when I was young. . . ."

Ron nodded briefly: "You didn't see him for some time before he died, you said?"

"Not for a year or so."

"And you said you loved him."

"Yes."

"Then . . ." He was looking at me.

"Yes," I said. "I'm queer."

"Sorry," Ron said. He got up from the chair. The momentary curiosity which his eyes suggested suddenly changed to embarrassment. He was standing now in front of the chair, not quite knowing what to do. "I'm ever so sorry," he repeated.

"I don't mind," I said. "It just happens to be true."

"I'll tell you everything," he offered, thinking that I needed pacifying. He resumed his seat. "I'll begin at the beginning," he said, but the phrase sounded strange coming from him. He paused momentarily, and I reflected what an enormous influence the cinema was, not only over looks, speech, gestures and action. Ron was now unconsciously aiming at "structure" and "dramatic unity".

"I met Julian about a year ago," he said now. "It was in July on the platform of Chancery Lane Station on a Saturday afternoon, that was. We were waiting for the train and got talking. He made me laugh. I liked him from the start. When the train came along and we got in, he asked me where I was going. Well, I was very fed-up that afternoon and thought I'd go to the park, just on my own; then maybe later I'd go to the pictures. I said I was going to Hyde Park to have a stroll round. Then we talked about other things. Just before we got to Marble Arch, he said did I mind if he came with me to the park, unless I was meeting someone, and then he said he'd been feeling fed-up too. I said I wasn't meeting anyone, 'I don't know Hyde Park very well,' I said. 'Sorry you've been feeling low.'

"So we went for a walk. We talked about the Army. He said he was in the Army all through the war. I asked if he was an officer. He said what difference did it make, but he laughed. He said he wouldn't have minded if he'd been a private, but his people made him. Then we talked—just about everything. I liked talking to him. He seemed to know a good deal. I'd never really met anyone like him before. You see people like me don't always meet people like him. And if we do they're never so nice, I can tell you that. And, do you know, he knew a lot about people like me. The way we live, how much we earn, all that. I told him where I lived, and he said he'd been to Islington. That's where I come from, Islington. Only now I've moved to another place.

"Then he said would I like to have some food and go to the pictures afterwards. I said yes; I was doing nothing. So we took the bus and went to some place in the West End off Shaftesbury Avenue, a foreign place—Italian, I think—first time I'd been there." He added as an afterthought: "Soho."

"Well, we had dinner and went to the pictures. We didn't have to queue because he took the best seats. Then we went to a pub just before it closed. It was the same place you saw me tonight. The *Treble Bob*. D'you know, by that time I felt as chummy with him as if I'd known him all my life. He told me he was a lawyer in the City. He said, 'You can't realise how grateful I feel to you. I was feeling pretty low till we met,' he said. I told him my end of the story. About the girl I knew. I wasn't going steady with her, but we used to go out. Only the day previous we had a ruck. Then as we walked up to Cambridge Circus to catch my bus, he gave me his card with his name and address on it and wrote down his phone number. 'Please ring me up soon,' he said. 'I don't just say this,' he said, 'for being polite, I'm not at all polite. I mean it,' he said. 'I've been feeling very fed-up lately and I like your company. Ring me any time. I'm always free after work.'

"Well, when I got home I thought a lot about him. You see, when I first met him I used to live with my mother, and I shared the same room with my two brothers. One's a clerk and we don't get on—Ernie, that's my brother. I couldn't go to sleep for quite a time, thinking about Julian. At first I thought I oughtn't to see him again, because—well, you know what I mean—I'm only a working man, haven't had much of an education. My father was a tool-maker, same as me, only he died. Then I thought Julian knew that and didn't mind. He said so. He said when it comes to friendship it doesn't matter where you come from, who your father is and how much you earn, he said. Besides, he said things were changing now and soon a toolmaker might earn as much as a lawyer. He thought it was only fair too. Well, I don't know much about that sort of thing—politics and so on.

"I thought I was daft to tell him all about my girl, because it was private, but then he told me about himself too.

"I thought quite a lot about him the next day also. I never thought I would, but perhaps it was because it was Sunday and I had nothing to do, no girl to take out, nothing. I didn't want to go to a pub before dinner. I never do. In the end I went to Petticoat Lane to pick up a valve for our radio. I could have bought it in a shop for about the same price, but I didn't want to stay indoors. Then when I came back to dinner my mother started getting on at me again; you know how it is. I don't know why I got so very fed-up, but I did, and after dinner I went for a walk by myself. I went to Hyde Park and listened to the speakers, but I didn't know anybody and felt pretty lonely and I thought I really ought to see Julian again. Then I went to the pictures. It was a rotten film.

"Well, next morning, just before I clocked in, I rang Julian. He was still at home. 'Is it all right to ring you this early?' But he said of course it was all right. 'Doing anything tonight?' I said. He said no. 'Let's go out,' he said. 'Let's have supper out.' Well, it would have been nice, but I didn't want my mother to know, so I said it'll have to be after we've eaten. He said that was all right and he'd meet me at the Dominion Cinema.

"We went to the Palladium, only I paid for my seat; then to a pub—the same one again. We sat down in the corner. It was practically empty and we had a long talk. I liked being with him as much as the first time—maybe more. I don't know. Then he asked me what I was doing at the week-end and I said nothing in particular. So he asked if I'd go down to Brighton on Sunday.

"I said that was all right with me, but I wanted to pay my share. Julian laughed and said O.K. Well, it was a nice day and we left early. He hired a car, a small sports car, pre-war, and we bathed in

the sea and had dinner. Then when we came back he let me drive
the car. It was still quite early and we went to have a drink at his
place. I wanted to see it.

"He told me he lived on his own. Well, you've been there; you
know it. It was smashing. We played the radiogram and we had a
few drinks. I said that's the kind of place I'd like to have. Only not
so smart, you know what I mean, but independent like.

"'On your own,' he said. 'Don't you want to get married?'

"I said, 'Well, after a time, I suppose, but not yet.' Julian said
it would be nice if we could take a place together, 'You and I,' he
said, and I don't remember what I said. I tried to afterwards, but I
couldn't think. Then all of a sudden he put his hand on mine and
said it would make him happy if we had a place on our own. Then
he put his arm around me and kissed my face.

"Well, I must have looked bloody silly after that, because Julian
said, 'Well, beat me up if you like. I wouldn't much mind,' he said.
'I can't help it. I like you very much, Ron. Perhaps too much.'

"Well, that was how it started. I suppose you know how it was."

He was silent now. The words had been spoken, the statement
made; there was no retreat. It was for me to speak now, I felt. It
was almost immaterial what I said as long as I was sympathetic.
But I had to speak.

I said, "Yes. I understand. You let him kiss you because you liked
him. But you didn't quite know why."

He was looking at me again. I was now sitting on the couch
quite near him, with my hands folded and resting on my knees.
His eyelashes were long and silky; the photograph didn't do him
justice. It only gave a hint, a bare suggestion of how attractive he
really was. But now he looked much older than his picture and
much older than his years.

"You had," I said slowly, "affairs with girls before you met him?"

"Yes; but that was different. It was different with girls."

I didn't ask him why it was different, because very likely he
didn't even know. It was quite probable that he'd never had real
sex with women. I made a note to check on that later if I got the
chance. It was, however, obvious that he wasn't an invert, and yet
he had become attracted to Julian.

"Had you never been kissed by a man?" I asked.

"No," he said. But he didn't look upset or angry. He was merely answering a question.

"How did you feel afterwards?"

"It was strange." He smiled for the first time. He didn't seem to me the sort of person who would smile frequently whatever mood he was in, and perhaps it was the fact that he smiled so infrequently that made him so attractive on the rare occasion when he did so. His teeth had almost suspiciously perfect shapes: lateral incisors small, a tiny space between the centrals, the articulation of the premolars exemplary. He showed almost the whole arch when he smiled. Then I saw the gum margin and knew the teeth were real.

"It was strange," he said. "Julian wanted to see me home, but I said I'd go alone. It wasn't too late. I could have taken the Underground easy, but I walked back all the way. I wanted to be on my own. If I came home early, Mother would still have been up and she'd have asked questions. So I waited till everybody was in bed like before I got back.

"I'd been feeling funny all the time. I wanted to laugh. But, you know, I didn't feel sorry for what happened. And the next morning I felt really pleased. It was only then I began to think what would happen if Mother and all the others found out. That was the only thing. And when I got to work, I thought again what would happen if other people knew about it. I mean, the blokes I work with. The funny thing was I wanted to tell somebody about it. Only there was no one. . . ."

"Haven't you any friends?"

"I used to go round with a few of the boys. You know how it is, but that was only after I left school. We weren't evacuated. Mother wouldn't hear of it. And the men I worked with first were much older. I had a friend who was at the place I first worked in, but he got married and moved away. I never much cared for the boys in our street or in Islington. Then I had a girl." He shrugged his shoulders, "Maybe I'm not the type that makes friends easy. I don't know. . . ."

He was silent now. I got up to offer him a cigarette. Knowing his background, the fact that he didn't make friends easily was surprising. In working-class life opportunity for privacy is rare, and collective action is an age-old tradition. There is usually an extraordinary solidarity among workers, who do everything in groups. In fact, there is perhaps in their friendships a stronger homo-erotic undertone than is generally recognised.

"The same morning," Ron went on, "I saw the girl I'd been walking out with. I saw her at the bus stop, but we didn't speak. I felt I could never make it up with her, not now. I went to see Julian the same evening. . . ."

There was another silence. I said, "I'd like to ask you a very personal question. It's not out of curiosity. I'm a doctor and it's important."

"All right," he said. His voice was very, very quiet. There was no resentment in his eyes and very little curiosity.

II

Ten minutes later I got up and brought over the whisky, the syphon and the glasses. "Very little, please," Ron said.

While we were drinking, I looked at him more closely. He was wearing black brogue shoes with a discreet pair of dark blue socks. I wondered if this was Julian's influence, as it was usually in the choice of shoes and socks that people like Ron made mistakes. There was a kind of barbarous cleanliness about Ron that was almost American. His large, strong hands seemed tortured with soap, hard brush and manicure, and under the handkerchief in his breast pocket I saw the end of the nail file. I had already noticed that his hands and fingers were shapeless, so ugly that they were attractive. But it was only now I realised that it was his habit to put out cigarettes by pinching them between his fingers.

"What happened afterwards between Julian and you?" I said. I put my glass on the writing-desk.

"We met practically every evening. Sometimes we went to the pictures or a play or just stayed indoors. We never got browned-off. Julian was saving up for a car and I'd been saving for a motor-bike, so we decided between us to buy a really smashing car. I mean a new Rover or a Riley. That was one thing we had in common. We were both keen on cars.

"Then one evening Julian said he wanted to tell me something.

'Maybe it's the daftest thing you've ever heard,' he said, 'but here it comes; I'm in love with you. I just can't help it, Ron.' I said why was it daft? But he didn't tell me. In fact he looked very . . . you know . . . embarrassed when I went on at him quite serious, to tell me why. He wouldn't. I still don't know. . . ."

Probably, I thought, Julian's experience in the past had been unfavourable. It's the most natural thing in the world to tell someone you love them if you do, whether you're normal or not, but it sometimes produces embarrassment. "What did you say to him?" I asked.

"Well, I told him I was very happy with him. I wouldn't be here otherwise, would I? 'I always think of you while I'm at the works,' I said. I said I'd never been in love before, and I didn't know I was now. Julian said I was."

He looked away for a moment. "But things were difficult at home. Mother used to nag a lot. She didn't know where I spent all my evenings, and I could see she wanted to know; but I didn't tell her. How could I? I expect she thought I was walking out with a girl. But, anyway, I got very fed-up living at home. D'you know why working people get married so early? Because they want to get away from the old woman."

This was an old half-truth. There was much I knew about the working class and much I didn't. I did know about the myth of the "restless energy" or "the ancestral vitality" of the masses. Ron's mother was a case in point. Always running about, always restless, always talking, always nagging. This was not actually evidence of energy or vitality, but purely and simply a form of neurosis, if not mild hysteria, partly induced by the fact that she couldn't afford labour-saving gadgets and because she wasn't intelligent enough to conserve her energy or to use efficient movements. "So you left home," I said.

"Well, not at once. We had a few rows and I used to walk out of the house. Then one day it was Julian's birthday and I gave him a present. I wanted to give him something nice. I had my eye on a cigarette-case in one of the posh places off Piccadilly. Solid silver. Engine-turned. Julian only had a very dirty old leather case, but he wouldn't let me buy the silver one. I was daft to tell him I was going to give it to him. He said no; we were saving up for the car for one thing, and he didn't want any presents from me. 'It's enough that you're a friend of mine,' he said. 'I can't have anything better than that.' But in the end I gave him a present just the same. I mean, it was his birthday and it wasn't proper not to give him something, was it? I gave him a cigarette box—just a cheap one you know, nickel, but it looked nice. I bought it in Charing Cross Road, and I put a card inside, saying happy returns. He was very pleased. I could see that.

"Well, that night we went out to have dinner and after that to a club. It was very swish. All old furniture and cut-glass lamps and pink shades and soft lights and a pianist playing on a white piano. Mind you, once or twice I'd told him I wanted to go and see a night-club. But I didn't like the people at this one. I've seen the type before in the West End. Julian was very nice to them, but I just couldn't be. He was talking to one of them, a proper weed he was, and then a mush came up and began talking to me. He asked me all sorts of questions, and in the end invited me out to dinner. I just didn't say anything. I could have knocked him down. Afterwards I told Julian about it and he said I shouldn't have been angry and that I should have thanked him and made some excuse like 'I'm busy with work and don't go out evenings,' he said. 'Why were you so chummy with them?' I said. He said because one must be civil to people, whether you like them or not. 'It doesn't cost you anything,' he said. Now I know he was right, but I couldn't see it then. He said he used to know that crowd of people before we became friends. But I was glad he'd dropped them. You ought to have seen them, proper sissies; and the way they talked and carried on—you ought to have seen them.

"Then we had a quarrel one day. I don't quite know how it started. I've thought about it quite a lot. It was partly that a man came to see him one evening when I was in the flat. He just dropped in. I didn't like him from the first. He stayed for quite a long time and Julian gave him drinks and I was left out of the talk. I didn't understand half of it, anyway. I could see that he looked down on me. He thought I was just dirt, because I was a working man. He was quite well-built, only he was very lah-di-dah and carried an umbrella and yellow gloves. And he was very keen on Julian. I could see that. He asked Julian to have lunch at the Savoy the next day. He was called Douglas. After he'd gone I asked Julian about him, and he said he'd known him a long time."

The name Douglas conveyed nothing to me. He was probably a man who was not attracted by working-class boys.

"I asked Jul whether he liked Douglas and he said, 'Yes. Why?' 'Oh, I just wondered. You're going to have lunch with him at the Savoy, aren't you?' I said. He said, 'Yes. But why do you want to know?' I said, 'There's no harm in asking, is there?' He said, 'Look, Ron, I have to see a number of people. They ask me to lunch. I ask them back. They're partly business friends, partly people I've known a long time. It doesn't mean that I'm having an affair with them or going to.' I didn't say nothing, but I was angry—I suppose because I had no other friends except Julian and he had dozens. Well, I suppose I was jealous, only I didn't tell him, but he knew it and yet he didn't say so. I have to admit he was nice about it. But that evening I felt very fed-up, and when he said, 'Let's go out and eat,' I said no. I was really angry. And soon after I went home.

"Well, I really was browned-off with everything. There was a row at home again about my sister. She'd been sacked from her job or something, and it was her fault, so I went out for a walk. I felt miserable. Well, the next time I went to see Julian I was sick of the old woman and the whole bloody lot of them and I said to him, what about moving together somewhere like we'd agreed before? He said it was difficult. The car ought to come first. He was already making inquiries. He had to think it over, he said. But I knew he'd changed his mind. I thought so, anyway. I thought he'd only said he wanted to share a flat in the beginning, but he'd never meant it. So in the end I said, 'We can't go on like this. We come from two different worlds and we can't really live together.'

"We had no real quarrel like, not a proper one. I just told him we couldn't go on and he said, 'Don't be mad. You have to discipline yourself, grow up; you're still young,' he said. I said that was beside the point. 'You really prefer your posh friends to me; that's about the size of it,' I said. Well, he got angry after that and shouted: 'You have no right to say that. Besides, you know it isn't true. The truth is that I'm in love with you and you're in love with me.' 'No, I'm not,' I said. 'That's where you're wrong. I'm not in love with you.'

"Of course what he said was true, only I was angry. I was very much in love with him, but I was ashamed of it. I didn't want him to know, see. So I walked out. I could have knocked anybody down, I was that angry. Two days later he sent me a letter asking me to forgive him. It was a very nice letter, but I didn't answer it. Then he sent me another. He said he loved me and I mustn't treat him like that. I didn't answer that either. I just didn't want to see him again."

"Why not?" I asked.

"I don't know. I was mad," Ron said. He shrugged a shoulder. "I'm not much of a writer. Then the day I got his second letter I saw my girl—the one I used to walk out with. We got on to the same bus. It was crowded. I don't know if she smiled, or if I did; I don't know; but we made it up. We started going out together again. I thought the row I'd had with her was my fault. Well, for quite a time we were steady. You know, going to the pictures, to cafés and the rest, kissing in doorways. For a time I thought it was the same as with Julian, only more natural, if you get me. Only I didn't see her as often as I used to see Julian.

"I went back to the gym some evenings: I was doing a bit of boxing, not serious like, just fooling around. But you know, some-how it wasn't the same with Val. She wanted to go out dancing for one thing and I don't like that much. I'm too heavy on my feet and it only makes me sexy. Besides, I found I could never talk to her the same way I could to Jul. She said I'd got very deep lately—I mean, since we had the ruck—and half the time she didn't understand me. But I expect I got very fed-up with her, because she never let me touch her. Not properly. Course, we had nowhere to go, only the parks. But there were other things too. I began to feel she was common; her people too. Then one day Val asked me point-blank if I'd marry her, and the way she asked, you ought to have heard it . . . I got so angry I said I wouldn't and that was the end of it. It was in the street too, just off Upper Street on a Saturday afternoon. She began to shout at me. I just walked away.

"Well, I didn't tell my mother anything about it, but she found out from the neighbours. She'd taken a fancy to Valerie—I don't know why—and there was another fuss. Fancy my mother taking her side; I mean, it's usually the other way round. And my sister

joined in too. She'd been at school with her. Well, we had quite
a fight. It was Sunday dinner. I knew if I didn't get up and walk
out on them I'd crown the old woman and there'd have been a
court case and all. So I just banged the front door. I didn't want any
food. I took the bus to King's Cross. There's a tobacconist who has
adverts for rooms in his window. I'd looked at them before. Only
this time I meant it. There were any amount of addresses and I
went round to see the rooms. I found one quite near the works, so
I don't have to hurry so much in the morning. It was quite a nice
room too, and private. There were only three people in the house.
The landlady's a widow. It cost more money, but I'd worked that
out before already. So I went back for my things and moved out.
My mother yelled at me, but I just didn't answer. I gave her ten
quid. She wouldn't take it, so I left it on the kitchen table. I walked
out on them, and a good thing it was too. That was nearly three
months ago."

His tone was no longer indignant when he continued: "Well, the
first week I felt all right. I spent some time in the gym and went out
with one or two of the boys who go there. But I didn't like them."

He was now addressing the carpet, as if I weren't in the room:
"I never really cared for them, but now I definitely decided to
have nothing to do with them. Not after I'd met Julian. They had
nothing to talk about, only women and horses and dogs and drink.
Well, I soon felt pretty fed-up again. I didn't want to go back home.
I never want to go back there. And I didn't want to meet another
girl. Not like Valerie, anyhow.

"So I began to go out in the evenings by myself. There were a
lot of places in London I didn't know. Places I'd never been to. My
parents hardly ever went to the West End even, only once or twice,
when they were young. Folks never moved out of Islington in the
old days. I went to places like Bayswater and round Regent's Park
and Mayfair—practically everywhere.

"Well, one evening I was just looking in the windows at Harrods
when somebody called my name. It was Julian. I wasn't looking
for him. . . ."

I was glad that Ron was still gazing at the carpet and not at me
when he said that.

"I knew he used to live near there, but it was a big surprise to me all the same. Not just seeing him, but him speaking to me and being nice about it. I mean, I thought he'd never speak to me again after I'd walked out on him and didn't phone him as he'd asked me to in his letters. 'Well, how are things with you, Ron,' he said. 'Still working at the same place? How's Mr. Purvis,' that's our manager; fancy, he even remembered that. 'Did you get the rise? What are you doing these days?' He couldn't have been nicer. Then he said had I eaten, had I had supper? I said yes; then he said he was going back to his place and he asked me up, as if nothing had happened. I mean I had a row with Val. and we made it up, but it was different with Jul. Well, I went back to the flat and we had a drink and he went on talking. He didn't say a word about our row, just as if nothing had happened and as if it were no time since we'd met. He had a new suit on, a grey one I'd never seen before. I asked him about it. I thought it was about time I had a new one. I had my other suit on that was a year old, blue hopsack. It had just about had it. I had some patterns in my pocket, so I asked him which to choose, and he picked on this one I'm wearing. He said double-breasted, and one button. Then I saw that he still had the cigarette box I gave him for his birthday.

"Well, in the end we made it up. We talked so much; I stayed the night with him. I didn't have to bother now I was living on my own. And he had an alarm clock.

"I saw there was a girl's photograph on his mantelpiece. He said she was a friend he used to walk out with. I told him all about Val. and that we were all washed up now.

"I saw him again the next day and he said the girl was keen on him, but he wasn't on her. 'I've always been straight with you, Ron. I can't help it,' he said. 'The thing is I only went out with her because you left me. I'm not blaming you, mind you. It was all my fault,' he said. I told him it was mine, but he shut me up and said it didn't really matter, it was forgotten and done with. 'Now you see, Ron, what a mistake it was to tell you I was in love with you. D'you remember?' he said. He told me he'd never want anybody else. He said that in the morning when he gave me breakfast. He had to get up very early too.

"He said he'd give the girl up, only it would take time and we couldn't meet every day because of that. He had to do it slow, like a gentleman, not to hurt her, see. I was very pleased, of course, but the next day at work I began to think about it and I felt it was wrong. Wrong to give up his girl on my account. Only I never told him that. I reckon I was selfish. He said we should definitely live together, but I said that wasn't so important now that I was on my own. Later perhaps. Well, after that I could only see him two or three times a week, but it was O.K. by me that way. He asked me to have some pictures taken. Well, it was then I had the one took you saw. It was only a cheap one, but Julian said it came out well. I gave him one and he slipped it behind the girl's picture. We laughed when he did that, and he said it wouldn't be long before he'd send the girl her photo back and have mine out instead."

Here Ron suddenly came to a halt and looked at me. I knew why. I nodded, and he went on: "Then one evening, it was just three weeks ago, on a Wednesday it was, we'd been out to dinner and had a drink at a pub not far away. Well, as we came into the hall, there was a gentleman waiting for him, only I didn't know at first. It wasn't very late, round about half-past nine or so. He was very civil to me, but I could feel he looked down on me. I had the same suit on I'm wearing now"—Ron pointed to his sleeve—"but you know how it is, I can always tell. The way he looked at me for instance. He just gave me one look, didn't say a word except, 'I hope you'll excuse us, I'd like to have a word with Captain Leclerc,' he said, and Julian said he wouldn't be long. Anyway, they went out of the house, leaving me in the passage like. It was some urgent business, I reckoned, else he wouldn't come so late. Maybe it was the man Julian was working for, the lawyer.

"A couple of minutes later Julian came back and said he was sorry to keep me waiting. We went into the flat, but I saw that he was all in. I mean he'd been quite happy the whole evening, but after he'd talked to the man, he changed badly. His face was white. 'Have a drink, Ron,' he said, but his hand was trembling. 'Was it your boss, Jul?' I said. He just looked at me at first, then he said yes. 'There's some misunderstanding,' he said. Then he said he'd have to lunch with him the next day. He tried to change the subject, but I could see he was worried. I admired him. People like us can't hold it back if we're in trouble. Sometimes we keep quiet and don't talk, but Julian went on being polite to me. He said he had no right to worry me with his personal affairs.

"'But it's all right, Jul,' I said. 'You can tell me all about it; it doesn't matter. I'd like to help you if I can.' I had my Savings Book on me. I showed it to him. I'd been saving up for the car and I had a hundred and fifty quid. 'I gave ten to Mother,' I said. 'You can borrow the rest any time you like; only you have to give the Post Office notice if you want to take more than three pounds out,' I said. He smiled and gripped my shoulder, and said he'd never had a better friend than me. He said everything would be all right. We had a drink.

"But he still seemed depressed, so I said: 'Do you want me to stay the night with you?' Well, he seemed to be thinking. I thought first he'd say yes, but he said no. But he asked me to dinner the next day. You know, I worried the whole night about him.

"Well the next evening we met again and he said things had turned out all right. But I didn't believe him. He was just trying to be nice. Then he said we couldn't meet the following evening, because he had to go out with his girl. I wanted to tell him not to break it to her that it was all over, but I couldn't. I suppose I was selfish, but what could I do? Now I knew what love was, and I was in love with him, especially since he was in trouble. He said he'd see me in two days' time. Then I remember he made a telephone call to you. . . ."

"To me?" I said. "Are you sure?"

"Positive. I'd forgotten your name. But when you came up to me tonight and said your name was Page and you knew Julian, I knew it was you."

"But what did he say?"

"Well, he didn't speak to you; you must have been out. He spoke to someone else on the telephone." Ron looked round. "He said he wanted to speak to Dr. Page, then a minute later he said it didn't matter. He'd ring tomorrow. Then he telephoned another doctor, only I forget his name. If you tell me some names, I'll probably remember." He looked at the ceiling for a moment. "It was a long name. Foreign, I think. Well, the man was in and Julian said he couldn't sleep nights and wanted some new stuff. 'I've tried everything,' he said. Then he said, 'Thank you. I'll see you first thing in the morning.'"

So that explained why Ron had come with me so readily tonight. And he confirmed that Julian was the man who had tried to ring me the night I was ill from the after-effects of my wisdom tooth.

"Then, what did he do afterwards?" I said.

Ron tried to think. "Not much after that," he replied after a while. "A little later I went home. I didn't know that was the last time I'd see him.

"I went to his place on Friday night, as he'd invited me, but there was no answer when I rang the bell. I waited a little in the hall after that, then I walked round as far as Harrods and looked at the windows. About twenty minutes later I went back, but there was still no answer. I thought he was late or couldn't make it and couldn't let me know because I've got no telephone at home, but just as I was standing there I heard somebody coming in. It was an old woman. She saw me there and looked at me. She said, 'Excuse me, are you looking for the Captain?' and I said yes and she looked at me and said 'You know he's dead—died this morning?' I must have looked silly, because she stared at me. 'The housekeeper'll be in in the morning,' she said and I thanked her and walked out.

"Well, if you ask me what I did that night, I can't tell you. I didn't go to a pub. That was the night after. I suppose I just walked round. I must have walked all the way home, because it was late when I got back and I felt very tired and didn't take off all my clothes—just my shoes and jacket. I slept till nine. The people where I live don't wake me and I forgot to set the alarm clock. Well, that morning I didn't go to work; just as well, because I couldn't have worked. Then I saw it in the paper. I walked about the whole morning, not doing anything, and then I went to a pub. In Warren Street. I'd never been there before. It was in the evening and I drank a lot. But it only made me sick. I was sick in the street and sick again at home. The next day I thought of doing myself in. Only I didn't. I reckon I didn't have the guts. It takes courage to die, you know. . . ."

"Yes; but it takes an even greater courage to live," I said.

He was looking at the floor. "Reckon so," he muttered, but there was no conviction in his voice.

"Did you go on drinking?" I said.

"Me? No. In the end I went back to the works. It was all right. I lost three days' wages. I said I'd been ill. Then I went to the gym, but it was no good. I was in a bad mood all the time. There's a boy who sometimes spars with me, same weight as me, thirteen stone, only younger. I practically broke his jawbone. I hit him too hard, see. Then almost every night I went to the *Treble Bob*, where you found me. But I don't like pubs much. I don't know why I go."

"You're still looking for him," I said.

"Maybe."

There was a pause. He was looking at my books without really seeing them. I had no more questions. I offered him a drink.

"No, thanks," he shook his head, but I saw there was a sudden wave of suspicion about his face. For a moment I could see his mother in him. "You said you haven't seen Julian for over a year. Well, didn't he ring you up the next day? You were out when he rang first."

"That's just the point. He didn't. I was ill at the time. But, of course, now you know what he wanted from me, why he tried to ring me, don't you?"

The suspicion went as fast as it had come, but Ron must have sensed something, because his voice suddenly became quiet, almost apologetic. "He wanted stuff to kill himself, I suppose."

"Yes," I said. "And not knowing his state of mind, I might have given him a prescription. Well, the man he rang after me may have been his own doctor, but Julian must have known what he was doing. He obviously got sleeping tablets from several doctors. He took a tremendous overdose. No single person would have given him so much."

"But why did he kill himself?" Ron said as if talking to himself. He suddenly raised his voice. "You know more about him than I do. I only knew him a short time. It seemed long, though. D'you think it was my fault? Perhaps he was too much of a gentleman to tell me, like."

"Certainly not. That's one thing I'm positive about. It wasn't your fault. I still don't know why he killed himself, what the final motive was. But one thing's certain: Julian was unduly sensitive. You mayn't have noticed it, but he was." I was now doing the bedside-manner stuff and I felt I must have been good at it, because Ron nodded while I talked. But I was as much in the dark as Ron.

He broke in suddenly: "Do you think it was money? I mean

sometimes people shoot themselves because of cheques. Officers
. . . I mean you read about them in the papers. If I'd known, I'd
have given him all the money I had in the Post Office. I'd have
worked overtime, done anything."

There was no doubt about Ron's sincerity. "I doubt if it was a
question of money," I told him. Then I remembered something.
"There's only one thing I haven't asked you," I said. "Was Julian
different after you went back to him? After your quarrel, I mean?"

He thought for a bit, then said: "If anything, he was happier
with me the second time. I know I was. There's no use hiding it,
is there? Of course, we didn't meet so often, not after I went back
to him, because of the girl. . . . Do you think she had anything to
do with it?"

"I shouldn't think so for a moment."

"Or his boss, that old man who came to see him that night?"

The old man! I looked up. That description didn't fit Mohill and
there was no other partner. I had a sudden idea; it made my voice
tremble.

"What did the old man look like?" I said.

"Oh, he was . . . I don't know, a little shorter than you or me,
but he was upright. Wore a bowler hat and had a white moustache.
You know, a sort of military moustache. He looked exactly like
an old officer you see on the pictures. Only he was in civvies. He
walks with a stick. There's something wrong with his foot. . . ."

"You mean he limped?"

"Yes. D'you know who he is?"

"No," I lied.

III

On the way to Islington I told Ron that he could come to see me
any time he was in trouble, and I gave him my card. But I didn't
expect him to return; he would probably be too shy. I also told him
he must try to pull himself together. I vaguely felt I was treating
him a little shabbily, just pushing him out after he'd given me the
information I wanted, but there was something else on my mind.

It was nearly two o'clock in the morning when I drove up to

the house. I was surprised to see the light in Terry's window. Why wasn't he asleep? I decided to go up to his room. He was in bed, wearing nothing under the blanket. There was a book in his hand and a burning cigarette in the ash-tray. Terry hardly ever smoked.

"Can't you sleep?" I said. "It's five to two."

"It's the heat," he said and smiled, but neither his voice nor his smile was convincing. I saw the handkerchief; then I looked a little closer. He had been crying.

He picked the book up from the blanket with his soda-red hand and put it on the night table. I suddenly knew what was on his mind: "Here I am slaving for you. Look at my hands. I devote my whole life to you because I love you, but you carry on with toughs, one after the other. You spend whole evenings with them." But what he actually said was: "Would you like some hot milk?"

"No, thanks," I replied. "I'm quite sleepy as it is." I knew of course that Terry had not been listening while Ron was in the room. He'd never have done a thing like that.

"You sure?" he said.

"Quite, thanks." I took one step towards him and looked into his face. "And there's no reason to cry, Terry. Absolutely none at all. You ought to know me better than that. Soon enough I'll tell you all about what's been going on. Now go to sleep." I placed my hand on his naked shoulder. "Go to sleep. It's all over now."

He touched my hand, gently, tenderly. His own hand was cold. Then, a second later, the pressure began to increase.

Seventeen

Sunday was dull and rainy. I felt a little dizzy when I woke up, perhaps because I'd gone to bed so late, perhaps because so much had happened the previous night. I looked at my watch. It was just after ten o'clock.

I put on my dressing-gown and went to the bathroom. Terry was washing my socks in the basin.

"Good morning," he smiled. "I'll be through in a second."

"What time did you get up?"

"Oh, I've been up ages."

"It's amazing how you can do with so little sleep."

"Perhaps it's because I haven't any brainwork to do."

He gave the socks a last rinse, then took them to the kitchen to dry.

As I ran the water and undressed, I finally decided to tell him about the case. It was the least I could do. . . . Except that . . .

A moment later I'd forgotten all about Terry. I took a very quick, cold shower, dried myself, then instead of having breakfast, I went to the consulting-room and telephoned Colonel Leclerc.

It was a woman who answered.

"This is Dr. Page speaking," I said. "Miss Ann Hewitt is my patient. . . ."

"Oh yes," the woman said suddenly, as if I'd dropped a coin into a juke-box, causing her to speak. "She told me about you some time ago. How is Ann?"

"I think she'll get over the shock," I replied. "What I really 'phoned for was to see if it was convenient for me to meet Colonel Leclerc."

"He's still very upset," she said, "and spends nearly all his time brooding. He never goes out. His brother wrote and asked him to go over to Ireland, but he wouldn't hear of it. All this is very bad for him. . . . His doctor told him so. . . . But do come, by all means. . . . Topping idea. What he really needs is company to take him out of himself. This afternoon? Certainly, if you wish. Any time after lunch. Now, if you're coming by car . . ."

I went to the kitchen to have breakfast. While I was eating Ann rang. I thought perhaps it might be Everard. I certainly owed him an explanation.

"Shall I tell her you're out?" Terry asked.

"No," I said. "I'd better speak to her." I got up. I mustn't be impatient.

"Good morning," I said. "You must forgive me for not ringing you, but if you knew what a time I've had these last few days. . . . Yes, I can see you tonight, if you like, but it'll have to be late. I have several calls to make. What about coming here after dinner? For coffee. I'd like to ask you for dinner, but I'm not sure what time I'll be back. Shall we say eight-thirty?"

When I returned to the kitchen, I said to Terry, "I'm going to the country for the afternoon, but I'll have to be back after dinner, because Miss Hewitt's coming to see me at half-past eight. But there's no reason why *you* should come back." On Sundays in the summer, Terry often went out cycling in the country. "It's a nasty day," I said. "What are you going to do?"

"If you don't want lunch, I think I'll go to Petticoat Lane. . . ."

"One day I'll go with you. I always say that, but this time I mean it. . . . What'll you do in the afternoon?"

"I expect I'll go to the Cinema Club. They're showing *Dr. Caligari*. . . ."

He may have said something after that. I was no longer listening.

Eighteen

Mrs. Tanner, the woman who had answered the phone, turned out more or less as I'd pictured her. I remembered Ann telling me she was a cousin who had come to keep house for the Colonel after the death of his second wife. She was about sixty and on the stout side. I confess I had rather expected her to be untidy and all over the place, hatpins falling out, stockings put on in haste, and colours clashing, but it turned out she seemed to pay careful attention to her appearance. She had a humorous face that nevertheless suggested past disappointment, and plenty of spirit.

The Colonel, apparently, had been annoyed at hearing of my impending visit. "I'll just tell him you're here," she said. "I think it'll be all right. You'll find him upset, but don't worry. Isn't it a nasty day?"

It most certainly was. It had been pouring with rain and the landscape looked gloomy. I had had difficulty in finding the house, since there had been hardly anyone about to ask the way. The only time I'd been here previously was before the war; I'd gone by train and Julian had met me at the station.

For some reason, I had thought the house was larger and that it had a Regency entrance with two pillars. Now I saw it was Victorian and rather neglected, the cream paint flaking off the front door.

I looked at the Colonel's portrait over the mantelpiece. The painter had somehow caught the expression of the eyes; I remembered that. Unlike Julian, the Colonel had blue eyes that were fixed on you all the time. There was arrogance in them and conceit, perhaps stupidity.

The nightmare picture was there too: possibly a Fuseli; his school anyhow, but less interesting than I thought. There were several engravings, late eighteenth-century ones which one usually sees in corridors of country houses.

The table was set for two, raffia mats under the faded plates, a bottle of barley-water in the Sheffield wine-cooler, a small jar of pills and none too clean napkins in green celluloid rings. The wallpaper showed the dampness of the house.

I saw the sideboard, a beautiful Georgian piece with a serpentine front, but completely out of place in the room. I thought perhaps I'd remind the Colonel that I'd spent a week-end in this house before the war. It was about the best conversational opening. A second later the woman returned.

"It's all right," she said, but her face was serious. "He's in the den. Come along." She led me across a dark passage into a smallish room overlooking the derelict garden. I noticed a few low bookcases and a television set.

"Maurice, this is Dr. Page," the woman said and withdrew at once. They had plainly had a row about my coming.

The Colonel was standing in front of a small writing-desk. He was shorter than I remembered, his hair now completely white and his moustache a little thicker. Only the intent, arrogant gaze in his eyes was the same. I began to wonder if it was partly short-sight.

"Good afternoon," he said, and gave me the briefest of nods. "What can I do for you?"

It wasn't exactly the words that took me aback, nor the fact that he didn't offer me his hand or ask me to take a seat. It was more the tone and the way he looked at me; at my face, my shoes, my face again. Nervous shock, I reflected; his bark is worse than his bite. . . .

His attitude decided me to change my approach. "I'm sorry to trouble you, sir," I said. "I fully realise how you must feel. I'm a doctor."

"Yes," he nodded. His right hand rose in an impatient gesture. He was talking to a subordinate: an N.C.O. or warrant officer who was taking liberties instead of getting to the point.

"Miss Hewitt is my patient," I said.

He seemed to bow. I took my eyes off him. "I met her a few months ago through Julian, whom of course I'd known since we were students. A couple of days after the tragedy she came to see me. She was on the verge of a nervous breakdown. She became my patient and I began to treat her. At the same time, she was extremely anxious to find out what had happened. . . ."

"That was quite natural," he said. It was impossible not to note the arrogant sarcasm at the corners of his mouth; "most natural under the circumstances. I can't quite see, however . . ." He cast a glance towards the clock on the mantelpiece.

It was then that I lost my temper. My bedside manner, my conventions, my sense of humour were gone in a flash. Nothing remained except curiosity and a very childish desire to give the Colonel as good as he gave.

"Miss Hewitt was in fact so anxious to find out," I said, my voice raised, but my gaze controlled, "that she decided to employ a private detective."

The shot went home. There was no doubt about it. Revenge was sweet. So that was how an arrogant colonel looked when alarmed and frightened.

I waited a few seconds. I was master of the situation now, but at what a price. I felt like a cad. I said: "I had the greatest difficulty in persuading her not to do so. Finally, she took my advice. . . ."

His relief was instant. I could almost hear him sigh, but he was too anxious to show he wasn't upset, in case I'd noticed anything. "I see," he said; the irony was in the forced smile and in the nod. "It was very good of you. . . ."

"I don't know whether it was good or just *wise*." I went on: "That's a decision I must leave to you, sir. I only persuaded Miss Hewitt not to employ a detective by offering to investigate Julian's death myself. And I did this because I felt I owed it to his memory. My work was easy. A couple of years ago he came to see me and asked my professional opinion on his particular condition, so I guessed at once what was likely to have happened. It was just a question of a few inquiries and a certain amount of luck. I found out that he was involved with someone else while still engaged to Miss Hewitt, and I actually found the man, who told me you'd been to see your son two days before his death. You asked Julian to lunch at your club. I am here now to ask you to help me. What shall I tell Miss Hewitt? She knows absolutely nothing."

I had deliberately looked away from him while I spoke, but now I turned slowly towards him, and I saw that his face was deadly white and his right fist was clenched. For a moment I thought he'd faint or throw something at me, but very suddenly his features

relaxed. All at once he became an old man. He even seemed to
shrink as he stood there in his single-breasted grey flannel suit, the
top button fastened. His head came slowly down, but his eyes were
still on me. His lower lip twitched slightly.

"I suppose you know everything." His voice was a little hoarse.

"Everything's a big word," I said quietly.

He suddenly looked away. He said, "Why don't you sit down?"
He limped to the armchair and pulled it across to face the settee,
which he indicated with his chin. As I sat down there came a fairly
loud, metallic creak from the broken springs, but I was sure he
didn't hear it. We were now close to each other. His eyes were
bloodshot, his head shaking a little. I saw his tie. It was Rugby. It
was so obvious he had tried to give Julian a step up in life, Harrow,
Oxford, the Guards. . . .

"I suppose," he said slowly, "in your own mind, you are accus-
ing me of having driven my son to suicide, aren't you?"

I shook my head. "No, sir."

Again he didn't seem to hear. "But you don't know the facts,"
he insisted. "All this is very painful for me. . . ." Suddenly he turned
away and looked towards the edge of the mantelpiece, looking for
something. I saw his medals in a small glass case, the cross of the
D.S.O. almost vulgarly white against the black velvet background,
between the *Légion d'Honneur* and the Mons Medal. There was a
signed photograph in a leather frame between the case and the
clock. It could have been Haig.

"You can smoke if you want to," he said. "I don't smoke myself.
The ash-tray's behind you on the table."

He waited till I'd lit a cigarette, his eyes impatiently closed. "I
must tell you," he said suddenly. "In the first year of the war an
old friend of mine, who was connected with the London District
Command, asked me to lunch one day. He told me in confidence
that Julian was frequently seen in the West End in mufti, entertaining men in the ranks and visiting places of bad reputation. I was
very shocked, all the more because at that time I was mobilising
my friends to get Julian a transfer to the Guards. I didn't believe
it at first, but I asked Julian about it. He told me point-blank that
it was all nonsense. He did entertain some men from his own
regiment and stood them a few drinks, and as for bad reputation,

during the war practically anywhere could have been so described. Those were the very words he used. I was greatly relieved, but I told him that what he had done was very unwise, because it was liable to misinterpretation. Besides, it just wasn't the thing." He shook his head. "An officer may stand drinks to his men at a regimental dance, but not on leave in London, and certainly not in a pub. He said the younger generation took a different view and this was the people's war.

"Well, I know things have changed since my time, but that sort of thing, standing drinks to men, is very bad for discipline. Besides they resent someone from our class going to their pubs. I shouldn't have sent Julian to Oxford in the first place; that's where his whole generation picked up Communist ideas: a regular breeding-ground. But he wouldn't hear of an Army career. That was my first blow. But let that pass. . . .

"Anyhow, I wasn't much worried, and soon after that Julian went abroad with his regiment, got his transfer to the Guards and to my great satisfaction was later awarded the Military Cross. After the war I was glad he settled down to the career of his choice, and he worked very hard at it. We had one or two disagreements. Immediately after the war I went abroad on official business, and when I came back I found him living in what was almost a slum. He was preparing for his examinations and said he wanted to save money. Well, times were certainly hard and England already had a Red government, but I gave Julian a decent enough allowance and there was absolutely no need for him to go on living off the Harrow Road. He moved after that, and later I bought him a partnership in a really first-class firm.

"When he finally became engaged to Ann I was very pleased. I thought he'd settle down. I met the girl and her people. They were in every respect the best one could wish for. And she was deeply in love with him.

"I was very upset therefore when Ann came to see me, less than six weeks ago. She told me Julian was behaving in a peculiar way. She wanted to discuss plans for the wedding, but he always tried to put things off. I couldn't understand the situation, but I must say I was suspicious. I was actually on my way home, but decided to stay in London. I tried to see Julian at once. I rang him in his office, but he was out on a court case the whole day. I didn't want to see him at the courts, but I asked them to give him a message. I stayed in all the time at the club waiting for him to ring me, but he didn't. I rang again, and they said the case had gone on so long that he was unlikely to return to the office, but would probably go straight home. I waited a bit; then I rang his flat. He was out. I rang again after dinner. Again there was no reply. I went out for a walk, then I thought he must surely be in by then, and I went to his house. But he was still out and I decided to leave a note for him to call me as soon as he returned. The housekeeper was out too, so I scribbled a few words on a piece of paper, which I meant to put under his door. Then he suddenly came in."

There was a silence now. Slowly, unobtrusively I looked at him. He was gazing at the floor. Then he spoke again:

"To my great surprise he wasn't alone, but in the company of a youth, obviously of the lower classes. It was rather late and I couldn't help putting two and two together. I must say I needed a great deal of restraint not to have it out with him there and then. I saw how embarrassed Julian was. He realised that I knew. I spoke to him alone, and he didn't even try to defend his conduct. He knew it was useless. I said, 'I want you to come and see me at lunch tomorrow at my club.'

"He came to see me the next day. I asked the porter to send him up to my bedroom as soon as he arrived, because it was obvious I couldn't talk to him in any of the rooms downstairs. At lunch-time nowadays my club is very full.

"Well, I'm afraid I was very angry, but you'll perhaps understand the circumstances. I hadn't slept the whole night, and a father has the right to be sharp with his son, especially as, in this case, the son was undoubtedly in the wrong. . . . I may as well tell you that neither Julian nor his mother had any money of their own. Before he got his job, he was entirely dependent on me, and I must say I've been extremely generous. My second wife left everything to me—it wasn't very much—and I'd decided to invest it in Julian's future.

"Under the circumstances it's easy to understand that I had to take a firm hand, all the more because Julian was no longer a child."

The Colonel was now feeling the strain. His whole voice and diction changed. He wasn't looking at me, and seemed to be speaking to his writing-desk. "It was only when I saw Julian arriving home with a guttersnipe—you should have seen his haircut—that I realised my old friend Burton had been right when he warned me, and that Julian had lied to me. To me, his father, who had given him everything. But that's not the point. . . ."

The head sunk and so did the voice, which was now little more than a whisper, a sob unaccompanied by tears: "That my own son, my only son should be a pervert. . . ." He was silent for a moment. I didn't speak. Then he suddenly looked at me again as if trying to brush my silent arguments aside. There came an impatient gesture with his left hand; an ugly, lined hand with a signet ring on the middle finger: "One knows that kind of thing goes on. One isn't blind, but one turns away from it with horror. I actually came across it twice in my military career. Two officers of my own regiment were found to have had . . . well, relations with their own men. Some people think it funny; they laugh about it. But I can't. It's a sign of a civilisation in decay. It's an unspeakable thing to do, especially with men serving under you. An officer should be an example. . . . Well, one of them was persuaded to leave, but in the other case there was a scandal and the chap went to jail. We were in India and I was quite young at the time. I must admit I had a share in the case. I was Adjutant at the time and the report came to me from the Company Sergeant-major. I insisted on an enquiry and on making an example of the man. He came from quite a good family too. I didn't believe in hushing things up. So you can imagine my feelings when I found out my own son. . . ."

His voice trailed off, and he paused. Then very suddenly he looked at me.

"Since the tragedy I've been going over and over the thing in my mind. There's such a thing as heredity, perhaps. People talk a lot about it, and I dare say there may be something in it. I'm sure there was nothing of that sort in my family, but I'm sorry to say Julian took after his mother—my first wife. Her people were . . ." He almost said "a bad lot", then he brought out the words in a voice that had no dimensions—". . . most unbalanced. My brother-in-law used to drink, my sister-in-law jumped in the river. . . ." There was a long pause; he looked away. ". . . Anyhow I was forced to divorce Julian's mother. . . ."

His expression was almost angry. I said nothing and wasn't even looking at him. "I told Julian that he'd lied to me. He wanted to speak, but I said, 'I don't want to listen. I'm not interested. You're not addressing a jury. The thing's just got to stop. There's such a thing as willpower and discipline. You're weak and you have no courage.' Oh, I didn't mean physical courage. He had that all right. I meant moral courage. 'I'm not asking you, Julian,' I said. 'I don't even want you to make a promise. I'm giving you an order. I want you to give up your undesirable associations and marry Ann as soon as possible. Do you understand?' I asked him. He didn't say a word. I was furious. I said, 'If you don't, I won't have anything more to do with you and I'll inform your partner.' I thought it was time for me to be firm. Julian said, 'Very well, Father,' and he left. Would you still say I was responsible for my son's suicide?"

"I never thought so for a moment, sir. You didn't know the circumstances. . . ."

"Surely he could have used his will-power."

"Oh, yes; but in certain cases it isn't enough. This is extremely difficult to explain, even for a doctor."

"It wasn't my fault." He was now quite childish.

"No, sir."

We were silent. After a time I looked at my watch. "You're staying for tea, aren't you?" he said. For a second he almost smiled. "Only we mustn't . . . I mean my cousin, Mrs. Tanner . . ."

"Sorry, sir. I must get back to Town."

"Incidentally," the Colonel said before I rose, "does anyone else know . . . ?"

"I shouldn't think so, sir."

"No," he said, and nodded. "What are you going to say to Ann?"

"That it was nervous depression resulting from his war injury, a thing that might have happened any time, sooner or later. A sudden nervous blackout. . . ."

II

It was all clear now, or at least as clear as it could be. I had discovered and could explain many things, but there was much, of course, I could never hope to explain. The mind is chaotic and the doctor's sympathy, understanding and skill are not always enough to come to grips with the chaos. Of the many causes that drove Julian to suicide, the number that could be superficially explained might perhaps be compared with the cold upper layers of the earth; below, among the masses of frothing lava, were the almost inexplicable, deeper motives. The rational explanation is superficial, even if it convinces us of its truth. The act of suicide, or any other act for that matter, is brought about by deeper instinctive forces which are unrealised and never admitted, and which the rational explanation merely supports or reinforces in advance or in retrospect. The act itself would take place without the superficial causes, just the same.

Julian was incapable of changing, perhaps because inversion was a deeply ingrained habit with him, but largely because he found love for a man a beautiful and exciting mystery; a kind of magic that, like most people in a similar position, he had never tried to explain. I myself had often tried to explain it, with the help of other qualified mystery-solvers and magic-analysers, but I had never got anywhere.

There was no doubt that Julian had experienced the full magic of real love with Ron, the type of man he liked; a real tough in looks who was at the same time capable of tenderness and affection. And Julian had probably realised he was getting on. Like most inverts, he had an agonising fear of an old age in which his physical attraction would diminish, but not necessarily as slowly as his ardour. He must have felt that Ron was somehow his last great love.

Basically, of course, social conditions may have had something to do with it. If Julian had been born into the working class or into the *petite bourgeoisie*, the problem would have been easier. There are several thousand working-class inverts all over the place; waiters, cooks, manservants, male nurses, hairdressers, shop-assistants, whose only fear is imprisonment or perhaps occasional violence. Many are tough and seasoned. There was the builder's foreman I'd seen in the pub recently; there was a bookie's runner I knew in Croydon, a market stall-keeper at Bermondsey, a radio-dealer in Camden Town, and so on. Their integration in society was perfect; although it may have been known they were queer, they were not regarded as other than normal.

Julian was not brought up in their surroundings and, even if he'd tried, could not have descended into them. It was far easier for him to climb the social scale. In fact, that is precisely what had happened to him: he had gone to a better school than his father, had served in a better regiment, and, had he married Ann, he would have been better off, apart from the fact that he'd have earned more and more money as he gained experience as a lawyer. Besides, Julian must have known that the main attraction in the eyes of his love-object was that he was a gentleman. And he also knew that a certain amount of money was essential.

Julian was in love, and he needed money. His father's threat would have meant him giving up his practice, and would have involved him in some sort of scandal. He might, of course, have taken up some ill paid job for which he was little suited. Several inverts have been faced with similar situations and have solved their problem. Julian could not.

III

Later I began to think about Julian's relations with Ann. When he'd been more or less jilted by Ron, he had no doubt become depressed. It was probably in such a state of mind that he welcomed her interest in him as a solution. She was young and not unattractive; she had plenty of money and made a fuss of him.

But when Ron returned, Julian must have known that in his own tongue-tied, shy way Ron had been in love with him even when in fact they had separated.

It was then that Julian had begun to sound Ann. Did she love him enough to share him with someone else? He'd found, of course, that she was uncompromising and jealous and he'd decided to give her up.

On the whole, I doubt whether he had been more selfish and grasping than others of his class and generation, whose egotism and greed had struck me so violently after the war. The results of the social revolution had brought many people to their "senses" with a vengeance. Having gone through the guilt complex of being middle class or upper class in the 'thirties and early 'forties, they had, after the war, become ambitious and mean and as careeristic as conditions allowed. All this was understandable, especially from a group of people who stood to lose so much, not to speak of the fact that Communism—with which many salved their consciences—had turned out to be a false god, and a dangerous one at that.

But his father had been completely wrong about Julian's political ideas and even about his past. Julian did not think and act in political terms. His interest in the working class had been romantic, emotional and sexual. He had no extra sense of responsibility towards the worker; he only had special interests. It has been said that the sexual attraction of the worker for the upper-class invert is an unrealised guilt complex. I find this explanation somewhat far-fetched, although there is some truth in it. A more acceptable explanation is that, to a man like Julian, the worker seems more masculine, which in some ways he is. But here again we come back to the old magic, the mystery.

More I shall never know.

Nineteen

"Do you know," Ann said, "you've been neglecting me." The pee-vishness of her tone was slightly relieved by her smile. I was not certain how much cynicism there was in the smile.

"I'm sorry," I said.

"I suppose you've been busy and all that," she continued, still smiling, but now the tone gave me an indication of what I ought to say.

"Yes, I have," I told her; "but that isn't exactly the reason I didn't ring you."

"Then why didn't you?"

"It was trial and error. I wanted to see exactly how long it would be before you contacted me. . . ."

"I didn't realise," she said. She held her breath.

"I had to check up on you. That's why I didn't ask you today how you were when you came in. I already knew. You're well on your way to recovery. The rest is now up to you. You've had a bad nervous shock. It was unfortunate, but perfectly natural. But you're recovering because you're a normal, healthy woman." The temptation to look in her face was strong, but I resisted it. I had to. I was Infinite Wisdom. "You must now stand on your own feet. You must forget Julian completely, or at least get to the stage where his memory no longer upsets you. You won't find that difficult."

It was then that I looked at her and I saw she wanted to say something, but I didn't let her. "You yourself," I said, "quite intelligently and wisely hit on the best and healthiest solution. A change of scenery, a change of atmosphere. You want to go abroad. As I told you, it's the best thing you can do. Now, when are you leaving?"

She suddenly looked at me, confused, angry. "You mean, you're not coming with me?"

"You don't have to be alarmed about that. I'm not going for two reasons. First of all, because you don't need me. There's not the slightest need for treatment. Secondly, because if I did go with you there's a strong chance you'd become desperately dependent on me. More than that, in fact. If we continue seeing each other, you might get a transference."

"What's that?"

"Love under false pretences. You fall in love with your doctor, because you think he's a kind of God Almighty without whom you can't exist. It's a very dangerous situation. . . ."

"Why is it dangerous? Why should it be?" I saw she was blushing.

"Because it isn't genuine. It leads to being an emotional cripple."

"But what about the man . . . the doctor?"

"What about him?"

"Wouldn't he have understanding, affection. . . ."

"Understanding is understanding," I said, "and love is love. They are two different things. The person who contracts transference may or may not want understanding, but she definitely wants love, and the doctor can't possibly give it to her. . . ." I almost added that love was not a medical function.

She remained silent for a time, then she said with an effort: "You're about the hardest man I've ever met."

"I don't know about that. If being professional and objective is hard, then I suppose I'm hard."

"You have to admit you treated me very differently in the beginning."

"The circumstances were different. If you have a temperature you should stay in bed; if you have no temperature you should get up. When you first came here you'd had a bad shock. I had to watch you; I had to see you often. Now I know you're all right."

"So now you can be cruel."

"Don't be silly."

She began to cry. This was one of the few occasions on which I didn't offer the slightest sympathy to someone crying in my consulting-room. I was taking a certain risk. It was still guesswork, but my view was that transference was mild in her case and that a little firmness might help. From the various signs, I rather thought my view was correct. On the other hand, if I'd made a mistake, I could easily have provoked a crisis. But this seemed unlikely. Ann was a spoilt, rich girl, but otherwise perfectly healthy.

I waited till she'd taken her handkerchief out of her bag and dried her eyes. I sat completely still in my chair. It was very quiet in the room.

Two minutes later, from Terry's bedroom window, I watched her walking away from the house. She did not look up as she reached the pavement, but began to hurry along the street as if chased by anger. I thought she would probably hurry back to her hotel and send me an abusive letter. At least, that was what I hoped she'd do.

Twenty

It had been raining since Sunday, but I hardly noticed it. In the early afternoon Cook's had told me on the telephone that the travellers' cheques were ready and that one reservation was certain and the other very likely for Friday; if the worst came to the worst, I could have two tickets for Monday next. Today was Tuesday. I had been busy ever since I had rung them. I had to re-read case histories and re-examine my patients, Miss Wilkins, Miss Mayhew, Mrs. Haynes, Mr. Gomersall, Gordon and a couple of others. I told them I was going away for three weeks. I had no worries, not even in the case of Mrs. Redfern. She was a near psychopath and very dependent on me, but I'd made an arrangement with Bunting at St. Gabriel's to keep an eye on her and see her if she got depressed.

Dighton had come the previous day and told me he was going on holiday himself—a week at Eastbourne, with his girl friend. He showed me her photograph. She had a humorous, good-tempered face and masses of hair. She looked the sort who probably had broad shoulders and a generous bosom.

There was only Ann left, and she rang up to say she was coming in the afternoon. From her tone on the telephone, I knew more or less what she'd say to me when she came. Professionally I was pleased, and privately greatly relieved.

I had certainly been very busy the last two days, but that was not the reason I hadn't yet told Terry I was taking him with me to France. The real reason made me rather shy. Because I'd been busy ever since I'd gone to his room after I'd given Ron a lift to North London, I hadn't thought much about Terry consciously, except momentarily, but the passage of time had had the same effect on me as it has on certain writers in whom the plot develops while they are asleep or occupied with some other work and not even thinking of their book.

I now knew that I was in love with Terry or, at least, I was as near to love as I had ever been in my life. I was a psychologist; I recognised the symptoms.

I was in love. Each of us waits for the miracle which will change his life. Sometimes it comes late. For me, this was it, and it had come mercifully early, just when I felt it was time for me to come to a decision and to settle down. Love can do great damage to the fabric of the mind, but I had always known that at times it can also cure and improve. I hoped it might cure me, for my weakness was that I had been suffering from an undeveloped heart. This had little to do with the fact that I preferred men to women, for there are thousands of people in the "normal" world whose hearts are small.

I had often heard people say that beauty and goodness and impulse are one. But I'd heard that in much the same way as, once or twice in a lifetime, we hear the warning of a kindly figure, half-familiar in the dim lights of the railway station, as he comes up to say we are taking the wrong train, then disappears. Now, for the first time, I actually felt it and believed it.

Love makes some people young and irresponsible, but I knew that I would mature under its influence. I should not be restless. I should no longer have that mad craving for excitement, the desire to "live" a novel. The case was finished, anyhow. I should have to live my own life. I should have a new sense of responsibility, and it would give me pleasure to be responsible. But all this was unimportant. It was so typical of me, so very typical, to think of the unimportant things first, investing them with an importance.

Terry was now on his way to the gym. He might go there less often in the future. It was so touching and beautiful that he had cried that night because he had felt that I had let him down. But when I told him that he ought to have known me better than think that, he had at once become happy. It was then—I realise it now—that I knew he was in love with me.

He was the first human being who had ever really fallen in love with me. And now I knew I could return his love.

At best, there were three more days before we could leave. All of a sudden I felt impatient. It seemed certain that the rain would continue throughout the week, and I had nothing to do. But that was immaterial. We must go away at once. Cancel the reservation and leave tomorrow. All it would mean was that we would have to get up an hour earlier and take a slow train to Dover. In France there was no need for reservations as long as one had second-class tickets. I decided to ring Cook's.

As I got up to look for the telephone directory, the front-door bell rang. I looked at my watch. It was not yet four o'clock. Ann was not due until half-past, but sometimes she came early.

It was Ron, however, to whom I opened the door. He was standing by the staircase as if in apology for ringing my bell. In his grey gabardine raincoat over the pinstripe suit, he looked younger than his years and rather menacing.

"Hullo," I said.

"I thought you'd be in," he said, not moving. "I hope you don't mind . . . I mean, you said I could always come and see you. . . ."

"Of course. Come in."

Slowly he moved. At the doorstep he quietly said, "Thank you": then he wiped his shoes on the mat. It was no use hiding from Ron that his visit had taken me by surprise. It so often happens that a stranger takes someone into his confidence, becomes enthusiastic for some reason, and pours out his heart without reserve, but as a result, he usually feels ashamed afterwards, and generally avoids his confidant. Usually he feels uneasy when they meet again and downright embarrassed or angry if the person makes even as much as a reference to the confession.

But there was no resentment in Ron's voice or attitude, no shame; only a certain shyness.

"Well, sit down," I said. He didn't remove his raincoat. "Aren't you working?"

"I'm taking the afternoon off," he said.

"Well, how are things?"

". . . Quite well, thanks."

"What's wrong then?"

He shrugged a gabardine shoulder, which seemed impossibly wide. He looked closely at me. "I don't know," he muttered. "I don't know what to do."

"Tell me this," I said. "Do you feel as down-hearted now as you did the other night?"

"No . . . but still . . ." He shook his head, and looked away.

"Do you still go to the *Treble Bob*?"

"I went there last night. Nothing else to do."

"You still miss him?"

He nodded.

"You really must make an effort to forget him. It'll take time, of course, but you must get away from it all. From Julian and everything associated with him. I'm going to tell you something, Ron, which may sound dreadful, but I think it was a lucky thing for you that Julian died."

There was fear in the eyes and he looked more than ever like a child. "Yes; I mean it," I said. "I'll tell you exactly what's happened to you. You've been infected, like hundreds of other people, but I don't think the infection has done serious damage yet. There are many chaps who've had the same experience as you. There must be several in Islington. Among the boys you know. You pass them in the street, but they hide their secret from you. Anyhow, most of them give it up. They get married to women and forget all about it. And so they should. It's not a good thing, Ron, to be queer. It suits very few people and on the whole it gives less happiness than normal love. . . ."

"I can't go back home . . ." Ron said.

"Who wants you to go back home? It was a good thing you left your mother. Sooner or later you'd have left her, anyhow. Everybody leaves home some time. Besides, it wasn't convenient to live there. And it was probably a good thing you gave up your girl friend, too. If she was the type you described, she wasn't suitable. After a time you'll find the right girl. Just take your time. But you must look. You're a normal person who's been infected. You must get it out of your system. Being queer's no good for you. It cost Julian his life."

"What do you mean?"

"What I say." This was pep talk. My assessment of Ron may have been faulty, but I knew I was doing nothing wrong; perhaps I was being helpful. "Yes," I said; "it cost him his life. Oh, I don't mean to say it was on your account in particular. You just happened to be with him at the time. It was bound to wreck him sooner or later."

Ron looked incredibly humble, and when he brought out the words "What about you?" it was more in the nature of childish curiosity.

"I'm different, Ron," I said. "I was born like that. You weren't and I can grapple with it. It's even useful to me because it gives me an extra insight into people. . . ."

"But it doesn't make you happy," he whispered, and nodded twice.

It was only then that I got the impression that he was, perhaps unconsciously, trying to seduce me. There was something in the way he looked and spoke. I was sure that wasn't the purpose of his visit. Realisation perhaps was not yet in his mind, but the idea would probably occur to him in a moment or two. There were almost too many reasons; all of them obvious. I was Julian's only friend known to Ron, and he might perhaps have thought I was a little bit like Julian. Ron was also desperately lonely and he may have been afflicted with that terrible and devastating emotion, pity. Pity for me or pity for himself; it was all the same.

How attractive he was; God, how attractive, as if nature for a brief season had lavished almost everything on him: good looks, strength, manliness. It would be so easy, so appallingly easy. I wouldn't make a mistake; I knew the technique too well. How often had I faced similar situations. One didn't need to be a psychologist, to know how to act; only an invert. One little move, the flicker of an eyelid, the tiniest gesture would be enough. He was already looking for encouragement in his own, shy way. In a second he would make a move. But it was I who moved first. I looked away; not too fast, not with fear, not brusquely or disapprovingly, and above all, not indifferently. I looked away quite naturally. Here again I understood the technique.

"No," I said. The word had slipped out. I had an uneasy feeling he might realise what it was meant to convey. Then, a moment later, I again felt myself in charge of the situation; I was Infinite Wisdom again. I shook my head. "You'll get over it, all right. In the first place, you must try to give up drinking, and if your will is strong enough you'll succeed. Then you'll soon forget the whole business." I felt my schoolmasterish attitude was convincing. "In a sense," I said, "although it's not a very kind way to look at it, Julian's death was a warning for you.

"Do anything that interests you, but do something. If you don't like the people around you, find others. . . . You can go to evening classes, for example"—this was the only thing I could think of at the time, because I remembered Dighton,—"where you'll meet people who are better company than the ones you broke away from. That's about the size of it."

A second later the door-bell went. It was obviously Ann.

"That's my next patient," I said. "I'm afraid you must go, but if you feel you need my help, even treatment, come and see me again. After September. I'm going on holiday in a couple of days' time."

He moved. He was a little confused, a little subservient. He didn't speak. I let him go ahead of me into the hall, where I opened the door to Ann.

"Good afternoon," she said. Ron glanced at her in the way an Islington boy usually looks at a well-dressed young woman. I asked her to go into the consulting-room and take a seat, then when the door had closed behind her, I held out my hand to Ron. "Well, good luck."

"Thanks." I thought he smiled for a second and I felt his large damp hand in mine.

Slowly, very slowly, I closed the door. He had obviously not recognised Ann from her photograph on Julian's mantelpiece, and she, of course, had never seen Ron. The meeting was all over in ten seconds. I was still facing the door, my hand on the knob like a child gazing after a shooting star. What would they have said to each other had they known, these two who each in their own way had loved Julian? It had been a highly dramatic situation in which the actors hadn't realised the parts they were playing. They will never know. They lived on two different planes. The distance between two parallel lines sometimes can be infinite.

Alone with the secret, exciting and terrible, it seemed I spent some time in the hall, but I only thought of this later. I suddenly remembered that Ann was waiting. When I returned to the consulting-room I was already a different man. I found her looking at a copy of *Psyche*.

"How are you?" I said.

She didn't answer immediately. She played a little with her cigarette-case, then she looked at me and replied very quickly: "I'm leaving for Italy in a couple of days' time."

"How long for?"

"I don't know yet," she said. I wondered whether her tone was meant to indicate that it was none of my business. I wasn't absolutely sure, but I had to know.

"You're feeling all right, I presume?"

"Very well, thanks."

She again replied quickly, blinking as she did so. The contempt in her voice, in the impatient blink, was unmistakable. She might just as well have said: "You're an arrogant bounder, Page, a little, upstart, unimportant doctor, living in a two-hundred-a-year flat, trying to give yourself airs. You think I was in love with *you* for one single second?" The diffidence, the hesitation, the frequent downcast looks of our first meetings were gone, and so were the confidences, the enthusiasm and the affection of last week. She couldn't have been more superior and sure of herself.

I was on the stage again, acting a part, a part I had never played before and which I had not even rehearsed. Like the actor who must be ready for any eventuality, I had to improvise. But I was, by nature, good at this sort of thing; and I was happy into the bargain. A second later I was already the humiliated, little bounder of a doctor, the none too successful charlatan Ann wanted me to feel. I knew that my impersonation was good, because for a moment I really felt crushed and couldn't utter a word. I couldn't even stammer.

A moment later, when I was wondering whether I wasn't overdoing things, she said, "I'm afraid I have to go now. Thank you for all you've done. I don't actually owe you anything, do I?"

"No," I replied as quietly as possible. "The cheque you sent me more than covered your appointments. I shall send you a proper receipt."

"Thank you," she said, and got up.

I followed her, like a shop-assistant, humbly, fast, apologetically.

"Goodbye," she called without looking back, and I closed the door slowly behind her.

So that was that. I felt relieved. Returning to the consulting-room, I took off my jacket like an actor undressing, and threw it on the couch. If there had been a transference, it was only very minor, and it had been nipped in the bud. Ann Hewitt would never return, as people always did whose transferences I had dislodged in the customary, slow, cautious way I had been taught. She would go on disliking me for a time, but she would soon forget about me, as she would about Julian, with whom she had been in love.

It was still not too late to call Cook's. They said it was perfectly all right to take a morning train and then sail by the early afternoon boat. I could pick up my tickets first thing in the morning.

Slowly I replaced the receiver, then I looked round in the room. This ought to have been a "great day". My affairs for the time being had been settled. The case was finished; I had not been involved, after all. I was going away on holiday with someone I loved, with someone who loved me. Indeed, it ought to have been a "great day" for me, if only I had not been the man I was. Unfortunately for me, and those like me, the battle must continue. In my case, love—the greatest, perhaps the only thing in life, must never be mentioned. It must stay underground, as it always has—apart from brief intervals—since the dawn of history. Ours is a secret love and a vulnerable one. It isn't its barrenness and sterility that kills it in the end, but the hostility and condemnation of a minority which for all we know may turn out to be smaller even than the underground. The real normal world is as neutral towards us as nature itself.

Terry returned a few minutes later. There was rainwater on his hair, and on his clothes. "What a day," he smiled. We were in the hall.

"Terry," I said, "I've got a surprise for you." This was a speech. "We're leaving for France sometime tomorrow. We'll spend a couple of days in Paris; then we'll go to the South for two or three weeks. Unless, of course, you don't want to?"

He was almost numb with happiness. "Thank you very much . . . wonderful," he stammered. The frightened, large dog eyes were suddenly sparkling in a smile. "I haven't been to France yet . . . Only Belgium, last year. . . . I really don't know how to thank you. . . ." He took a sudden step towards me.

To my embarrassment, I was momentarily overcome by a combination of emotions, and I was anxious to be alone.

"May I have your passport?" I said quickly.

Then, as he ran to his room, I realised that it would no longer matter if he saw that this was one of these rare occasions when I had been near to tears.

ALSO AVAILABLE FROM VALANCOURT BOOKS

FRANK BAKER	The Birds
WALTER BAXTER	Look Down in Mercy
CHARLES BEAUMONT	The Hunger and Other Stories
DAVID BENEDICTUS	The Fourth of June
PAUL BINDING	Harmonica's Bridegroom
JOHN BLACKBURN	A Scent of New-Mown Hay
THOMAS BLACKBURN	A Clip of Steel
	The Feast of the Wolf
JOHN BRAINE	Room at the Top
	The Vodi
MICHAEL CAMPBELL	Lord Dismiss Us
ISABEL COLEGATE	The Blackmailer
HUNTER DAVIES	Body Charge
JENNIFER DAWSON	The Ha-Ha
A. E. ELLIS	The Rack
BARRY ENGLAND	Figures in a Landscape
RONALD FRASER	Flower Phantoms
GILLIAN FREEMAN	The Liberty Man
	The Leather Boys
STEPHEN GILBERT	The Landslide
	The Burnaby Experiments
	Ratman's Notebooks
MARTYN GOFF	The Plaster Fabric
	The Youngest Director
	Indecent Assault
F. L. GREEN	Odd Man Out
STEPHEN GREGORY	The Cormorant
JOHN HAMPSON	Saturday Night at the Greyhound
THOMAS HINDE	The Day the Call Came
CLAUDE HOUGHTON	Neighbours
	I Am Jonathan Scrivener
	This Was Ivor Trent
JAMES KENNAWAY	The Mind Benders
	The Cost of Living Like This
CYRIL KERSH	The Aggravations of Minnie Ashe
GERALD KERSH	Fowlers End
	Nightshade and Damnations
FRANCIS KING	Never Again
	An Air That Kills
	The Dividing Stream
	The Dark Glasses

FRANCIS KING	The Man on the Rock
C.H.B. KITCHIN	Ten Pollitt Place
	The Book of Life
	A Short Walk in Williams Park
HILDA LEWIS	The Witch and the Priest
JOHN LODWICK	Brother Death
KENNETH MARTIN	Aubade
	Waiting for the Sky to Fall
MICHAEL McDOWELL	The Amulet
	The Elementals
MICHAEL NELSON	Knock or Ring
	A Room in Chelsea Square
BEVERLEY NICHOLS	Crazy Pavements
OLIVER ONIONS	The Hand of Kornelius Voyt
J.B. PRIESTLEY	Benighted
	The Other Place
	The Magicians
	Saturn Over the Water
	Salt Is Leaving
PETER PRINCE	Play Things
PIERS PAUL READ	Monk Dawson
FORREST REID	The Garden God
	Following Darkness
	The Spring Song
	Brian Westby
	The Tom Barber Trilogy
	Denis Bracknel
ANDREW SINCLAIR	The Facts in the Case of E.A. Poe
	The Raker
COLIN SPENCER	Panic
DAVID STOREY	Radcliffe
	Pasmore
	Saville
JOHN WAIN	Hurry on Down
	The Smaller Sky
	A Winter in the Hills
HUGH WALPOLE	The Killer and the Slain
KEITH WATERHOUSE	There is a Happy Land
	Billy Liar
COLIN WILSON	Ritual in the Dark
	Man Without a Shadow
	The Philosopher's Stone
	The God of the Labyrinth

Lightning Source UK Ltd.
Milton Keynes UK
UKOW03f0317020217

293361UK00004B/111/P